the
baby
snatchers

BOOK THREE OF THE SYDNEY HARBOUR HOSPITAL SERIES

CHRIS TAYLOR

LCT Productions Pty Ltd
18364 Kamilaroi Highway, Narrabri NSW 2390

ISBN. 978-1-925119-28-2 (Paperback)

The Baby Snatchers is a work of fiction. Names, characters, places, brands, media and incidents either are the product of the author's imagination or are used fictitiously. Any resemblance to actual persons, living or dead, events, or locales, is entirely coincidental.

Published in the United States of America.

Books by Chris Taylor

THE SYDNEY HARBOUR HOSPITAL SERIES
(in order)

The Perfect Husband
The Body Thief
The Baby Snatchers
The Final Bullet
The Debt Collector

THE MUNRO FAMILY SERIES
(In order)

The Profiler
The Investigator
The Predator
The Betrayal
The Deception
The Negotiator
The Christmas Vigil
The Ransom
The Defendant
The Shooting
The Maker

Find out more about all of Chris Taylor's books, including the hugely popular Munro Family series by visiting her website at:
www.christaylorauthor.com.au/about/books

DEDICATION

*This book is dedicated to my friends Sue Ricardo,
Ally Thomson and Pru Knight for reminding me
that every now and then, I need to drag myself away
from my keyboard and enjoy some "girlfriend time."
Thank you for your friendship and support.*

And as always, to my wonderful husband, Linden. I love you.

Acknowledgments

As usual, no book comes into being without a lot of help and support by my friends and family. A world of thanks must go to my wonderful editor, Pat Thomas. Thank you for everything that you do to make my stories even more amazing than I could ever dare to dream. To Detective Superintendent Michael Kilfoyle, thank you for lending my story credibility. Any mistakes are wholly my own.

To Damon, Alisha, Grady and all of the staff at damonza.com, thank you for yet another fantastic cover. To my sister, Nicole Guihot and to my friend, Ally Thomson, thank you for your excellent editorial comments, proof reading skills and suggestions. I hope you like the final result.

To Amy Atwell and her dedicated staff at Author EMS who are so much more than book formatters. Amy, once again, thank you for your magic.

To the fantastic writer organizations such as Romance Writers of Australia, Romance Writers of

America and Romance Writers of New Zealand for all the help, support and encouragement they offer new and aspiring writers, including me.

To my readers, thank you for your support and love for my stories. Your encouragement and enjoyment make this journey all worthwhile.

And lastly, to my friends and family, especially my husband and children. Thank you for putting up with late dinners and even later conversations as I've emerged day after day from the sometimes scary but always enthralling world I've created on my computer.

PROLOGUE

6th May, 1973

Dear Diary,

Matron approached me tonight, just as I was pulling on my coat. The storm that had raged for most of the evening was still fierce in its intensity. My trusty Toyota was parked at the far end of the hospital car park. By the time I reached its safety, my hair was plastered to my face and my uniform was drenched.

But that's not what has kept me up way past the time I should be in bed, snatching whatever hours I can before my alarm clock and the demands of a busy country hospital once again intrude. It's what Matron said as I was leaving the maternity ward that has my thoughts in a frenzy and my body too tense for sleep.

She spoke to me about the newborns—or more precisely, their mothers. Their young, unwed mothers. She painted a terrible picture of the awfulness of these innocent babies' lives. They've been born out of wedlock to mothers too young to know what it means to care for a child; to mothers with no means of providing for them— not to mention their total absence of morals.

Matron's harsh and desperate whisper still echoes in my ear. 'If something isn't done, these babies will grow up as bastards, forever labeled, forever maimed. Unloved and unwanted, treated like trash.' Is that what I want for them? The very thought makes my heart ache with sadness, anger, helplessness.

What can I do to save them, these innocent babes in arms? It's the very question Matron posed to me as I made my way outside. The question has been racing around and around inside my head, keeping me from sleep. I don't know what I can do to save them! I am a young, single female. What is it Matron expects me to do?

I'll talk to Marjorie. She'll know what to do. She always knows what to do. Until I know the answer, I won't sleep comfortably again...

CHAPTER 1

Present day

Georgina Whitely finished her internal examination of the young woman who lay on the bed in the birthing suite of the Sydney Harbour Hospital. The midwife removed her gloves and smiled at her patient.

"I have good news, Cynthia!" she said. "You're fully dilated." A surge of adrenaline rushed through the nurse, but she kept her voice calm. "We're going to get ready to push now." For better or worse, this was where things got interesting.

At Georgie's announcement, the patient's hands fisted around the steel bedrails. Barely sixteen and terrified, with her hair plastered to her face, her breaths came fast. As Cynthia's midwife, it was Georgie's responsibility to see the girl through the final stages of labor and ensure a successful outcome for both mother and baby.

"Slow it down, Cynthia. That's it. Big breaths. In

and out. You're almost there." She kept her voice soft and hypnotic, yet firm, hoping to penetrate the fog of apprehension and pain that filled most women at this point. She'd been no different.

"It hurts!" Cynthia gasped and tears ran down her cheeks. "Please, nurse! Can't you make it stop?"

"You're doing wonderfully, Cynthia. Not much longer, now. Think about your baby and slow down your breathing. In through your nose and out through your mouth. That's it. Well done! Keep going."

Georgie grabbed the wet cloth she'd left on the nightstand and swiped it gently across the girl's flushed face. It wouldn't do anything to ease the pain, but at this point in time, that was all Georgie could do. It was too late for an epidural or any other kind of drugs, apart from the laughing gas. The baby would arrive any minute.

"Ow! Bloody hell! Please, nurse! You have to make it stop! Please!"

"It's all right, Cynthia. Use the gas. Breathe through it. You're almost there."

The contraction that had gripped the teenager's body finally eased its relentless hold and the girl gasped and groaned and cried out in relief. Fresh tears slid down her cheeks. She turned to Georgie, her eyes desperate with fear and pain.

"How much longer? How much longer is this gonna take?"

"You're nearly there, Cynthia. Keep on going. Your baby's going to be here any minute!"

The girl stared at Georgie, her expression one of anxiety and distrust. Georgie didn't blame her. Cynthia had been in labor for more than fifteen hours. No doubt it was hard for her to believe the pain and torment was ever going to stop.

Most of the time, Georgie's patients had someone beside them, offering support. Whether it was the father of the baby or someone else, not many women chose to go through labor on their own. Georgie couldn't help but wonder if the poor girl had anyone; if there was a single soul who cared about the teenager or the baby. It was a sad and depressing thought.

"Ow! Ow! Ow! It's coming again! Please! Nurse, help me!"

Georgie's chest went tight, but she did her best to remain calm through the girl's desperate pleas. "Cynthia, I want you to listen to me. Pull up your legs and bend your knees. Keep your chin down on your chest. As the contraction builds, I want you to try and push."

"Ow!" The girl screamed and gasped all at once, putting more effort into voicing her pain than she had moving her baby along. Georgie moved closer to the bed and turned the girl's head to face her.

"Listen to me, Cynthia. We need to get this baby out. It won't happen without your cooperation. Do you understand?"

In the aftermath of a contraction, the girl nodded and let out a soft sob. "I'm trying! I'm doing the best that I can!"

"I know you are, Cynthia, but you need to

concentrate on pushing. Don't waste your energy on crying out. Keep your chin down and your legs up and when you feel that contraction building, I want you to push down with all your might. I'm going to count to ten. I want you to keep on pushing for as long as you can, all right?" She smiled down at her, hoping to reassure her, and was rewarded with a wobbly smile.

"All right."

Glancing across at the monitor, Georgie noticed another contraction was on its way. "Okay, Cynthia. Here it comes. Bring your legs all the way up, drop your chin down on your chest. Here it comes, Cynthia. Breathe in and *push!*"

Georgie began the countdown, keeping one eye on the monitor. The baby's heartbeat was still strong and regular. They were almost there.

"That's it, Cynthia. Keep pushing! Eight…nine…ten. Relax."

The girl collapsed back against the pillows and sucked in mouthfuls of air.

"Take it easy, Cynthia. Big, deep breaths. Slow it down. That's it, honey. One more big push like that and I think the head will crown. Your baby will be here before you know it." She smiled and moved around to stand between the young girl's legs and glanced at the monitor again. "Okay, Cynthia. Here it comes. Big breaths, like I told you. Chin down, legs up. Let's go! One…two…three…"

Lifting the girl's hospital gown out of the way, Georgie watched the baby's head appear and quickly donned a fresh pair of gloves. "I can see the head, Cynthia! I can see a whole mop of black hair! Keep going! You're nearly there!"

"Ow, it's stinging! Nurse, it's stinging!"

"Big, slow breaths, Cynthia. The pain will soon disappear. One more push and it'll all be over, I promise."

The girl frowned at her with a narrowed gaze. "You promise?"

Georgie shot her a big smile. "I promise. Now, here comes the contraction, keep your head down and push!"

The girl groaned through her clenched teeth and pushed with all her might. Georgie held her gloved hands at the ready.

"That's it, Cynthia! Keep going! Your baby's nearly here!" The head cleared the opening. Quickly, Georgie felt around the baby's neck for the cord. It wasn't there and she breathed a quiet sigh of relief.

"Another second or two, Cynthia. Take another deep breath." Georgie twisted the baby's shoulders and it slid into her waiting hands. The cord was free from entanglements and the baby looked as it should.

"It's a girl! Congratulations, Cynthia! You have a little baby girl!" Quickly clearing the baby's airway with suction, Georgie wrapped her in a clean towel and placed the baby upon her mother's chest. Skin to skin, the tiny infant gave only the slightest of murmurs and then closed her eyes, content.

"She's not crying. Why isn't she crying?" Cynthia asked, her voice rising in panic.

"Not all babies cry at birth." Georgie hurried to reassure her. "She's happy where she is. She'll cry when she's ready. Her color's good and she's breathing fine. There's nothing to be worried about."

"Are you sure?" the girl asked, her eyes still filled with uncertainty.

"Yes, honey. I'm sure," she said and offered her another smile. "Say hello to your daughter. You've waited a long time to meet her."

The girl pulled back the towel and studied her baby. It took awhile, but at last, Cynthia cracked a smile. "Hello, sweet baby," she whispered. "You've taken Mommy to hell and back and I bet this is only the beginning."

Georgie listened to the girl's murmurings and tried to dispel her disquiet. Quickly and efficiently, she delivered the placenta, taking care to check that it was intact. Satisfied, she disposed of the waste and peeled off her gloves.

After washing her hands, she opened Cynthia's hospital chart and began writing up a report of the birth. Flicking through the sparse pages, she noticed there was no one listed as an emergency contact or even as next of kin. She couldn't help but wonder what support system the girl had in place and how she'd cope with a newborn once she left the hospital.

"Have you got someone at home who can help you out with the baby over the next few weeks?"

Cynthia kept her gaze fixed firmly on the baby and shook her head. "No, there's just me."

Georgie frowned. "You live alone?"

"Yeah. Ever since my asshole of a boyfriend took off. As soon as I told him I was pregnant, he couldn't get out of the door quickly enough. I haven't seen hide nor hair of him since."

"Where do you live?"

"Here and there," the girl replied evasively. "I move around a lot."

"What about your family? Are they able to help out? The first few weeks are always the hardest, while you're getting to know your baby and working out how to cope. It can be overwhelming for all new moms."

Cynthia shook her head again. "Nope, just me and...Josephine." She stroked the baby's tiny cheek. "Yeah, Josephine. That's what I'm gonna call you."

Georgie bit her lip in indecision. At the beginning of her shift, she'd noticed Cynthia's general air of neglect. Her hair was lank and unwashed. Her bare feet were stained with dirt. The smile she gave her little daughter showed a decided disregard for her dental health and now that the stress of the birth was over, Georgie detected the unmistakable smell of body odor.

Surely she couldn't send a newborn home to what could very well be substandard living conditions without drawing it to someone's attention? She flipped through the hospital notes again, looking for some indication social services had been involved, but there was nothing. The girl had presented to the emergency department of the Sydney Harbour Hospital late the night before with signs she was in active labor.

She'd been admitted to Ward Seven. Georgie had taken over her care from the night nurse hours earlier. The labor was long but uneventful, and she'd assisted in the delivery of a healthy baby girl. Georgie grimaced and couldn't help but wonder how long the baby would stay that way if her living conditions weren't up to grade. With mounting concern, she sighed.

Cynthia turned her head to look at her with fear in her eyes. "There's something you're not telling me! What the hell's wrong with my baby?"

Forcing a smile, Georgie set aside the chart and moved closer to the bed. "Your baby's perfect. There's nothing wrong with her."

The girl continued to stare at her with mistrust. "Then why do you keep sighing?"

Georgie drew in a deep breath and eased it out. "I'm a little worried about your living arrangements and the lack of support at home. Taking care of a new baby is difficult. I'd feel more comfortable if I knew you and Josephine had some help."

Cynthia lowered her gaze to the baby in her arms. "We don't need any help. We'll get by just fine on our own. Won't we, Josephine?" She pressed a kiss upon the soft, dark hair that covered the infant's head. "Just you and me, baby. That's the way it's gonna be."

Georgie chewed her lip in indecision. There was no doubt the girl had bonded with her child and would take care of her the best she could, but from the look of things, she was barely able to look after herself, let alone a newborn. Tactfully, Georgie tried again.

"Cynthia, you're sixteen. There must be someone I can call to let them know about you and Josephine. Your mom, perhaps?"

The girl stared at the bed covers. "I never knew my mom. I was adopted at birth, like Cameron."

"Who's Cameron?"

"My brother. Well, my adopted brother, but I don't think of him like that. He might be eleven years older than me, but he's as real a brother to me as flesh and blood."

Georgie seized on the possibility that Cameron could provide Cynthia with some support. "Does Cameron live in the city?"

The girl shrugged, her eyes still downcast. "Maybe. Last I heard he was a cop, stationed in the city."

"How long has it been since you've seen him?"

"Ten years."

Georgie started in surprise. "Ten *years?*"

"Yes," Cynthia replied, her jaw jutting out at a stubborn angle, as if daring Georgie to question her statement.

Georgie curbed her curiosity and said simply, "I don't understand."

Anger flashed in the girl's eyes. "My family's a fuck up, all right. Surely you've figured that one out already."

A moment later, the girl's shoulders slumped on a heavy sigh and her anger seemed to dissipate. She pressed a kiss against the soft hair that covered her baby's head. When she spoke again, her voice was calmer.

"Mom and Dad couldn't have kids, so they adopted. First, Cam and then me. I don't know why they bothered. Mom never took to motherhood. Some of my earliest memories are of her yelling at me for something or other. I could never do anything right."

Her lips twisted. "She hated my brother even more. He grew into a big kid. By the time he was fifteen, he towered over her. She hated that he dominated her physically. It only made her more malicious. Of course, Cam used to give back everything she doled out, and more. It wasn't like she didn't deserve it. She treated him like little more than hired help, only there wasn't any payment involved."

Georgie's heart filled with sadness at the thought of what the two of them must have gone through. "What about your dad?" she asked softly.

Cynthia smiled sadly. "Dad was the only good thing in our lives, but he was no match against the viciousness of Deirdre Dawson. I was five when she ordered him to throw Cam out. I'm sure Dad didn't want to do it, but she gave him an ultimatum."

Cynthia ran her hand gently over her daughter's head. Her fingers stroked the petal-soft cheek. "Dad chose her. He took the easy way out. He chose to keep the peace between him and his wife and let his son fight his battles on his own. Cam went to live with the family of one of his high school friends on the other side of town. I haven't seen him since."

"How do you know he's in Sydney?"

"We might have lived in a small country town, hours from the city, but news filtered back over the years. I heard he went into the Police Academy straight out of high school. A couple of years ago, I overheard one of Dad's friends telling him Cam was doing pretty well as a police officer in the city."

"Is that what brought you here?"

Cynthia lowered her gaze and slowly nodded. "Things were getting worse at home. For a little while after Cam left, Mom seemed happier. There were even odd moments when she'd treat me kindly. I missed Cam, but life was bearable. Then I grew up." She grimaced at the memory and pain flickered across her face. Georgie's heart clenched.

"When I hit puberty, things changed again and it wasn't for the better. I filled out, grew taller; attracted the attention of the boys. It wasn't like I encouraged them," she added defensively and Georgie nodded in understanding.

"Mom started accusing me of all sorts of things, calling me awful names. I couldn't even walk out the front door without her screaming obscenities at me. Dad used to tell me to ignore her; that she was going through the change of life." Cynthia shook her head in disgust. "As if that excused everything."

The young girl's breath came faster, harsh in the silence of the room. Her baby slept against her mom's chest, oblivious to the tension that held

Cynthia's body taut. Georgie stepped closer. Her patient had not long ago given birth after a long and arduous labor. She didn't want her upsetting herself unnecessarily.

"It's okay, Cynthia. We don't need to talk about it anymore. I understand—"

"You understand *shit*. You want to know why I'm here, alone in a labor ward with no one to call on for help? I'll tell you why! Two years ago, I came home after spending an evening with my friends at the movies. Mom met me at the door. I'd hardly stepped foot inside before she started in on me, screaming about how I'd been out all night, spreading my legs for every boy in town. I did my best to ignore her, like I'd been doing for years. She followed me into my bedroom." Her voice cracked. Her expression was distant and filled with fear. Once again, Georgie tried to intervene.

"Don't talk about it anymore, honey. I don't want you to get upset. It's not good for you, or for your baby."

Cynthia stared down at her daughter, still blissfully asleep. "I want to tell you. I want you to understand."

Georgie nodded, but tension knotted her insides. Though the girl mostly spoke with a refined tongue that evidenced a sound education, it was obvious she'd been living on the streets for some time. There had to be a good reason why.

Cynthia drew in a ragged breath. She looked up at Georgie with eyes that were filled with agony.

"I asked Mom to leave me alone, but she refused. Instead, she pushed me hard down on the bed and sat on me. She prised open my thighs, digging her fingers into my skin. She kept screaming at me, calling me names. She said she was going to prove I was a slut."

Georgie swallowed a gasp of horror. Anticipating where this was going, dread poured through her veins. She prayed in silent desperation that she was wrong about what Cynthia was about to reveal.

"She tore off my panties," Cynthia said in a voice dull with pain. "I think she was surprised I wore any, but it didn't stop her. It was like she'd gone crazy, possessed with something so evil, I couldn't bear to look at her. She forced two fingers inside me, crowing all the time that she could tell I wasn't a virgin." Cynthia gasped and shuddered. Tears ran down her cheeks. "It hurt so much."

The girl's sobs now came in earnest, shaking her tiny frame. Georgie stepped forward instinctively, her heart breaking. Gathering the girl and her baby carefully in her arms, Georgie held them.

Murmuring wordless sounds of comfort against Cynthia's hair, Georgie waited out the storm. Her anger boiled out of control. With an effort, she clenched her jaw, forcing it down. She didn't want the girl to misinterpret her anger.

When at last Cynthia's sobs quieted, Georgie slowly pulled away. Brushing the matted hair out of the girl's eyes, Georgie offered her a reassuring smile.

"Is that why you left?"

Cynthia lowered her gaze and nodded.

"Did you speak to your dad about what happened?"

"No. I saw what happened with Cam and nothing had changed over the years. Dad was weak. He always took her side over mine. There would be no support from him."

"You've been living on the streets since you were fourteen?"

"Yes."

"You came to Sydney, looking for your brother."

"Yes."

"Have you made any enquires as to his whereabouts?"

Cynthia looked down at herself. Though she wore a clean hospital gown, the ground-in dirt and filth on her hands and feet was clearly visible.

"I arrived in Sydney with nothing more than a few personal items in my backpack and the clothes I wore. I had a total of twenty-nine dollars and thirty cents in my purse. It didn't take long for the money to run out. I moved around from shelter to shelter and all the time, I thought of Cam. I wondered if it were true that he was a police officer and that he was stationed in the city. I wanted to go to him, to find him, but I was scared."

"Of what?" Georgie asked gently, even though she had a fair idea.

"That he wouldn't recognize me. That he'd refuse to acknowledge who I was." Her voice lowered to a whisper. "That he wouldn't want to have anything to do with me. I was part of the past—a past he'd long left behind. I was scared he wouldn't take kindly to being reminded about where he'd come from."

Cynthia sighed quietly and settled herself and her baby back against the pillows. Idly stroking the infant's soft cheek, she continued: "For months, I went back and forth, scrounging up the courage to approach him and then being too terrified to try. Once, I even got as far as the front steps of the city police station, only to turn away. By then, it had been a long time since I'd taken a shower and I was embarrassed by my appearance. A few weeks later, I met Albert."

"Who's Albert?"

"Josephine's father."

"Tell me about him."

The girl's expression softened and a small smile played on her lips. Georgie listened while Cynthia spoke about a boy a few years older than her who she'd met living on the street. They'd struck up a friendship that turned into love. All had been going well until Cynthia became pregnant. Albert reacted badly to the news of his impending fatherhood. The day after she told him, he walked out on her, abandoning her and their unborn baby. She hadn't seen him again.

Georgie listened and bit back a sigh at the desperateness of the girl's circumstances. Unfortunately, it was an all too familiar tale. Ward Seven was a public maternity ward and it catered almost exclusively to the several hundred, mostly young, pregnant girls who arrived there every year without health insurance. Many of them were drug addicts, alcoholics or both. Most were without stable homes or reliable family support. The enormity of the problem saddened Georgie almost to the point of despair, but she refused to give up on the desperate women and their babies in her care. Cynthia and her daughter were no different.

"I have a colleague who's married to a police officer who works in the city. I could make some enquires and see if we could find your brother," she said. "What do you think?"

The girl shrugged, but Georgie caught the brief flash of hope in Cynthia's eyes and resolved to do what she could to find the girl's brother before she was discharged.

"I could also put you into contact with someone from the Department of Family and Community Services. Would that be okay?"

Cynthia was shaking her head back and forth even before Georgie had finished. "No way! There's no way in hell I'm letting those interfering, old bitches steal my baby."

"They're not going to take Josephine away from you, honey. All they'll do is try and help you and your little girl. She'll need special things like clean clothes and water to bathe in and a safe, warm place to sleep—and unless you're going to breastfeed, you'll need bottles and formula. The people from social services might help you find a better place to live and give you some assistance until you get back on your feet. If you don't want to do it for yourself, think of your baby. Do it for Josephine."

Cynthia averted her gaze, but a moment later, she offered Georgie a shrug, which Georgie took as a yes. She breathed a quiet sigh of relief. At least the girl was prepared to accept help. If not for her sake, then for the baby's. It was something.

The door to the birthing suite opened and Georgie's mother appeared in the room. As head of the labor ward, Marjorie Whitely was Georgie's boss. It had taken five years of persuasion, but her mother had finally convinced her to leave her beloved pediatric nursing and retrain as a midwife. It meant that Georgie took orders from her mother, but so far, their professional relationship was working.

"Is everything all right in here, Georgina?"

"Yes, thanks, Marjorie," Georgie replied, calling her mother by her given name, like the rest of the staff did. "Cynthia's just given birth to a healthy baby girl. I'll have them cleaned up and returned to the ward shortly."

Her mother nodded her approval. "Very good." She cast her gaze in the direction of the young mother. "Congratulations, Cynthia."

Georgie's patient smiled and ducked her head. "Thank you."

Marjorie returned her attention to her daughter. "Georgina, do you mind if I have a word with you outside?"

Georgie glanced up in surprise, but nodded. "Of course." She looked over at Cynthia. "I won't be a moment. When I get back, we'll get you into the shower. How does that sound?"

"Great. Thanks," Cynthia replied, and threw her a grateful smile.

Georgie smiled back and then followed her mother out of the room. "You wanted to speak with me?"

"Yes. That girl in there. What's her story? Where are her parents?"

Georgie's shoulders slumped on a heavy sigh. "She's a runaway. Terrible family life. She left home when she was fourteen."

"Where's she living? From the look of her, it's not somewhere I'd be happy sending a newborn. They're so susceptible to disease and illness at this age."

"She didn't give me an address, but she said she lives there on her own. She thinks her older brother is working somewhere in the city. I'm going to try and locate him. I also spoke to her about contacting FACS and she's agreed to let me make the call."

Georgie's mother pursed her lips. "That's something then. I guess we can be grateful for small mercies."

"I'll call them as soon as I get Cynthia and the baby settled back on the ward."

Marjorie nodded. "Good. Let me know how that goes."

"I will."

With that, her mother turned and headed toward the nurses' station. Georgie slipped back into the room. The baby had wakened and Cynthia smiled down at her, a look of delight and wonderment on her face.

"You're so beautiful, Josephine. My beautiful little girl." Another round of kisses were pressed against the baby's head.

"How about I take her for a while and let you have a shower? It's been a long, hard day and you deserve a break. There's a bathroom right through that connecting door. You'll find soap and towels on the shelf. There are clean hospital gowns there, too, unless you'd rather change into clothes of your own. I could go back to the ward and collect something for you, if you like?"

A flush of embarrassment slid across Cynthia's cheeks. She averted her gaze. "No, that's okay. A gown will be fine. I... I didn't leave anything on the ward."

Georgie looked around the room for Cynthia's belongings. A brown paper bag containing the cheap dress and sandals she'd arrived in were all that Georgie could find. She bit back another sigh. Things were even grimmer than she'd thought.

How on earth was the girl going to care for a baby?

CHAPTER 2

It took awhile, but right before Georgie's shift was about to end, she received a call from a FACS employee. The woman, who identified herself as Cheryl Stuart, opened her monologue with an apology.

"I'm sorry it's taken me so long to phone you back, but we're absolutely snowed under. Two of the people in my office are away sick and another one's on annual leave. It leaves me and one other—and believe me, she's as overworked as I am."

Georgie wanted to commiserate with the woman about the never-ending issue with government resources that just wouldn't stretch as far as they were needed, but time was running out. Cynthia would be discharged within a day or two. Something needed to be set in place quickly.

"I'm sorry to hear about your rough day," she said in a mollifying tone, "but I have a young girl who gave birth a few hours ago and I'm concerned about her living arrangements. She's been estranged from her parents for two years and has good reason not to want to contact them. I understand she has a brother living in Sydney and I'm trying to track him down, but so far, I haven't had any luck."

Her announcement was met with silence and then a loud and heavy sigh. "How old is she?"

"Sixteen."

"So she isn't that young."

Georgie felt a wave of anger. "She's young enough, and certainly in need of your help."

"Yeah, yeah, yeah, same old story. But it's not like she's eleven or twelve. I had a twelve-year-old the other week. New baby, living out on the streets. Nowhere to go, no one who cared. It kills me."

Georgie drew in a deep breath and eased it out in an effort to release the tension in her shoulders and neck. Cheryl wasn't telling her anything new. She saw the same on Ward Seven every day.

"If everything's fine, this girl will be discharged tomorrow or the next day," she said. "We'll lose any chance we have of helping her and her baby."

"Yep, I know how the story goes." Another heavy sigh and then, "What's her name? I'll see what I can do, but it won't be before tomorrow."

"Cynthia Dawson. I'll do my best to keep her here until you arrive, but please put her on the top of your list. We're short of beds and if someone else comes in overnight, I'm not sure there'll be anything I can do."

"Yeah, yeah, yeah. Same shit, different day," Cheryl muttered. "I'll do the best I can."

After thanking her, Georgie hung up the phone and made a record of the conversation in Cynthia's notes. She'd looked in on the girl a few moments earlier and had been pleased to see both Mom and baby were asleep.

"How did things go with Cynthia Dawson?"

Georgie looked up from the desk and acknowledged her mother's question with a nod. "I got onto FACS. They're overloaded, as usual, but they've agreed to come and see her tomorrow."

Marjorie grimaced. "Let's hope she's still here. We have a full house at the moment."

Georgie compressed her lips in silent agreement. "Let's pray we don't get anyone else in."

"How did things go with locating the brother? Did you find him?"

"I've made some calls. I'm waiting to hear back."

"What are the chances you'll locate him?"

Georgie shrugged and refused to acknowledge the wave of despair that threatened. "Who knows? But I have to try. That poor girl won't cope on her own. It's a simple fact."

Her mother's expression softened. "Don't take it personally, Georgina. You're doing the best you can."

Tears pricked Georgie's eyes. She hurriedly swiped them away. "Why does it feel like I'm never able to do *enough*?"

Marjorie patted her gently on the back. "What's enough? When is it *ever* enough? We can't blame ourselves for the situations these girls find themselves in. They've made bad choices. They have to live with the consequences."

Georgie stared hard at her mother and shook her head. "It's not always that easy, Mom. Don't you remember—?"

"Of course I remember!" her mother snapped. "But your situation was different."

"How?"

"You weren't living on the streets, for one. And that boy took advantage of you. He—"

"Jason didn't take advantage of me, Mom. I know you find that hard to believe. I wanted it as much as he did. We were in love. It was as simple as that."

Her mother's expression hardened. "You were a child, Georgina!"

"Mom, I was seventeen!"

"And he was twenty-three! He took advantage of you, Georgina. Fair and square."

Georgie opened her mouth to protest again and then closed it. There was no use arguing with her mother. Not about this. She'd learned that a long time ago. With a sigh of resignation, she pushed away from the desk.

"I'm going to head home and put my feet up. It's been one hell of a long day and I'm on again first thing in the morning."

Marjorie nodded and offered her a tight smile. "I'll see you then."

———

Georgie tucked an errant strand of chestnut-colored hair behind her ear and headed for the staff parking lot. The rustle of dried leaves beneath her feet reminded her they were well into the fall. Winter would be upon them any minute. Georgie didn't mind. She loved the cold.

Not that it got really cold in Sydney. Not like when she was young, tucked away in a cottage in the Upper Blue Mountains. She had fond memories of drinking hot chocolate by the open fireplace at the cottage, and having snow fights with her sisters. Though it only snowed about a week a year there, it was more than what fell in Sydney. As far as she knew, Sydney had never seen snow.

While her parents had also relocated to the city, they still maintained their mountain hideaway and when time and the demands of their jobs allowed, they escaped the noise and mayhem of the city and spent some quality time surrounded by the peace and tranquillity of the beautiful Australian bush. Georgie made a mental note to make an effort to take a few days off over the winter and join them there.

Her phone rang, distracting her from her thoughts. Tugging it out of her handbag, she glanced at the screen and smiled.

"Chanel! Thanks for calling me back."

"Of course! Why wouldn't I call you back?"

"I don't know. You're always so crazy busy, between work and your new promotion to senior resident. Congratulations, by the way, Doctor Sutcliffe. Then there are the triplets and that demanding husband of yours!" she joked. "How is Bryce, by the way?"

Chanel took the gibe in the spirit it was intended, and laughed. "He's great. I don't know how he manages to keep going. People tell me I'm amazing, juggling work with three small kids, but at least I only work part time. He works sixty hours a week and then comes home and helps out with the girls. The man's a saint!"

Georgie giggled and forced down the tiny pang of envy. Chanel was a good friend. It wasn't her fault she'd hit the jackpot in the husband stakes. Georgie could only hope she'd be just as lucky some day.

"How have you been, Georgie? I haven't seen you for ages!"

"Flat out, like everyone. Lately, it seems all I do is leave home, go to work and then come home again."

"We must organize a girls' night out. I'll confer with my dear husband and see when he's scheduled for days off. He can spend some quality time at home with his daughters."

Georgie smiled. "That sounds like a great plan. Let me know when we can do it. I might even see if Isobel can make it. I'm sure Mason would be happy to do daddy duty, too."

"He's such a sweetie," Chanel agreed. "After that horrible stuff Isobel went through with Nigel... I'm so glad she found someone special."

"Yes," Georgie agreed, remembering the traumatic events of a couple of years earlier when nurse Isobel Donnelly, had left her violent and abusive husband. Getting away from him had been difficult; and complicating matters further, her ex had been a prominent doctor at the same hospital. Things had been very tough on Isobel for a while. Georgie couldn't be happier that she'd found love and contentment with someone else.

"So, what can I do for you?" Chanel asked, interrupting Georgie's musings.

"I had a young girl in the birthing suite today. Sixteen-year-old runaway. She's had a tough life."

"Haven't they all?" Chanel said without rancor.

"Yes, you're right and this girl's no different. She's living God knows where and has no family support, except for a brother, and she doesn't know where he is."

"Okay. What do you want me to do?" Chanel asked, sounding uncertain.

"Actually, she told me her brother's a police officer and she believes he's stationed in the city. I was wondering if you could ask Bryce if he knows of him."

"Sure, I guess so. Do you know how long it's been since this guy worked there? They tend to transfer around a fair bit, especially if they're young."

"He's not that young. Cynthia said he was at least ten years older than her."

"Okay, so he's not straight out of the Academy, but he's still not old. Anyway, there's no harm in asking. I'll call Bryce right now."

Georgie sighed in relief. "Thanks, Chanel. I hate to trouble you or Bryce, but I couldn't think of a faster way to find out."

"Hey, it's no trouble. I'm happy to help out. What's the brother's name?"

"Cameron Dawson. At least, I assume they bear the same surname. I didn't think to ask."

"You never know, you might get lucky. Even if he has a different last name, it's unlikely there'll be more than one Cameron, aged approximately twenty-six or twenty-seven, at the same precinct. I'll call you right back."

After thanking her again, Georgie ended the call and made her way to her car. The cherry-red Mazda CX-3 was parked where she'd left it. She'd barely sat down in the driver's seat when Chanel rang her.

"Wow, that was quick. How did it go?"

"No good. Bryce's not answering his phone. He might be out on a job. I've left a message for him to call me. I'll let you know once I actually speak with him."

Georgie's shoulders slumped in disappointment, but she forced herself to reply with a level of optimism. After all, with a bit of luck, Chanel would talk to her husband about it before the night was over and Georgie would have the information she sought.

"Thanks, Chanel, I really appreciate it."

"No problem. I'll speak to you later and I'll let

you know when I can escape from here and have a night out on the town with you!"

Georgie laughed and after a round of fond farewells, ended the call. Turning the key in the ignition, she headed for home.

Detective Sergeant Cameron Dawson typed the last sentence of the report he'd prepared on the drug bust that had gone down earlier that day. A moment later, he saved his work and logged off. With a sigh, he stretched his arms above his head and leaned back in his cheap, government-issue chair. It squeaked in protest against his weight, but he was beyond caring. His eyes drifted closed with fatigue.

It had been a helluva tough day. The bust had been a culmination after months of surveillance and long hours undercover, deep in the bowels of a drug cartel. Cameron had been only one of several detectives involved in the sting.

More than a thousand pounds of methamphetamine had been confiscated in the raid, along with vast amounts of the chemicals and other drug paraphernalia required to make more. A dozen criminals involved in the extensive meth operations were now behind bars, charged with a string of offenses. It would be a long time before any of them saw the light of day. All in all, it had been a good day's work and Cameron felt justifiably satisfied.

"You did good today, Cam."

Cameron opened his eyes and managed a tired smile in Bryce Sutcliffe's direction. "Thanks, mate. Appreciate you saying so."

Bryce had been caught up in a complex homicide case and hadn't been part of the meth investigation, but like all of their colleagues, they were a team first and foremost and they cheered each other on. Some days the support and encouragement from his fellow officers was needed and sometimes it wasn't, but it warmed Cam through to know the men and women who worked at the City of Sydney Police Station were devoted to each other as much as they were to their jobs.

"You're the talk of the town," Bryce added. "Every media outlet in the city wants a piece of you. Good thing you're kind of pretty. You'll grace the cover of every magazine. Who knows? Hollywood might even come knocking on your door!"

Cam grinned good-naturedly. "You're full of shit, Sutcliffe. I think you've gotten way too close to the hundred or so diapers your girls must go through each week."

Bryce laughed and shook his head. "It just goes to show what you know about kids. The triplets are three-and-a-half. They stopped wearing diapers a year ago."

"Really? 'Cause that sounds awfully young. I had a little sister once. I was eleven when she was born. I remember she was still in diapers, at least at night, right up until she turned four."

"Yeah, well maybe I exaggerated a little bit, but Zoe's mostly toilet trained and the other two won't be far behind." Bryce paused and then frowned. "What do you mean you *had* a little sister? What did you do? Disown her?"

Cam swallowed a gasp, feeling like he'd just taken a punch to his stomach. Bryce's chuckle came to a sudden stop.

"Oh, shit. I'm sorry, Cam. That was stupid of me. She... She didn't die, did she?"

Cam shook his head and ran a hand tiredly over his face. Squeezing his eyes shut against the sudden surge of pain, he clenched his jaw and tried to come up with an answer.

"No, mate, nothing like that. At least, not that I know of. My dear old dad kicked me out when my sister was just a kid." He shrugged. "I haven't seen her since."

Bryce's expression grew more troubled. "Jesus. I had no idea! Shit, I'm sorry, mate. I was only joking. Me and my big mouth. Chanel's always telling me to think before I—"

"Don't sweat it, Bryce. You weren't to know. No one knows. That's the way I like it. I did it tough for a few years, but who doesn't? There wouldn't be many people who go through their childhood without picking up a few scars along the way. That's just the way it is."

"So you haven't seen your sister since—?"

"I left home at sixteen. Cynthia was five. I remember she stood near the front gate and waved good-bye to me until I was out of sight. It was the last time I saw her."

"You never thought of looking her up or finding out where she was?"

Cameron shrugged and did his best to keep the emotion out of his voice. "What's the point? I assume she's still living at home and I have no inclination to see my father ever again. Besides, she probably wouldn't even remember me."

Bryce stared at him in silence, a strange expression on his face. Cam frowned up at him. "What's the matter? You look weird."

Bryce averted his face, but Cam could see he was gnawing on his lower lip—as if he had something to say, but didn't know how. Cam cursed under his breath. What the hell. His secret was out there now. *Did it matter if Bryce knew all the sordid details?*

"I can tell you're bursting to know more," Cam said, forcing a grin. "Ask away."

"It's not that. I... I was speaking to Chanel a few minutes ago. She... She called to ask me if I knew a cop by the name of Cameron Dawson."

Cam frowned. "Why would she ask about me?"

"She was asking on behalf of someone else. A friend of hers who works at the Sydney Harbour Hospital. Georgie Whitely. She's a midwife."

Cam watched Bryce curiously, wondering what point his colleague was trying to make. He raised an eyebrow. "And?"

Bryce looked away and then began to pace. Cam's frown deepened. *What the hell had gotten into the man?* He asked Bryce as much.

"Shit, mate. I'm sorry. It's none of my business, but I promised Chanel I'd speak to you about it."

"About what?" Cam said, not even bothering to hide his exasperation.

"About... About someone who claims to be your sister."

Shock held Cam momentarily immobile. At last, he found his voice though he was filled with a growing sense of unease. "My sister? What the hell would your wife know about my sister?"

"Not Chanel. Her friend. Georgie. The midwife."

"You're not making any sense, Sutcliffe. For Christ's sake spit it out!"

"Georgie Whitely helped deliver the baby of a young girl by the name of Cynthia Dawson. She said she was your sister."

Cam gaped, his jaw slack with shock. It couldn't be *his* sister. *His* sister was barely sixteen. "She must be mistaken," he said, his voice not quite steady. "My sister lives in the country and she's still in high school. Way too young to be having a baby."

Bryce stared at him, his expression solemn. "I don't think so, Cam. Chanel told me the girl was young. A teenager. She insisted she had a brother who was a cop and was stationed in the city. His name was Cameron—"

A loud buzzing noise started in Cameron's head and blocked out the rest of what Bryce had to say. Shock and disbelief rendered him speechless. His heart pounded. *How could his little sister be in a hospital in Sydney, having a baby?* She was still a child! How the hell had their parents let it happen? And where the hell were they?

The thought that his parents might be in Sydney

for the birth sent panic rushing through his veins. As much as he wanted to see his sister, he couldn't risk running into them, especially his father. The rage he'd felt for so long against the man who'd been responsible for throwing him out hadn't abated with time. If anything, the possibility that Ray Dawson was a few mere miles away sent renewed anger surging straight to his brain.

For his mother, he felt nothing but contempt. Right from the beginning, she'd treated him like a slave, but as far as Cam was concerned, it was his dad who bore the blame for putting him out. His dad could have stood up to his mother. His dad could have told her no. But he hadn't. Instead, at his mother's insistence, he'd turned his back on his son. He'd taken the coward's way out and had asked Cam to leave...

A hand on his arm startled him and brought him crashing back to the present. He blinked rapidly in an effort to clear his mind of the bitter memories.

"Are you all right, Cam?" Bryce stared at him with a look of concern and tightened his hold on Cam's arm.

"Yeah... Yeah, I'm fine." Cam pulled away from Bryce's hold and turned away, making an effort to calm his breathing and slow his racing heart. "You surprised me, that's all. I was a little taken aback when you mentioned my sister. And a baby..." He shook his head. "It's a bit much to take in."

"Of course, I understand. I'm sorry. I didn't know. When Chanel asked me if I knew you, of course I told her yes. She asked me to pass on the information about your sister. Georgie's concerned about her. She indicated you were her only family and with her being so young with a new baby... I guess Georgie and the other hospital staff wanted to make sure she and the child were going to be okay."

Cam nodded, his lips compressed. His anger had once again been stowed away in the dark pit of his gut, where he'd kept it hidden for so long. "It's all right, Bryce. I get it. She's sixteen with a newborn. She needs help."

Bryce shrugged. "I'm just the messenger. Do with it what you will."

Cam's thoughts suddenly snared on something Bryce had said. He frowned at his colleague. "Did you say Cynthia told this midwife I was her *only* family?"

"Yeah, I'm sure that's what Chanel said. That's why it seemed so important to let you know. Apparently, she's likely to be discharged tomorrow or the next day at the latest and Georgie wanted to know she had someone looking out for her and the baby."

Cam's frown deepened. If Cynthia told the nurses she didn't have any other family, perhaps his parents weren't at the hospital, like he'd assumed. Surely if they were, the midwife wouldn't have any reason to ask his sister about family. Yes, the more he thought about it, the more he was sure Cynthia had gone to the hospital alone.

A pang of distress ripped through him at the thought of his little sister going through something as momentous as the birth of her child all alone. At least, he assumed she'd been alone.

"What about the father of the baby? Surely, he must be in the picture?"

Bryce shook his head. "I don't know anything about the father. Chanel didn't mention him."

Cam drew in a deep breath that expanded his chest, and then exhaled. More than a decade ago, he'd vowed never to revisit the past. He'd mourned the loss of his little sister, but she'd been collateral damage. She'd been too young to take with him. At the time, his only hope had been that she'd be treated better than he had and that perhaps their adoptive parents would show her a little more love and kindness than they had their only son.

But what if it hadn't worked out that way? What if that bitch of a mother had transferred her wicked attitude toward Cynthia? And what if his father still hadn't found the guts to stand up to the woman? What if Cynthia's teenage years had been as dark and depressing as Cam's? *Had she been kicked out of home, like he had? Was that the reason she was pregnant and alone at sixteen?*

The questions kept coming, racing around and around inside his mind and he had no answers. With gritted teeth, he pressed his hands against both sides of his head in an effort to slow down his thoughts. Bryce threw him another concerned look and with a gargantuan effort, Cam managed to calm himself enough to reassure his colleague.

"It's all right, Bryce. I'm okay. I am. I probably don't look like it, but I'll be fine. I have so many questions about how this came to be. Having no answers is frustrating."

"I understand. You've had a shock. Is there anything I can do?"

"No. I appreciate your offer, but this is something I'm going to have deal with on my own. I'm glad we brought that meth investigation to a close. The boss owes me a few days off. I'll go and see him now and tell him I need to collect. I have to visit with my sister and work out what the hell has gone wrong with her life. A baby at sixteen?" He shook his head, feeling grim. "It's not the best way to get ahead."

"I'm sure between the two of you, you'll be able to work something out. Who knows? Things might not be as bad as they sound. I'm only getting the information secondhand, remember?"

Cam nodded, his gut still heavy with dread. As far as he could see, there was nothing good about a teenage girl who might have been kicked out of home and now had a baby in tow, but maybe he was reading too much into it? Maybe it was like Bryce had said. Maybe it wasn't quite as bad as it sounded.

There was only one way to find out.

Chapter 3

Present day

Dear Diary,

'We're all put on this earth for a purpose.' It's what Matron kept saying to me. It wasn't the first time I'd heard those words. The nuns at my high school had said them, too. It was like they were supposed to instil some kind of fervor in the students to work harder and to excel; to seek out our higher purpose; fulfil our destiny.

Now, so many years later, I don't know if I believe the words or not, but one thing is for sure: I've dedicated my life to finding out. From that very first moment, so long ago, when Matron pulled me aside and whispered to me of her plan, I was sure I'd found my purpose and I've spent many years striving to get it right. I only hope my efforts will one day be recognized.

Not everyone will agree with my methods, but no one will argue with the outcome. Each time, I did what was necessary and right... And THAT I do believe...

Georgie stowed her handbag in her locker and made her way to the staff tea room. A handful of nurses rostered on the morning shift sat around a kitchen table, most of them holding steaming cups. Nodding and smiling in greeting, she went to the small counter and poured herself a cup of coffee. Adding cream and sugar, she took a grateful sip and sighed in satisfaction.

"Ah, there's nothing quite like that first taste of coffee," she murmured and took a seat at the table.

Her mother glanced up from the newspaper spread before her and frowned. "You look a little tired, Georgina. I hope you got some sleep?"

"Yes, but it was fitful. I kept thinking about Cynthia Dawson. I hope Cheryl or someone else from FACS gets here in time. Did we have any patients come in overnight? Is there still a rush for the bed?"

Her mother shook her head. "No, thank goodness, but we have four women due in today. Whether they go into labor on their due date is anybody's guess, but we still need to be prepared." She glanced around the room at the other nurses and then returned her attention to Georgie. "It won't be an issue for Cynthia Dawson. She'll be discharged this morning."

"Marjorie!" Georgie protested. "You can't do that! We need to keep her here at least until she's been seen by FACS. Cheryl promised me she'd drop by to see her today. We can't let the poor girl leave with a new baby without doing something to help."

Marjorie's expression turned grim. Slowly and methodically, she folded the paper and then, with a heavy sigh, she turned to Georgie. "I'm sorry, Georgina, you've misunderstood me. Cynthia Dawson's baby died last night. It was very sad and unexpected, but as you know, these things can happen. The girl is understandably upset, but otherwise in good health. She'll be discharged this morning."

Georgie's heart pounded. She stared at her mother in shock, trying hard to take it in. Cynthia had given birth to a healthy little girl. Georgie had run the newborn tests on the baby herself. They'd all fallen within normal ranges. There had been no indication there was something wrong, and she'd told the young mother so. She shook her head, trying to come to terms with the news the infant was dead.

"H-how... How did it happen?" she stammered.

Her mother shrugged. "Who knows? The baby was taken to the nursery late last evening so Mom could get some sleep. Four hours later, someone checked on the child. She was due for a feeding. The baby was found in her in the crib, cold and unresponsive. CPR was performed, but to no avail. We'd lost her."

Marjorie's voice hitched on the final words and Georgie's heart clenched in pain. The baby might have only been a few hours old and Georgie barely knew the little girl's mom, but knowing the infant had died so suddenly and without explanation... This was the part of her job she hated.

"Who was on duty last night?" she asked quietly.

Her mother's gaze sharpened. "Preliminary cause of death is SIDS, Georgina. Nobody is attributing blame."

Anger flared to life inside her. "I'm not blaming anyone, Marjorie. To the contrary, I wanted to offer my commiserations to the staff involved. I can't imagine how they must feel."

Her mother's expression softened marginally. "Rosemary Lawson and Tammie Sinclair were on duty. Rosemary found the baby."

Georgie absorbed the news somberly. "I'll go and see Cynthia," she said, her voice dull. "She must be distraught. She might have had a tough life, but she loved that little baby. She would have been a good mom, if she'd been given the chance."

Marjorie sent her a pointed look. "She's sixteen, Georgina. What sort of life could she have given a child? I hate to say it, but the death of this baby might be a blessing in disguise."

"No!" Georgie protested on a gasp. "How can you say such a thing? It's not our place to judge." A couple of the other nurses nodded in agreement, looking just as distressed as Georgie. Marjorie eyed each of them solemnly.

"I want you all to listen to me. We work in a hospital. Not everyone gets to go home. It's tough, and every single time it happens, it's hard to accept, but we have to because we're nurses and that's what we do. We try our very best to help the sick get well, but sometimes, no matter what we do, it doesn't work out that way."

"That baby wasn't sick, Marjorie," Georgie said quietly, staring at her mother.

Her mother held her gaze and replied just as quietly. "Apparently, she was."

Tears burned behind Georgie's eyes, but she frantically blinked them away. What her mother said was right. They were professionals—nurses who gave it everything they had—but every now and then, they lost one.

The thought of little Josephine, dying in her crib, all alone, filled Georgie with so much sadness, she wanted to find a quiet place to cry, but this wasn't about her. She had to pull herself together and tend to Cynthia's needs. As awful as Georgie felt, Cynthia had to be feeling a hundred times worse. It was up to Georgie to give her comfort and understanding and whatever else the poor girl required. She refocused on her mother.

"Did anyone hear from Cynthia's brother?"

Marjorie frowned. "I thought you were going to look into that? I assumed he would have been in last night, if he was interested at all."

"I did try to contact him, but I haven't heard anything back."

"I haven't seen any visitors this morning, but I guess it's early yet," one of the other nurses offered.

Georgie acknowledged her comment with a nod. As soon as she'd spoken to Cynthia and offered her condolences, she'd call Chanel and see what she'd learned. With a heavy sigh, she pushed away from the table and headed out the door.

Georgie found Cynthia in a bed that was placed against the far wall. The curtains were drawn, shielding her from the rest of the ward. Sliding the curtains open just enough so that she could slip inside, Georgie approached the girl who was curled up in a fetal position on the bed.

"Cynthia?" she called softly and laid a hand gently on the teen's shoulder. Cynthia tensed and curled herself tighter, covering her head with her hands.

"Cynthia, it's Georgie. I'm the midwife who was here yesterday. I helped you through your labor."

A torrent of sobs shook the young girl's shoulders and were quickly followed by a harsh gasp of pain. Cynthia lifted her head momentarily and stared at Georgie with eyes that were dark and desolate. Tears streamed down the young girl's cheeks and dripped onto the bed. Georgie couldn't remember when she'd seen anyone looking more wretched.

"M-my b-baby! M-my J-Josephine! They t-told m-me she was d-dead! You told me she was fine. What h-happened?" Another howl of pain twisted the girl's face and she once again buried her head in her hands.

Feeling more helpless than she ever had in her life, Georgie perched on the edge of the bed and stroked the girl's matted hair. Even after a shower, the faint stench of body odor and ingrained dirt hovered in the air. Georgie's heart broke at the thought of the life Cynthia had led—and more than likely would continue to lead if help and better fortune didn't come her way.

"*Why?* Please, nurse! Tell me *why!*" The anguished cry was muffled by the bedclothes, but Georgie's eyes filled with tears. She had no answers for the young girl and the knowledge pierced her heart.

Indeed, why did some babies suffer sudden and unexplained deaths? That question had been asked many times in the past, and would no doubt be asked again. Regardless, each time it was howled or screamed or gasped or whispered, it was always difficult to answer.

"Sometimes things happen," she whispered. "They can't be anticipated. I'm so sorry you lost Josephine, Cynthia." With her lips pressed tightly together in an effort to stem her emotions, Georgie murmured more words of reassurance and continued to offer comfort with every stroke she gave Cynthia's hair.

Gradually, the girl's sobs quietened to hiccups. Georgie stood and went into the nearby bathroom. Taking a washcloth, she dampened it under the faucet and came back to where Cynthia lay. Wiping it across her face, she did her best to soothe the pain away, knowing that nothing would remove the feeling of emptiness and devastation, but doing all she could.

"Excuse me. I'm looking for a patient by the name of Cynthia Dawson. Can you tell me where she is?"

The low rumble of a male voice sounded somewhere in the open ward. Georgie set the cloth aside and pulled the curtains back. A man stood a few yards away, talking to one of the other nurses. At Georgie's approach, the nurse looked up, relieved.

"You'll need to speak to Georgie Whitely. She's the nurse looking after Cynthia today."

The man turned his attention to Georgie and lifted a single dark eyebrow in silent query. Her heart skipped a beat. He was tall and broad shouldered and looked about her age. His hazel eyes captured hers for a heart-stopping moment and then dipped lower, raking her slowly from head to toe.

Georgie tensed reflexively, even as heat trailed in the wake of his gaze. Her nipples tightened. As if aware of her contradictory emotions, a mocking expression glinted in his mesmerizing eyes.

He was good looking enough to warrant a second look by any woman with a pulse and his casual air of confidence told her he was well aware of his sex appeal. Annoyed at her body's unwanted reaction to his attractiveness, she cleared her throat.

"I'm Georgie Whitely. I'm a midwife on this ward. How can I help you?"

The gleam of amusement left his face. "I'm looking for my sister, Cynthia Dawson. I've been told she's a patient here."

Georgie's fists clenched reflexively. *So, she hadn't misheard.* He was looking for Cynthia—his sister. As his words registered in her brain, she swallowed a surprised gasp. Chanel had obviously spoken to Bryce.

"You must be Cameron Dawson," she said and was pleased her voice remained steady. At least the poor girl now had a family member to help her through her grief. Georgie couldn't help but feel relieved. At the same time, she wondered where he'd been over the past ten years.

From the look and cut of his charcoal-gray suit, crisp, white business shirt and tastefully matching maroon tie, he'd done well for himself somewhere along the line. *Why hadn't he shared some of his good fortune with his little sister?* She didn't know, but was more than curious to find out.

"Yes, I am. How do you know?"

His question broke into her thoughts and she forced herself to pay attention. "Cynthia gave me your name last night when I asked her about her family. You're a police officer, right?"

"Yes, I'm a detective stationed at the City of Sydney Police Station. I've been there nearly three years."

"Just as Cynthia said."

He frowned as if about to say something, but then appeared to change his mind. Georgie took his arm and led him out of earshot of Cynthia's bed.

"Where are we going?"

Georgie put a finger to her lips. Shooting her another suspicious look, but taking her cue, he followed along beside her in silence. Releasing his arm, she entered a small room off the ward that was used as the patient kitchen. Grateful to find it empty, she waited for him to enter and then moved to close the door.

"What's going on? Why all the secrecy? I'd like to see my sister."

Georgie nodded. She could understand the confusion and mistrust that now filled his eyes. "Mr Dawson, I'm afraid I have some very sad news."

The man's face turned ashen. "Oh, Christ, please don't tell me it's too late! I haven't seen her since she was a little girl and now that she's here, in Sydney..." His voice filled with urgency. "Please, nurse, tell me she's all right! What happened? I need to know what happened."

"Your sister's fine, Mr Dawson, at least, she will be in time. It's her baby I'm talking about. Cynthia gave birth to a little girl yesterday afternoon. I was present for the delivery. Unfortunately, for reasons we can't explain, the baby died in her sleep last night."

Shock replaced the look of desperation that had previously clouded his expression and he reared back. "*Died?* What the hell do you mean, she died? Was there something wrong with her?"

"Not as far as we know. There certainly didn't appear to be anything wrong with her when I saw her last, but the fact is, sometime during the early hours of the morning, the baby stopped breathing."

Cameron shook his head, disbelief and anger flashing in his eyes. "This is bullshit! How could a baby just up and die? This is the twenty-first century and we're standing in a hospital. Babies don't die in hospitals in this day and age!"

His voice had risen by several decibels and

Georgie did her best to remain calm. It was her only hope of soothing his temper.

"I understand your shock and confusion, Mr Dawson, but I don't know what else you want me to say. The truth is, your niece died of cot death, also known as SIDS—Sudden Infant Death Syndrome."

"I know what fucking SIDS means! What the hell do you take me for? An imbecile?"

"I'm sorry, Mr Dawson." She stared at him, trying desperately to find the right words. The truth was, there were never any right words in this kind of situation. She was only grateful over the years she'd spent nursing, she'd rarely been put in this position.

With a muffled curse, he turned away and dragged a hand through his thick, dark hair. Georgie crossed her arms over her chest, praying for the uncomfortable moment to end. When he spoke again, his voice was calmer, more controlled.

"Where's Cynthia? I assume she's been told?" He turned back to look at Georgie and the bleakness in his eyes tore at her heart.

"She's still on the ward, in bed. And yes, of course she's been told. I was with her a moment ago, right before you came in."

"How… How is she?"

"How would you expect?"

"Christ! She's sixteen! She's little more than a child! How the hell is she going to cope with something like this?"

Memories of Georgie's own experience

crashed into her, but she forced them away. Now wasn't the time to remember how it had been for her, pregnant and scared at seventeen. With her jaw clenched, she managed to respond.

"With all due respect, Mr Dawson, I don't think it matters how old you are. The loss of a child is devastating for anyone to endure. It's a tragedy that will take a long time for her to get over. She's going to need a lot of love and support from her family."

His eyes narrowed. "Have you met them? Have you met our parents?"

"No," Georgie replied, eyeing him steadily. "I was referring to you."

"Oh." His mouth closed with a click and a frown marked his brow. A moment later, he spoke again. "What about the father of the baby? Where is he?"

"I don't know. I haven't seen him. We only ask the necessary questions, unless the patient volunteers the information. Cynthia said she hasn't seen the baby's father since she told him she was pregnant."

"Great. That's fucking great. He sounds like a real keeper. She's probably better off without the prick, especially now she doesn't have the baby."

As if suddenly becoming aware of what he'd said, Cameron dragged a hand across his face in anger and frustration. "Shit! What a mess! What a fucking mess!"

Georgie frowned and put her hands on her hips. "Mr Dawson, I'd appreciate it if you'd mind your language and your bedside manner could definitely use some work. At sixteen, your sister has not only given birth on her own, without any support from her family, but in the space of twelve or so hours, she's gone from getting to know her new baby to being told that her perfect little baby's died. She's understandably traumatized and you need to curb any feelings you might have one way or the other about the subject of who and how and why and focus on your sister's needs."

Georgie's breath came fast, but she wasn't finished yet. Stepping closer, she got into his face. "Your little sister's hurting and she doesn't know where to turn, what to do, or how to cope. What she needs right now is your unconditional support and love. Keep your questions to yourself. When she's strong enough and when she's ready, I'm sure she'll tell you what you want to know. Until then, you need to keep your mouth shut and just be there for her. Do you understand?"

Cameron stared at her, looking more than a little taken aback. Gradually, the tension eased from his face and he stepped back, giving both of them some space. Georgie drew in a few deep breaths and tried to get herself back under control. Despite her best intentions, her actions hadn't exactly been those of a calm and collected professional. Her cheeks heated with embarrassment. She owed him an apology.

"I'm sorry, I shouldn't have said that. I was out of line. I—"

"No," he said, cutting her off. "I'm glad you did. I... I probably needed to hear it." He blew out his breath on a heavy sigh and once again turned away. As if unable to stand still, he began to pace the small room.

"When my colleague first mentioned Cynthia last night and the fact that she'd just had a baby, I was shocked and angry. I'm eleven years older than my sister. I left home when she was a small child and she was still in the care of our parents. Discovering she'd become a mom at sixteen confused the hell out of me. I was bombarded with questions, but had no answers." He shook his head and Georgie felt his frustration.

He spun on his heel and planted his hands on his hips, staring at her. "Where were my parents when this was happening? How did my baby sister come to be in Sydney, miles from home, pregnant and alone? I couldn't help but think maybe, just maybe they'd treated her as poorly as they'd treated me and the guilt of that possibility has been eating me alive." His breath came harsher and his hands clenched into fists. Renewed anger flashed in his eyes.

"The very thought that Cynthia's been forced out on the streets makes my blood boil. I don't want to believe it, but nothing else makes sense. If they were supporting her through her pregnancy, they'd be here, to support her through the birth. Wouldn't they?"

Once again, he turned his fierce gaze on Georgie and she could barely manage a nod. She was trying to keep up with the outpouring of past anger and hurts. She could understand his reaction. She'd feel the same way if this happened to one of her sisters.

"I-I probably shouldn't tell you this," she started hesitantly, "but you'll find out soon enough. If I had to guess, I'd say your sister's been living on the streets. She was very evasive about her living arrangements, apart from saying she lived on her own and there are other signs—physical signs that she's been doing it rather tough."

"*Fu—*" His jaw clenched and Georgie could see the effort it took him to control his temper. "I'm going to kill him. I'm going to track down that cowardly, sorry excuse of a father and kill him with my bare hands."

The coldness in his voice sent a shiver up Georgie's spine. She could only hope it was anger and desperation talking, and that he didn't really mean it. Dismissing his declaration, she turned the conversation back to the matter at hand.

"Let's talk about Cynthia. Is there somewhere she can stay? Do you have room at your place? I think it might be best if someone keeps a close eye on her for the next little while. It's hard to know how she'll react or if she'll be debilitated by her grief. Everyone's different, but there's no doubt she'll be grieving for a while. I can recommend a counselor at the hospital who specializes in this kind of thing, but there is a rather long waiting list, unless you can afford to have her see someone privately."

"I live alone in a three-bedroom condominium. I'll do and provide whatever Cynthia needs. Just tell me what that is, and I'll make sure it happens."

Georgie held his gaze and in that moment believed the integrity and determination she saw in his eyes. She hid her relief. So many of her patients had no one to turn to for support. Even those who left the hospital with their newborn in tow still worried her when she knew they'd be battling with the hardships of child rearing on their own. She'd never raised a child, but she knew enough to know it wasn't easy and was made harder still when you were running solo.

"Cynthia's lucky to have you," she said and meant it. Her first impression of Cameron hadn't done him justice. It was obvious there was more substance to him than that of the self-absorbed, arrogant ladies' man he portrayed.

He shrugged off her praise as if it were unnecessary and even more, unwanted. She tightened her jaw and curbed her irritation. She didn't say things like that just for the sake of it, but what would he know? He didn't know anything about her and was unlikely ever to find out, either. After his sister was discharged, she'd never see him again. The thought was a little disappointing.

"Can I go to her now?" he asked, breaking into her musings. His voice held more than a hint of impatience.

"Of course, but if you don't mind, I'd like to have a moment alone with her to let her know you're here. I'm guessing your visit will be as much a surprise for her as the news about her was for you."

He compressed his lips, but gave her a brief nod of understanding—appreciative and almost friendly. She brushed past him on her way out the door. A whisper of his expensive cologne tickled her nose and she deliberately refused to think about how nice it smelled.

She couldn't help but wonder how he felt about adoption in general, but it was obvious his relationship with his adoptive parents was less than amicable. Given her past, it would be beyond unwise to fall for a man who appeared to have issues with at least part of the adoption process. He might be good-looking, and smell nice, but she didn't need a complication like Cameron Dawson in her life, no matter how tempting.

Pushing the unsettling thoughts aside, Georgie strode across the polished linoleum floor until she reached the end of the ward. She eased open the curtain, calling out softly to the young girl who remained curled up in the bed.

"Cynthia? How are you doing?"

The girl rolled over and stared at her. Georgie was relieved to see the majority of Cynthia's tears had subsided. Red, swollen eyes and the occasional sniffle were the only reminders of her recent distress.

"You have a visitor, someone who'd like to see you," Georgie said.

Cynthia frowned and Georgie could tell the teen was trying to process Georgie's words. "A visitor? For me?"

"Yes. You mentioned yesterday afternoon you had a brother. I made a call and managed to track him down. He's waiting outside. He'd like to see you."

Cynthia's eyes went wide with disbelief. Hope

and fear warred on her face. "You found Cameron? He's *here*? At the hospital?"

"Yes."

"Does he know about...Josephine?"

"Yes."

The girl closed her eyes and fresh tears welled up beneath her lids and slid slowly down her cheeks. She lifted a hand and brushed them away and then opened her eyes again. She looked at Georgie and most of the fear had gone. Instead, her expression was filled with hope.

"Would you like to see your brother, Cynthia?" Georgie asked quietly.

"Yes! Yes! Oh, my goodness! Yes! Please, ask him to come in."

Georgie opened the curtain and beckoned to Cameron who stood waiting a short distance away. No doubt he'd heard their conversation through the thin fabric. He muttered a few cursory words of thanks and pushed past her. Georgie moved out of the way and closed the curtains after him.

"Cam, oh, Cam! I can't believe it's you! Oh, my goodness! You're so huge! I barely recognize you!"

"How are you, little sis? It's so good to see you, all grown up! I've missed you so much!"

Their voices were filled with laughter and tears and most of all, love. Georgie sighed quietly in relief and walked away with a much lighter heart. With time to heal and the love and support of her brother, Cynthia would be fine. For that, Georgie couldn't help but be grateful.

CHAPTER 4

Cameron helped his little sister into the passenger seat of his second-hand, silver Audi R8 Coupe and closed the door behind her. His head spun with a million frantic thoughts. *What the hell was he supposed to do now?*

After her initial joy at reuniting with him, Cynthia had slumped into a daze of sullenness and depression. Each question he threw at her received monosyllabic answers and he was fast running out of patience. Knowing his short temper was the last thing she needed, he did his best to suck in a few deep breaths and ease the tension from his shoulders.

He'd signed the discharge papers and had effectively agreed to take on the responsibility of his minor sister, but he wasn't quite sure where to start. He hadn't been responsible for anyone but himself from the moment he'd left home, and the knowledge that Cynthia was now depending upon him for her welfare, scared him. Most days he was lucky to keep himself stable and heading down the right path, and that was before taking on the burden of a teenage sister and seeing to her needs.

Physical needs he could manage. Like he'd told the cute nurse, he had plenty of room in his condo. It was the emotional stuff that was in much shorter supply. He'd learned a decade ago to shut down that side of him. It was safer and a whole lot less painful if he kept his feelings under control. But his little sister was hurting badly, dealing with the traumatic loss of her baby, and it was up to him to help her.

The thought that she was no longer alone surged through him, fierce and strong. By some stroke of luck, karma—whatever—he'd reconnected with her and he was determined to be there for her for as long as she needed him. She was a child dealing with one of life's toughest lessons. There was no way he'd let her go through any more on her own.

Climbing behind the wheel, he glanced across at her. Her head was turned away from him. She stared out the window. Her hands were twisted in her lap and fresh tears slid slowly down her cheeks. Sadness flooded through him, but there was nothing he could do.

Feeling helpless and totally inadequate, Cam switched on the ignition and kept his focus on the road. The sassy midwife had been right. There would be time enough for questions later. Right now, his baby sister needed to be left alone and given time to heal.

"Cam?"

Cameron started at her husky question. Weaving in and out of the burgeoning midday traffic, he'd let the silence between them lengthen and had been lost in his heavy thoughts. It took him a moment to realize Cynthia had spoken. "Yes, honey?"

"Could you... Could you stop by a K-Mart?"

Cam frowned with uncertainty. "Now?"

She nodded and kept her eyes lowered.

"You want to go shopping?"

"No! I mean...yes... That is..." A blush stained her cheeks crimson.

Cam shook his head, still confused. "There's a mall not far from where I live, but... Are you sure you're up to it? You've only just come out of hospital. I thought you might want to go home and rest. I could fix us some lunch and get you settled and then—"

"I need some things," she blurted out, still refusing to look at him.

"What kind of things? I have spare toothbrushes in the bathroom and you're more than welcome to borrow my—"

"Women's things."

"Oh." Now it was his turn to blush.

"Could we just go to a drugstore?" she said quietly.

His lips compressed and he nodded. "Sure."

In the end, he gave her a handful of cash and told her to go and buy what she needed. She'd taken the money gratefully and had headed into the store. Cam waited for her in his car. There were some things even an older brother shouldn't be forced to do and this was one of them. Not for the first time, he wondered what the hell he was going to do.

Georgie scanned her list of patients and tried to suppress a sigh. She was back at work after a couple days off and had hoped to return feeling rested and rejuvenated, but it hadn't worked out that way. Her mother's mention of Georgie's teenage indiscretion had stirred up painful, old memories and had played on her mind night and day until she was all but consumed by thoughts of the baby she'd given away.

She'd given birth to a little boy and he'd been perfect in every way. Not that she'd been allowed much time with him. Her mother had seen to that. Marjorie had assured her it was for the best; that adoption was the only sensible thing to do. Georgie was seventeen with the world at her feet. A baby was the last thing she needed.

Over the months of her pregnancy, her mother had slowly worn her down until Georgie finally agreed to sign the papers, but the knowledge that she had a child—a son—living somewhere in the world was never far from her thoughts.

Hearing Cynthia talk about the horrible home life she and her brother had endured with their adoptive parents had brought the whole awful time back and Georgie couldn't help but wonder if her son had fared better than them. She could only hope and pray he'd been adopted by loving parents who treated him with kindness and respect, but she couldn't shake the dreadful feeling that things might not have turned out like that.

What if he'd been adopted by people like the Dawsons? What if he were being mistreated and would one day be forced out on the street?

The knowledge that she couldn't do anything about it was slowly driving her mad. Though the laws now allowed a birth mother to seek contact with her child, she was torn about whether it was the right thing to do. Her son was now a twelve-year-old. Presumably, he was settled and comfortable in his life. She had no way of knowing if he'd been told the truth about his adoption, or how he'd react if he hadn't.

She'd agreed to give him up and it had been the hardest thing she'd ever done. *Was it fair to either of them to seek him out again? Would he even want to see her?* No, she had to believe he was happy; that he was better off without her in his life. Making contact with him now would only scare and confuse him and he might struggle with the fact she'd given him away. He might even blame her, *hate* her...

A shaft of pain tore through her at the thought and she pressed a hand against her mouth to hold back a gasp. She hadn't wanted to give him up... She *hadn't*! And yet, she had done just that. With the slightest movement of her hand, she'd signed all her parental rights away...

"Hey, Georgie, are you working on the post-natal ward tonight?"

Blinking away her heavy thoughts, Georgie turned to greet the nurse who strode up beside her.

"Hey, Julia. Yes, I'm looking after the moms and bubs in beds ten to thirteen."

Julia grimaced. "You're in for a tough night. Two of the four are heroin addicts. Both of them used constantly during their pregnancies. The woman in bed twelve's addicted to methamphetamine and the one in bed eleven's a chronic alcoholic. Her baby's been born with a severe case of fetal alcohol syndrome."

Georgie's heart sank. Mothers withdrawing from long-term drug and alcohol addictions were often rude and demanding and their newborns usually also had serious issues. While still in utero, the babies had become used to regular drug and alcohol fixes. Now that they'd been born, the drugs had come to a halt. It was imperative they withdraw from them slowly.

"I've been on a couple of days off. I'm not familiar with any of these patients," she said and continued to walk toward the nurses' station. Julia kept pace with her.

"Keep an eye on the woman in bed ten. Her partner smuggled in heroin last night. Unfortunately, she'd already taken the hit before we discovered it."

"Had she already been given her methadone dose?"

"Of course. A few hours before. She'd even attended a therapy session earlier that morning."

Georgie shook her head in despair. While inpatients, both mothers and babies received treatment for their addictions in the form of voluntary counseling and prescribed medication in strictly controlled measures. It was hoped the regulated dosage of methadone would aid both patients in a steady, controlled withdrawal with fewer side effects, but it was meant to be taken *instead* of the illicit opiate, not in addition.

The biggest problem the staff faced in the hospital wasn't dealing with the withdrawal symptoms, it was ensuring the patients remained drug free while they were in the hospital's care. While drugs and alcohol were strictly prohibited, it didn't stop the women and even the babies from craving another fix.

Some of the mothers promised to stay clean, but Georgie had learned the hard way their promises often meant nothing. If they weren't getting a fix outside the hospital boundaries, their partners brought it in, like in the case of the woman in bed ten, and they were getting high right on the ward, behind the seclusion of their privacy curtains.

It was incredibly sad and frustrating for Georgie to watch the women destroy themselves over and over again. They were mothers. Their babies were as dependent upon them as any newborn could be. It was beyond difficult to watch the little infants, already addicted to drugs, knowing that in a few days they'd be discharged along with their mothers and their lives would become something Georgie couldn't even bear to think about.

"How is her baby doing?" Georgie asked quietly.

"About as well as you'd expect. He's suffering many of the usual signs of withdrawal: sweating, fever, shaking, vomiting and diarrhea. Poor thing."

"When's his mother due to be discharged?"

"Tomorrow. FACS have been notified, but so far, no one's made an appearance on the ward. Let's hope someone assesses her before she leaves."

A tension headache made itself known behind Georgie's eyes and she squeezed them shut in an effort to dislodge it. Her shift had only just begun and already a familiar sense of hopelessness and dread churned inside her.

It was hospital policy to notify the people from FACS when the staff identified a baby at risk, but the social workers were overworked and understaffed and there just weren't enough of them to follow up on every case. Georgie hated to think how many children were suffering because of a lack of government resources.

With every drug-addicted mother who left the hospital with her baby in her arms, a tiny piece of Georgie died. She wanted to take each and every baby home and raise it herself—and that wasn't merely a response to her ever-present yearning for her own son.

But even if it were possible, it could never happen. There were simply too many. She could never take care of them all. That was the reason she'd felt so happy when Cynthia Dawson's brother had been found.

It had been a fortnight since the pair of them had left the ward, hand in hand, and Georgie had been almost overwhelmed with relief. Cynthia might not have a baby to care for, but she was still a child herself. And for the moment, grieving deeply over the loss of her newborn, she needed a lot of love and support. Although she hardly knew him, Georgie was confident her brother could provide that. His words and actions showed how much he cared. From the moment he'd arrived on the ward, much of his attention and focus had been on his sister.

Georgie thought of his slow and tantalizing once-over and a shiver of remembered heat swept over her. He was a very attractive man and one she wished she could spend more time with, despite the potential minefields surrounding the issue of adoption. Still, just because he had attitude concerning his adoptive parents, that didn't mean he was against adoption, period. *Did it?* She couldn't help but wonder if she'd ever be given the opportunity to find out.

CHAPTER 5

The month of May had all but evaporated and soon winter would set in. Pale morning light filtered in through the tinted windows that lined two walls of the squad room. Cameron sat at his desk, methodically going through files and feeling less than enthusiastic.

"Cameron, have you got a minute?"

Cameron looked up from his computer screen and nodded toward his boss. "Sure, Holt. I'll be there in a minute." He saved the work on his screen and then pushed away from his desk. He met Holt in his office.

"What can I do for you, boss?"

Detective Superintendent Holt Denman's expression was troubled and he took a moment to answer. It looked like he was trying to choose his words with care. Tension slowly took hold in Cam's gut. "Is everything all right?"

Holt gave a brief nod and pursed his lips. "Yes. I've just had a rather disturbing phone call. It's taking me a moment to get my head around it."

"What is it?"

"The New South Wales Police Commissioner just called me. He's had a visit from the premier. The man's accusing the staff at the Sydney Harbour Hospital of either stealing or murdering his grandson. It appears he can't quite make up his mind. Apparently the child died suddenly at the hospital a couple of days ago, within hours after his birth."

Shock ricocheted through Cam's body. *"What?"*

"Yeah, I know. It sounds ludicrous and the commissioner's inclined to believe it's nothing more than shock and grief talking, but the premier's insisting he has proof."

"Wow."

Holt grimaced. "Tell me about it."

"I can't wait to hear," Cam said, breathing a little more freely. His initial shock at Holt's announcement had worn off.

The New South Wales Premier, John Jamison, was known for his over-dramatic and somewhat paranoid ways. He'd once accused a cleaner of spying on him from the bathroom adjoining his office. After a comprehensive internal investigation at the expense of the tax payer, it was decided the cleaner, who barely spoke a word of English and had been in Australia less than six months, was merely there to replace the supply of toilet paper and had been oblivious to the premier's presence.

"I told him you'd be available to interview him within the next half hour. I understand he's making his way down from Macquarie Street as we speak."

Cam threw his boss a wry grin. "Gee, thanks, boss. What did I do to get on your wrong side today?"

Holt laughed off the question. "What can I say? I guess you got lucky. You've had a bit of free time on your hands since that meth investigation wound up. You might as well put your time to good use. The premier's interview ought to provide you with an interesting diversion, if nothing else."

Cam grimaced and made his way out of Holt's office. He detoured via the staff tea room and poured his second cup of strong black coffee. It was barely nine in the morning, but, more often than not, he relied on a regular intake of caffeine to get him through the day. It probably wasn't healthy, but there were a hell of a lot of other vices which were worse. Besides, ever since his sister had moved in, he'd found it hard to sleep and the shot of caffeine lifted him out of the miasma of fatigue.

Most nights, he'd wake in the middle of the night to the sound of his sister crying. It broke his heart to listen to her distress. He'd found an excellent psychiatrist by the name of Ava Wolfe who'd come highly recommended by the cute midwife at the hospital, but so far, his sister seemed to be making very little progress. It worried him that it had been more than a fortnight and she still cried herself to sleep.

Was that normal? Perhaps he should be doing

more to help her? The problem was, he had no idea what to expect, or what to do. If it were a guy, he'd get him busy with sports, like football or car racing or even hiking in the mountains, but Cynthia was a girl—and a teenager at that. He had no idea what teenage girls did to distract themselves when things got tough.

Maybe he should contact the midwife? She'd introduced herself as Georgie Whitely and had seemed to care what happened to his sister. Perhaps Ms Whitely could help give him some ideas about what to do. She was a woman and a baby nurse, experienced in dealing with young mothers. She probably knew better than he did what they needed to help them heal when life took an unexpected and tragic turn.

Thoughts of the spirited midwife suddenly filled his head. The fire in her dark brown eyes and the passion in her voice when she'd spoken to him about his sister remained fixed in his memory. She'd only met Cynthia the day prior to his arrival and yet it was clear the nurse already cared a great deal about what happened to her. Georgie Whitely had a generous heart. She also had a sweet ass and lips that looked so full and soft he couldn't help but wonder what they'd taste like.

He could phone her on the pretext of needing advice. It wasn't really a pretext... After all, she already knew he'd agreed to take care of Cynthia. A fortnight down the track, it wasn't a stretch to imagine he might be experiencing difficulties. Grief was such a personal thing. Everyone dealt with it differently. A teenage girl, mourning the loss of her baby, was not the run-of-the-mill variety.

Besides, his request for advice wouldn't be deceitful. He was struggling to know just what it was Cynthia needed. The feeling of helplessness was so foreign to him, frustration was raising its ugly head along with increasing fatigue and the last thing his sister needed was to be living with an irritable brother. He needed to get a handle on things and understand what it was she was going through. Then he might be in a position to help her more effectively, beyond his lame efforts, to date.

Glancing at his watch, he noticed he still had fifteen minutes before the premier was due to arrive. He reached across his desk for the phone and called directory assistance, seeking the number for the Sydney Harbour Hospital. He didn't know if Georgie would be at work, but he was willing to give it a shot. Without her private phone number, the hospital was his only way of contacting her.

He listened while the robotic, computer-generated voice gave him the information he sought. Scrawling the number on a piece of paper for future reference, he ended the call and then dialed again, this time to the hospital. The phone was answered on the second ring.

"Sydney Harbour Hospital. May I help you?"

"Could you put me through to Ward Seven, please?"

Cam waited while the phone rang out again, this time for much longer than before. At last, it was picked up and a woman answered.

"Ward Seven."

Cam cleared his suddenly dry throat. "Ah, I'm wondering if Georgie Whitely is available."

"Yes, she is. May I ask who's calling?"

"Cameron Dawson. My sister was a patient on your ward a fortnight ago. Nurse Whitely took care of her. I was wondering if I could speak with her."

There was a slight pause and then the woman answered. "I'll see if she's free. I won't be a minute."

Silence greeted him on the other end. Cam knew that at any moment Georgie could pick up the phone to talk to him and his guts twisted with nerves.

What was he going to say to her? Just come right out with it and ask her for a date? No, that wouldn't do. He'd play it cool, ask her for advice about Cynthia and gage her reaction; work his way up from there.

"Georgie Whitely."

The sound of her earthy, no-nonsense voice brought back a rush of memories of his all-too-brief encounter with the pretty midwife. Once again, he cleared his throat.

"Georgie, it's Cameron Dawson. I'm—"

"Cynthia's brother," she interrupted. "Yes, I remember. Is she okay?"

The concern was back in her voice and Cam felt warmth spread through him. Georgie Whitely was just as good and kind as he'd guessed. Throw in the fact she was sexy as hell and he couldn't help but be interested. He only hoped she was single and that she might be open to getting to know him better.

Realizing she was still waiting for him to respond, he answered in a rush. "Um, kind of. The thing is, I don't really know. Cynthia's been seeing that psychiatrist you recommended and some days she seems all right, but she still cries herself to sleep all the time and I wake up and hear her crying through the night. The truth is, I'm not sure what else I can do to help her. I was hoping you might have some ideas."

"Poor Cynthia! She's so young to be dealing with this kind of stuff! It would get an adult down, let alone a teen! It sounds like you're doing all the right things. It's only been a fortnight. It's going to take some time."

"So a fortnight's not too long to still be completely in distress... Is that what you're saying?"

"Grief is a personal thing," the woman on the other end of the phone explained in a gentle voice. "Some people take longer than others to find their way back to the way they used to be. Give her time. Other than the things you're already doing, that's all you can do."

Cam swallowed his impatience. "I get that, I really do. But I'm a guy. We fix problems by *doing* things. It's the only way we know how. But Cynthia isn't interested in any of my suggestions to do things and I was hoping that you might have some of your own... Being a woman and all..."

His words drifted off and he cursed under his breath. Heat crept across his cheeks. But when she spoke again she didn't sound offended; rather her tone was amused and he was relieved.

"Well," she began, "being a woman and all, I'd probably want to be left alone. It's what *we* do to fix problems. We turn inward and examine the issue from every angle, analyzing, dissecting, going over it again and again. It's probably not the best way to deal with grief. In fact, it's probably the worst thing we can do, but that's the way it is for many of us."

"That's exactly what Cynthia's doing!" he exclaimed. "She spends hours in her room with the blinds drawn, sitting alone in the dark. I try and talk with her, to engage her and interest her in other things, but she just keeps shutting me down."

"You're giving her everything she needs right now. A safe place to live, food in her stomach, unconditional love and support. Don't be too hard on yourself. Losing a loved one, particularly a baby, is tough on everyone. Don't forget, she's only sixteen. Like I said, you're going to have to give her time."

"And then what?" he pushed, needing something more concrete to focus on. "Can you suggest anything I can *do* to help? I can't stand by and watch her in distress without *doing* something."

Georgie chuckled quietly in his ear. "There you go, wanting to do something again. Men and women are different. We don't think about things the same way, but if you really do want to *do* something, how about taking her to the movies, or to a concert given by her favorite local band?

What are her hobbies, her interests? What did she do in her spare time, before the baby, before her life took such a tragic turn?"

Cam frowned and tried to think of anything his sister enjoyed. The truth was, he didn't know. She'd been a kid when he'd left home and if he were honest, he'd been shocked at the changes in her since he'd last seen her. The physical signs of her grief were difficult to take, but the other signs of the life she'd lived beforehand jarred him even more.

The first time he'd seen her, her hair looked like it hadn't been washed for longer than he cared to think. Her fingernails were chipped and broken and stained with what looked like years of dirt, despite the fact he was almost certain she would have been given a shower prior to giving birth. She'd worn a clean white hospital gown that day, but still the unmistakeable stench of body odor had permeated the air. Apart from her big blue eyes that had filled with tears upon seeing him, she looked nothing like the little girl he remembered from his unsettling past.

Though he was burning to know what had happened in the years since he'd been tossed out of their family home, he accepted her need for solitude and for time to come to terms with the death of her child. The little information he'd been able to glean from her was that she'd run away from home. He could only assume relations had deteriorated even more between her and their parents after he'd left.

A few nights earlier, they'd both been unable to sleep and found themselves out on the balcony. She hadn't offered any details why she'd left home, but she'd told him about the father of her baby and how she'd met him on the street. Albert, the baby's dad, was a little older than her and kind of cute and most of all, he'd made her laugh. For nearly a year they'd been sharing space and comforting each other in an abandoned warehouse. And then she'd realized she was pregnant.

Cam was secretly horrified that she'd risked her health in such a dangerous way by having unprotected sex—even if it was with only one partner—but he forced his anxious thoughts away in an effort to concentrate on what she was trying to share with him about her past. She wasn't stupid, by any means, but it wasn't like she was in a position to head to the nearest drugstore and purchase what was required.

It was obvious she'd been needy, starved for love and affection. Albert had come along and offered her the comfort she so desperately wanted. At the time, getting pregnant was probably the least of his sister's worries.

He wanted to ask if she'd been tested for STDs, but didn't want to say or do anything to disturb their fragile connection. He could only hope the hospital had a policy and tested the young moms for those things as a matter of course.

Now, he waited for answers from another woman and wondered what she'd say. He only hoped that it would be something he could put into practice to ease the suffering from his little sister's face.

"What if *I* take her somewhere?" she suggested.

Georgie's question broke into his thoughts and he snapped back to attention.

"I could take her to a spa," she added. "We could have a facial or a massage. We could even do our nails. I've been planning to do that anyway, as a way to relax on a day off. Do you think she'd enjoy something like that?"

Cam blinked. It had never occurred to him that Cynthia might like a day of pampering and relaxation, but the more he pondered it, the more he thought she would. He still remembered when she was a little girl, how much she loved painting her nails. She'd prance around the house with a different color on every finger and proudly wave them in front of his face.

'Look, Cam! Aren't they pretty? Don't you just love the colors?' she'd say. Then she'd giggle. He couldn't help but smile at the memory.

"I think it's a great idea!" he said. "But I can't expect you to take her. I mean, you barely know her. I get that you care, and I think that's great, but—"

"Cameron, I'm happy to do it. Can't we just leave it at that?"

Cam's gut clenched at her use of his name. It was the first time she'd called him anything other than Mr Dawson. The name had never sat well with him. As far as he was concerned, Mr Dawson was his father. One of the things Cam liked about being a police officer was that he was forever introduced as Detective Sergeant Dawson. No more Mr Dawson for him and that's just the way he liked it.

Now, indecision gnawed at his gut. He wanted so much to accept Georgie's invitation, but was it fair to have her do this for them?

No, not for *them*. For his sister. He had to remind himself she was offering to do it because she was kind and good, not because she wanted to get inside his pants. A guilty flush swept over his cheeks, but he refused to pay it any heed. *So what if he found her attractive?* It wasn't a crime and it wasn't like he could help it. If she didn't feel the same way about him, then so be it. At least he would have given it a try. And in the meantime, she might just be able to help his little sister, and for that, he'd do anything.

He released the breath he hadn't been aware he'd been holding and blew it out on a relieved sigh. "Okay. Thank you. I... I really appreciate what you're doing."

She laughed. "Well, I haven't done anything yet, but let's hope Cynthia responds. It's important for her to embrace the world again and every good thing in it. She's young. She's resilient. Be patient. All she needs is—"

"Time," he interrupted with a smile. "Don't worry, I get it."

"When do you think I should call on her?" Georgie asked.

"I'm at work at the moment, but I'll speak with her tonight. I'll phone you later, if you like. Are there any days you aren't available? When's your next day off?"

"I have a couple of days off coming up. If you let me know in the morning whether she's keen, I'll have time to book an appointment at the day spa."

Cam nodded in satisfaction. "It sounds like a plan."

"I'll give you my cell number. That way you can reach me when I'm away from work." She gave Cam the details and straight away he added them to his phone.

He'd achieved even more than he'd set out to, having not only obtained her help with Cynthia, but he'd gained the promise of her company, too. Okay, so he wouldn't be accompanying them to the spa, but she still had to come to his home to collect his sister and then return her again. That presented an array of opportunities, limited only by his imagination.

Once again, Georgie interrupted his thoughts. "It'd better go. I have babies due for a feeding."

"Of course," he replied and then remembered his earlier question. "I was wondering if you could tell me whether Cynthia has been tested for STDS? I'm concerned because of her lifestyle and..."

His voice petered off in embarrassment, but Georgie appeared to take his question in her stride.

"Of course. You have reason to be concerned. And yes, to answer your question, it's hospital policy to run blood tests for STDs. Cynthia's results came back clear. It's only the HIV and Hepatitis results that take longer. She'll need to be retested in three months and then again at six months, to be sure."

Cam compressed his lips, but nodded. "Thank you. I appreciate you letting me know."

"No problem. I guess I'll see you in a couple of days."

With a surge of anticipation and heartfelt thanks, Cam smiled and ended the call.

Holt strode toward him. "The premier's waiting downstairs. I'll bring him up and put him in Interview Room Two."

Cam's pleasant thoughts scattered like the wind and once again, he focused on the job at hand and got down to business.

CHAPTER 6

Cam stared across at the premier and tried hard to hide his disbelief. The portly, balding leader of the State Government got redder and redder in the face as he continued to blister Cam's ears.

"I'm telling you, Detective Sergeant Dawson, there's something evil going on in that hospital! My grandson was born perfectly healthy. I was right outside the birthing suite when he drew his first breath. My daughter spent hours holding him and marvelling over every little thing. Both the midwife and the doctor gave him the all clear. When I left that hospital a little after eight, there was absolutely nothing wrong with him. And now he's dead—from SIDS, apparently. At least, that's what they're telling us. I don't believe it for a minute."

Premier John Jamison's legendary piercing gaze settled with uncomfortable intensity on Cameron who did his best not to squirm. So far, the man had insisted the hospital was involved in everything from stealing innocent babies and selling them overseas to outright murder. At the moment, he appeared to have returned to his earlier conspiracy theory that staff members of the maternity ward were involved in procuring children to sell on the black market.

"It's big business, Detective," the premier continued matter-of-factly. "I've read about what happens in countries like the Philippines. Everything's up for sale, including children. Why would Australia be any different? My grandson was a normal, healthy newborn. The next day, they said he was dead."

"Did you see his body?"

"No. I wasn't there when they brought my daughter the news. They told her very early in the morning."

"What about your daughter? Did she have time with her deceased child? I understand many hospitals allow that kind of thing."

"Not as far as I know. Danielle's understandably in shock. She can't remember a lot of what was said even though it only happened two days ago. She's still having trouble with the whole thing. I had to call my doctor and have him prescribe something to help calm her down. She's been inconsolable." Once again, he turned his steely eyed gaze on Cameron.

"I demand that something be done, Detective. I want that hospital closed down and the management arrested!"

Cam sucked in a deep breath and exhaled on a heavy sigh. He knew all about supporting a loved one through the loss of a child, but this circumstance still didn't mean that the hospital was to blame. The premier's demands to shut down the largest and most prestigious hospital in the country—based on not a scrap of evidence of wrongdoing—was almost laughable, but Cam knew better than to give the man any indication his concerns weren't being taken seriously.

"Mr Jamison," he said quietly. "How old is your daughter?"

The man looked down at his hands, where they were twisted in his lap. "She's eighteen."

Cam hid his surprise and asked his next question. "Do you think she'd be well enough to come to the station and make a statement? With all due respect, you've admitted you weren't there when she was told about her baby's death. It might help clarify a few matters if I can speak with her directly."

The premier kept his gaze averted. "I told you, she isn't handling things very well. She's still grieving deeply for the loss of her child. We all are."

"I understand, Premier, but if you want me to investigate, I still need to speak with her while her memory is fresh. The longer we wait, the more likely she'll forget certain details and it could be something important."

This time, a dark red flush started at the premier's neck and spread across his face. His fidgeting got worse and Cam couldn't help but wonder why he appeared to be so uncomfortable.

"The thing is," the premier began, "Danielle's

not the most reliable of witnesses. She's... She's had a drug problem for the past few years. Her mother and I have been doing what we can to find her help and get her off the stuff, but it's been an uphill battle. The truth is, right now she doesn't want to get clean."

Cam stared at the premier in surprise. He'd had no idea the politician's daughter was a drug addict. He shook his head in silent commiseration. It just went to show, no matter where someone fit in society's hierarchy, no family was immune to stress and heartache. He could only be grateful Cynthia hadn't gone down that track.

"I appreciate what you're saying, Mr Jamison and I'm very sorry to hear about the difficulties your family have faced, but I really need to speak with Danielle and find out what she knows. I assume there was a funeral?"

"Yes."

"Who made the arrangements?"

"I did."

"Where was it held?"

"A staff member of the hospital gave Danielle a business card with the name of a funeral home printed on it. The *Peaceful Passing Funeral Parlor and Crematorium* on the corner of Booth Street and Parramatta Road. We held a private service on site. The baby was cremated."

Cam nodded. Cynthia had done the same thing and at the very same venue. At the time, Cam hadn't thought to ask her about her choice of funeral home. Now, he could only assume she'd also received a recommendation from the hospital. He admired their thoughtful and sensitive approach during such a difficult situation. It was kind of them to smooth the way at such a distressing time. Many young patients, lost in their grief, wouldn't know where to start or even to have anywhere to turn.

Cam sighed softly. Sometimes life just handed out shit and you had to deal with it as best you could. There was no other way around it. Wishing he had something better to offer the premier, he leaned his elbows on the desk and shot the man a sympathetic look.

"I'm sorry for your loss, Premier, and I wish I could help you with this, but until I speak with Danielle, I don't even know for sure the true facts. You've admitted you weren't there when the baby died. You think your daughter wasn't given time with her son after he died, but you're not certain of that, either." He dragged in a breath and continued, keeping his gaze on the premier's, trying to make the man see.

"I'd appreciate if you'd call me so we can set up a meeting—when Danielle is feeling up to it. I understand she's still grieving and her memory might not be up to scratch, but unfortunately, I do need to hear her side of the story before I can proceed."

The premier's gaze narrowed and another angry flush climbed up his neck and spread across his face. "So, until then, you're going to do nothing. Is that what you're telling me?"

Cam bit back a sigh. *What the hell did the man expect of him?* He opened his mouth to pose the curt question and then closed it again. Aggravating the premier wouldn't get him anywhere and would only exacerbate the man's already raw nerves.

In exasperation, he said, "If you like, I can speak with Deborah Healy. She's the General Manager of the Sydney Harbour Hospital. I'll see what she knows about your grandson's death."

"Ha! Deborah Healy!" he scoffed. "After everything that's gone down at her hospital over the past few years, I'm surprised she's still in a job. Besides, I've already spoken to her. You're wasting your time. She looked me in the eye, offered a few meaningless platitudes and then toed the party line."

The premier's voice cracked with emotion, as if the situation had finally gotten to him. Suddenly the tension went out of his shoulders and he leaned over the interview table with his head in his hands. A harsh sob escaped him, quickly followed by several more. Cam glanced around him, feeling helpless.

What the hell was he supposed to do now? The State's leader was crying like a baby right in front of him, with no apparent end to his distress in sight. Where was the man's assistant or someone else who could come to his aid? Cam didn't have a clue how to go about offering him comfort.

The door to the interview room swung open and Holt filled the space. Cam didn't bother to hide his relief. "Superintendent, it's good to see you. Is there something I can help you with?"

"You're needed in the squad room, Detective. I'll finish with Mr Jamison."

Cam flashed his boss a look of gratitude and got the hell out of the room. Flinging himself down at his desk, he replayed the scene in his head. Though what he'd said to the premier was correct, the thought of another dead baby sent a trickle of unease down his spine. His niece had died a fortnight ago. Now, a second baby had died. *How many more had there been?*

The thought was so sudden and awful, he didn't know where it had come from. It was followed quickly by another: *Had Cynthia been given time with her dead baby?* The day he'd reunited with her, a matter of hours after Josephine's death, it hadn't occurred to him to enquire after her child. He'd still been struggling to come to terms with her discovery in a Sydney hospital and the fact that she'd recently given birth.

Her surprise and joy over their reunion had dissipated all too soon and her grief over the loss of her child returned with a vengeance. It was all he could do to arrange for her discharge from the hospital and settle her in his home. He hadn't dared ask her any questions beyond what was necessary, for fear of upsetting her. Now, he couldn't help but wonder once again if she'd been given the opportunity to say good-bye to her baby.

His sense of unease grew stronger. He had nothing whatsoever to base the feeling on, but he knew with increasing certainty that he'd have to look closer at the occurrence of newborn deaths at the Sydney Harbour Hospital.

Earlier, he'd been eager to dismiss the premier's claims as farcical, but the more he thought about it, the more he felt he owed it to Cynthia and the premier to dig a little deeper and be certain that what they'd been told was the truth. Then all of them could put the matter to rest and focus on the future.

He hadn't asked the premier what ward his daughter had been admitted to or the names of any of the staff members she'd come into contact with, but Cam could always obtain that information from the hospital records—if it came to that. He only hoped it hadn't happened on Ward Seven and that Georgie Whitely wasn't involved. Losing two babies in as many weeks would be devastating for anyone, let alone someone who cared for her patients as deeply as she did.

He remembered her recent promise to help his sister. It was just another example of her kindness and compassion. With a soft sigh, he reached for the phone that perched in one corner of his desk and dialed his home number. It rang out. He dialed again and received the same result.

He cursed quietly under his breath. Either his sister was asleep, or she couldn't be bothered answering the phone. He was depressed by the knowledge that either scenario could be the reality—yet another reason why he needed to do something more to penetrate her lethargy.

Replacing the phone in its cradle, he forced

the problem of his sister's mental status from his mind. Despite what the premier had said about Deborah Healy, Cameron had a healthy respect for the general manager. It was true her hospital had come under fire in recent years. One of the hospital's reputable doctor's had been found guilty of domestic abuse, but Cam didn't lay the blame for this at Deborah Healy's feet. No one knew what went on behind other people's closed doors. He'd been in the police service less than six months when he'd realized that.

There was of course, the matter of the head of the Organ Donation for Transplantation Unit being arrested on charges of human-tissue harvesting and several other related offenses. The fact the doctor had been using Sydney Harbour Hospital patients for his tissue supply had been an awful discovery and had been given serious air time in the media. And then there was the doctor who'd been playing God and murdering patients. The hospital and the general manager had rightly come under fire, but still...

Being the head of such a large, prestigious hospital was a task of mammoth proportions. She was responsible for the actions of thousands of staff members, from the cleaners and kitchen staff, right through to the head surgeons. She was expected to be aware of each and every little thing that went on in her hospital, but was it really feasible that one person could find enough hours in the day to do so?

Cam shook his head, feeling grim. There was no doubt about it: Deborah Healy had a tough gig. It was a job he wouldn't want for all the money in the world. But he'd told the premier he'd talk to the general manager about the sudden and unexpected death of Jamison's grandson, so he reached for the phone again and this time, dialed the number for the hospital. It was answered after the first ring.

"Good morning, the Sydney Harbour Hospital. Can I help you?"

"I'd like to speak with the general manager, please."

"I'll put you through to Deborah Healy's assistant."

A moment later, the call was picked up again. "Deborah Healy's office."

Cameron gave his name to the receptionist and was put on hold once again. He waited on the other end of the phone for so long, he was almost convinced the woman had hung up on him. He was just about to disconnect and redial when the call was answered.

"Deborah Healy."

"Ms Healy, it's Detective Sergeant Cameron Dawson. I'm making enquires about the recent death of the infant son of Danielle Jamison."

The woman's tone sharpened. "The premier's daughter?"

"Yes. I met with the premier a short time ago. He expressed a number of...concerns."

"My staff informed me about the death of his grandson. I expressed my deepest sympathies to his family. Incredibly sad. It's hard for any of us to accept that unexpected and unexplained deaths sometimes happen, particularly when the victim is a baby."

"You think that's all this is? A reaction to profound grief?"

"We all deal with grief in our own way, Detective. Lashing out and blaming those around us, particularly those who had the child in their care, is a natural response. It doesn't mean there's anything of substance to his claims."

"Did the baby undergo an autopsy?"

"No. I understand one was offered, but Ms Jamison declined, as is her right in these circumstances."

"When did the premier speak with you?"

"He demanded to see me immediately after he'd been informed of the baby's death. I, of course, made time for him. I hadn't had the chance to be fully briefed by my staff at that point, but I knew the basic facts and I wanted to reassure him the hospital was there for him and his daughter.

"Naturally, he was upset. I let him have his say. I offered my condolences. He... He didn't appear interested in accepting them. He left my office in a great deal of distress. I let him go. There was nothing I could do to bring the child back. Though we don't like when it happens, babies still sometimes die for sudden and unexplained reasons. Only time can heal the pain."

"It's very sad for everyone involved, but if you don't mind, I'd like to obtain a copy of Danielle Jamison's hospital records."

Her tone grew a whole lot more frosty. "Whatever for?"

"I'm curious."

"About what?"

Cameron thought for a moment. He had no idea what he was looking for and certainly wasn't ready to disclose anything yet. For all he knew, there was nothing to investigate. Best to make sure before he made anything public or put the general manager offside unnecessarily. He kept his answer purposefully vague.

"I promised the premier."

From her disgruntled response, it was obvious she wasn't pleased with his reply, but for now, it was all he was prepared to give.

CHAPTER 7

Georgie swung her little Mazda into the driveway of the garage beneath her apartment block and parked in her designated spot. After another long day at work, she couldn't wait to slip off her shoes and kick back on the couch with a drink in one hand and the TV remote in the other.

She lived on the third floor of an older style block of units surrounded by ancient fig trees and many smaller varieties of shrubs and bushes. The greenery shaded most of the building, reminding her of her childhood home up in the Blue Mountains. Though her parents had been prepared to advance her additional funds from her trust account in order to upgrade to more modern lodgings, she'd turned them down in favor of the unit on Bellevue Road.

Now, climbing the stairs with her arms laden with groceries, she thought wistfully of a newer standard apartment that came with elevators, but as soon as she turned her key in the lock and stepped over the threshold, any thoughts of leaving her spacious unit evaporated.

With her modest nursing wage only stretching so far, she'd used a small amount of money from her trust fund to purchase tasteful, but expensive furniture. She'd spent more money than she probably should have, but she was well pleased with the result.

Custom made, dark leather couches with a matching coffee table and corner stands filled a good portion of the living room. The hand knotted, charcoal, cream and red contemporary rug provided a splash of bright color and added to the luxury of the room. Her large, flat screen TV was centered on the brick wall above the fireplace and was perfectly positioned for her to indulge her passion of watching reruns of her favorite comedy shows, even from the kitchen. She was currently satisfying a *Seinfeld* fix.

Dumping the grocery bags onto the countertop, she quickly unpacked them and then headed straight for the small bar that stood perched in the far corner of the room. Scooping up ice from the inbuilt ice machine, she filled a glass and then added a healthy dash of vodka. A slice of lime kept fresh in the bar fridge was added to the drink. With a sigh of contentment, she headed to the couch.

Sinking into its smooth leather comfort, she sighed softly again and took a sip from her drink. The day had been long and trying, with a difficult lineup of patients. The only bright moment in her day was when Cameron Dawson had called. She smiled at the memory.

She still hadn't heard from him about her proposal to spend some time with his sister, but he'd told her he was at work and would get back to her. Police officers usually did twelve-hour shifts. Depending on where he lived, he probably wouldn't be home before seven and then he had to speak with Cynthia before he'd try to reach her.

Georgie thought of the sexy, broad-shouldered policeman and couldn't help the skip in her pulse. Not only was he good-looking, but it was also apparent he had a soft heart. He hadn't seen his sister since she was a young child and yet he'd taken her in without question and was doing the best he could to see to her needs. It made Georgie feel all warm and gooey inside to know how generous and loving he was. She could think of a number of men who would have done things differently.

All of a sudden, she imagined having someone like Cameron as her boyfriend; a man who wasn't afraid of tender emotion or of exposing his heart. Okay, the girl in question was his sister and she'd been having a tough time of it, but no one had forced him to claim her and take her under his protection with a promise to do all he could to help.

Georgie knew only too well a man like Cameron Dawson didn't come along very often. Her disastrous, short-lived affair with Jason had ended in an unplanned teenage pregnancy.

Though she didn't doubt for a second he'd loved her, the pressure of impending fatherhood coupled with the mountain of disapproval from her parents, had sent him running. She didn't blame him. She'd wanted to run, too.

In the years since, she'd dated casually on and off. Her mother disapproved of the fact men came and went, in and out of her life with monotonous regularity, but for Georgie, anything more serious required a commitment and an honesty she wasn't ready to give.

It was only recently that she'd begun to feel the need to seek out a partner she could connect with on more than a superficial level. In the dark of night, when she'd lie awake tortured with thoughts of her son, she yearned to have someone special to share her heartache and to understand; to hold her close, to reassure her; to love her.

It was the reason why Cameron kept returning to her thoughts, time and time again. Men with his endearing mix of honesty, caring and compassion were rare. To add to his appeal, he was one of the sexiest men she'd ever met.

Her parents would frown on the fact he was a police officer. With her father a respected obstetrician and her mother a Nursing Unit Manager (or NUM as they were known to the hospital staff), they had high hopes for their daughters and the men they would eventually marry. Lawyers, doctors and company CEOs were the kinds of men they preferred for their daughters, but the attitude of her parents was the last thing Georgie cared about. It wasn't like they'd cut off her trust fund.

One thing her mother had promised her when she was doing her best to convince Georgie to sign the adoption papers was that they'd ensure she was always provided for and their high expectations for their offspring were because they loved their girls more than anything else. Georgie was confident if a police officer made her happy, they'd eventually accept and embrace him into their fold.

She shook her head ruefully at the thought and took another sip of her drink. Here she was, daydreaming about calling Cameron Dawson her own, and apart from his appreciative glance at their first meeting, he hadn't given her the slightest hint he was interested.

Okay, so he'd called her for advice about his sister, but Georgie was familiar with the whole sad situation and had connected with the girl. It wasn't surprising that he'd reached out to her for help, on a professional level. The key to moving things forward, if they were to move forward at all, would be to make him see her in a different light. Not as the midwife who'd cared for Cynthia, but as an interesting, intelligent and desirable woman...and maybe even a potential girlfriend.

Her mind raced through various scenarios where she could draw his attention to her assets and she couldn't help but smile. The first thing to do was to buy the right dress. After that, she'd look for some killer heels. Her smile widened in anticipation. She'd hit the shops tomorrow, right after she finished work. If there was one thing in the world she did enjoy, it was shopping.

Cam shook some oyster sauce into the stir-fry that was cooking on the stove and glanced across at his sister. They'd been talking quietly for the past hour and had now lapsed into a companionable silence. It was the most conversation they'd shared since she'd arrived and it gave him hope that she might finally be getting on top of her debilitating grief.

Earlier, he'd arrived home to find her in her usual state of solitude. The blinds and curtains in her bedroom were drawn against what had been another beautiful late fall day. He'd hesitated about intruding upon her voluntary isolation, but then thought of Georgie's offer and knocked firmly on the half open door.

Cynthia didn't respond to his knock or his quiet greeting and a moment later, he ventured inside the room. It was dank and musty and the air was stale. The smell of body odor reached him. He realized he couldn't remember the last time he'd heard her in the shower and he had yet to see her in any of the new clothes he'd purchased for her the day after she'd moved in.

A flash of irritation coursed through him. She was living with him, in a very nice apartment, not out on the street. It was time they got a few things straight. At the very least, she was going to abide by some rules relating to basic personal hygiene.

There had been a few tears and a bit of shouting, but she finally conceded he was right. She'd been living like her life was over and it was time to remember she was still alive. Not only alive, but young and healthy, with her whole future in front of her. Cam was willing to help in any way he could, starting with re-enrolling her in school.

She'd looked horrified at the thought until he assured her he'd enrol her in a TAFE college. Among other things, these colleges catered to a number of students who, for one reason or another, had been unable to complete their schooling on the traditional timeline. He promised they'd talk about it further, after he'd made some enquires and then he mentioned Georgie's offer.

It was then his sister gave him her first real smile and he'd sent up silent thanks. He wanted to call Georgie right away, but decided to wait until he could speak to her in private. He'd told her he'd call her that night and he would—after Cynthia had gone to sleep.

Now, he reached for two plates and loaded them with food, enjoying the spicy aroma that wafted toward him. Setting one plate in front of Cynthia, he took a seat opposite. She'd recently showered and he couldn't help but notice how pretty she looked with her clean blond hair shining softly under the overhead light. The fact that she looked even younger than her sixteen years pulled at his heartstrings.

She'd been through so much in her short life. More than she ever should have had to face. But it was over now and he hoped she could put it behind her and get on with living her life. He thought of Danielle Jamison and was once again grateful that his little sister hadn't gone down that path. Drugs were an altogether different beast and one he was glad they didn't have to fight.

"I was wondering if I could talk to you about what happened at the hospital?" he asked quietly, his thoughts still on the premier's daughter.

Her gaze flew to his and her fork paused on its way to her mouth. Alarm flashed in her eyes. A moment later, she shrugged and put the fork to her mouth, but lowered her gaze to her plate.

He kept his tone gentle. "This is probably the last thing you want to talk about, honey, but I'd like to know what happened. I came in right at the very end and I feel like most of the story's missing. If you don't mind, I'd like to hear what happened the night you gave birth to your baby and then...afterwards."

Cynthia was silent for so long, he was sure she wasn't going to answer. He forked more stir-fry into his mouth and almost missed her whispered reply.

"Her name was Josephine."

"Of course," he said quickly, relieved she'd responded. It could help with Danielle's investigation if he heard about his sister's experience. After all, there were many similarities and he wasn't yet prepared to dismiss them. "Tell me about little Josephine," he added and reached over to squeeze her hand. "I'd really like to know."

Cynthia began quietly and hesitantly, but gradually her voice picked up strength. She talked about the tiny baby she'd had for such a short time and Cam couldn't help but tear up. Knowing he never got to meet his young niece saddened him beyond words. He couldn't imagine how his sister felt—she who had carried the little girl inside her for so long.

"She had so much dark hair, just like Albert," Cynthia murmured with a sad smile. "And the cutest little rosebud lips. She was the most perfect thing I'd ever seen."

"Did any of the staff give you any indication there was something wrong?"

She shook her head, looking mystified. "No, that's why it came as such a shock when the nurse came in early the next morning to tell me Josephine had...died. I had no idea she'd been born with problems."

Cam squeezed her hand again. "From what Georgie told me, she was born perfectly healthy. They've put her death down to SIDS. Sometimes terrible things like that happen and nobody can explain why. It makes it so much harder to deal with, but it's just the way it is."

Cynthia nodded sadly. "Yeah, that's what Ava says."

Cam lifted his eyebrow in question and then remembered Ava Wolfe was the psychiatrist his sister was seeing. "Who told you Josephine had passed away?" he asked gently.

"I don't know her name. She was an older woman, a nurse, but I think she was the one in charge. I heard her giving some of the other nurses orders."

Cam nodded. If necessary, he'd be able to get a copy of the staff rosters which would tell him who had been on duty over the relevant time. "What did she say to you?" he asked.

"I can't remember the exact words. Everything from that day's a bit of a blur. She said something about finding Josephine in her crib and discovering she was no longer breathing. I... I started screaming at her. I needed to know my baby was all right. It was then that she shook her head and told me... She told me that she'd died."

Cynthia's voice hitched. Tears filled her eyes and ran slowly down her cheeks. Cam's heart clenched with pain and he wished he could make things easier, but the truth was, he needed to know. "Did you get to see Josephine again?"

His sister shook her head. "No. When I asked if I could, the nurse told me it wouldn't be wise. Apparently, by the time they found her, Josephine had been...gone for a while. The nurse told me she...didn't look so good. She urged me to remember my baby the way she'd been the night before—beautiful, tiny, perfect. She said it would be better that way."

Cam pressed his lips together, thankful that his sister had at least been spared the pain of seeing her baby cold and dark and still in death. If the baby had been deprived of oxygen for an extended length of time, she might even have turned black. It happened sometimes and it wasn't pretty. The nurse had made the right decision.

"I'm sure she was right," Cam said, wanting to reassure his sister. "This way, your memories of the time you had with your beautiful baby remain perfect and untarnished for the rest of your life."

Cam picked up his fork again and resumed eating. He was relieved to see Cynthia do the same. It couldn't be easy to dig up the painful memories from that day, but she seemed to be handling it, and for that, he was glad.

"The same nurse gave me the card with the details of the crematorium. I took it from her, not knowing what else to do with it. I hadn't even thought about disposing of…Josephine's remains. The nurse must have seen something in my eyes because she reassured me the crematorium staff would know what to do. All I had to do was contact them and they'd look after my baby."

Cynthia looked up at him and gave a small shrug, her expression filled with sadness. "That's about it. You found me not long after."

"You gave me the card and I called the crematorium. It was all done very quickly and efficiently. I must admit, it's the first time I'd had to do something like that, so I wasn't quite sure what to expect, either."

Cynthia nodded. "I was still in a daze, but I remember listening while you discussed the details with that man at the funeral parlor. We chose a tiny white casket with white and gold bows around the sides and a gold cross on the top."

Cam nodded and another wave of tears

pricked the back of his eyes. "It was beautiful, honey. Just like your beautiful Josephine."

As Cam reached out to cup his sister's cheek, she gasped aloud on a sob. Her face crumpled and she buried her face in her hands.

"I didn't even get to take a photo of her!" she sobbed. "If only I'd had a phone! It didn't even occur to me to ask one of the other patients. I'd only just given birth to this perfect, tiny person. I had no way of knowing it was the last time I was going to see her."

Her tears now fell in earnest and Cam's heart broke at the sight of her pain. Pushing away from the table, he closed the distance between them and pulled her upright so he could hold her close. Her arms went around his waist and she buried her face in his shirt.

Her sobs were desolate and heartbreaking. She cried like she'd never stop. The tears Cam had tried so hard to hold back slowly ran down his cheeks. He tightened his arms around her and let her weep. When at last her sobs quieted, he pressed a gentle kiss against her hair.

His little sister had been through so much and she still had her whole life to live. He couldn't help but pray the toughest days were behind her and from that point on, she could begin to look ahead. Georgie had told him time was the greatest of healers and he knew she was right. He only hoped Cynthia would give herself the time she needed and learn to accept the inevitability of what had happened.

It was a sad fact that SIDS sometimes

happened and nobody could explain why. Even still, he couldn't help the fresh wave of unease that had crept into his gut as he listened to Cynthia's story. The similarities between her experience and Danielle's were too many to be discounted. He was more curious than ever to discover just how many babies had died of SIDS at the Sydney Harbour Hospital.

It was much later when Cam finally found a moment to call Georgie. He was disappointed, but not surprised, when his call went through to her voicemail. It was after eleven and she'd told him she was rostered on an early shift the next morning. He left a message, thanking her again for her kind offer and confirming Cynthia was looking forward to spending the day with her. He ended the call by asking her to call him back with the details. Tossing the phone on his bed, he sighed softly and headed for bed.

Chapter 8

Dear Diary,

Every once in a while, I stare down at yet another tiny scrap of squalling humanity and wonder if this baby wouldn't be better off with its birth mother. Then I listen to the torrent of abuse that spews forth from the mouth of that same mother who is coming off opiates or the loud snores that erupt from the one who's sleeping off the enforced withdrawal from meth and I know that I made the right decision.

So many babies born to so many unworthy and ungrateful women. It turns my stomach to watch them. They don't deserve those babies. Most of them don't want them and can't conceive of what it takes to raise them. It's all about their next fix, their next high and the wholly selfish pleasure that comes with it.

It is the barren ones I feel sorry for. The women who yearn with quiet desperation to hold and love and nurture a baby of their own. It is for them that I do this. Them, and the children...

Georgie checked the monitor beside the woman's bed and then adjusted the straps over her enlarged belly. They had slipped a little low and for a few moments, Georgie couldn't find the baby's heartbeat. A minute later, the monitor picked it up again, and she sighed quietly in relief. The labor had been progressing nicely and even though the woman had been at it for more than six hours, it was still early days.

The patient was giving birth to her first child and first labors often went for at least twelve to fourteen hours. Some went a lot longer. Georgie had examined her twenty minutes earlier, and judging by the dilation of the cervix, they still had some time to go. Reaching for a washcloth, she dampened it under the faucet and then handed it to the girl's partner who stood by her side near the bed.

"Here, Wes. Use this on Sandra's forehead. She's perspiring and this will ease her distress."

The boy, who barely looked legal, took the cloth and stared at it a little uncertainly. Georgie nodded her encouragement and he swiped it hesitantly over his girlfriend's face. The cool fabric seemed to calm her and she blew out her breath on a grateful sigh.

"How much longer?" she rasped. Georgie told her.

"You're kiddin' me!" Wes responded. "You mean we ain't even halfway through?"

"It's a little hard to tell," Georgie said calmly. "Everybody's different. But if I had to guess, I'd say

Sandra is about halfway there. But you're doing fine, honey." Georgie smiled her encouragement, directing her comment to the patient.

"No one told me it'd hurt so much." The woman gasped around another contraction.

"I can arrange for an epidural, if you like," Georgie offered. "It will take away the pain."

Wes nodded enthusiastically, but Sandra looked less convinced. "I've been clean for three months, now. I don't want no more drugs."

"But, Sandy, this is a hospital drug. It's different and you won't feel no pain," Wes said with a hint of urgency.

Sandra's jaw set in a stubborn line and once again, she shook her head. "No more drugs, Wes. I made a promise to our baby."

Wes made a sound of impatience and scrubbed a dirty hand through his lank and greasy hair. "You're bein' stupid, Sandy. Take the fuckin' drugs! It's not like you're gonna get addicted. These ones are comin' from the doctor."

Georgie stepped forward and intervened. "It's all right, Wes. She's doing great on her own. If she doesn't want the epidural, that's fine. There are other things we can use—hot cloths on her back and massage are other great pain relievers." Georgie directed her attention to her patient. "Would you like Wes to rub your back, Sandra?"

"Yes, please." The girl moaned and turned further onto her side.

Wes looked even more uncertain, but placed his hands on Sandra's back. With awkward movements, he did his best to attempt a massage.

"Lower, Wes." Sandra gasped. "You need to move lower."

"Fuck, Sandy, I don't know what to do! I've never given anyone a fuckin' massage! What do you expect me to do?"

Sandra responded with another moan that escalated in volume and depth for the length of the contraction. When it was over, she gasped in relief.

"Big, slow breaths, Sandra," Georgie murmured. "Just like we talked about. You're doing great. Take it one contraction at a time."

The girl relaxed and Georgie moved closer to the monitor and checked that the readings were satisfactory. Her thoughts wandered to Cynthia, who was only a few years younger than Sandra, and then, of course, they landed on Cameron.

She was disappointed she'd missed his call the previous night, but he'd phoned after she'd gone to bed. Still, she was filled with anticipation at the thought of seeing him again, even if she'd be spending most of the time in the company of his sister. As soon as her shift was over, she intended to hit the shops in search of a dress that would be sure to capture his attention. She had no idea if he could become romantically interested in her, but she intended to give it her best shot.

"Ow! Ow! It hurts, nurse! It hurts!"

Sandra's distressed cries broke into Georgie's musings and she once again focused her attention on her patient. Glancing at the clock on the wall, she swallowed a sigh and returned to the job at hand.

Cameron reached for the phone that sat on his desk and dialed the number of the Sydney Harbour Hospital. As agreed, Deborah Healy had sent over the hospital file belonging to Danielle Jamison and he'd spent the afternoon going over it. The information seemed straightforward. The girl had presented to the hospital with her parents by her side. She was already in labor and at 1500 hours, after an uneventful delivery, her baby boy was born. He noted the use of twenty-four hour time. Like the military and the police service, its use was common practice in hospitals. Reading further, his heart had skipped a beat when he discovered the midwife who delivered the child was Georgie Whitely.

The birth report noted that routine tests were carried out by the midwife and the findings fell within normal limits. The patient and her baby were returned to the ward within the hour. They'd been left in the company of the new mother's parents.

The information was matter-of-fact and straightforward and gave no indication of the tragedy that was to come. Less than twelve hours later, the night nurse would discover the child had died. Flipping over a few more pages, Cam found the relevant report. It had been written by the

Nursing Unit Manager. Printed underneath the signature in a small neat script was the name *Marjorie Whitely* (NUM).

He frowned. *Marjorie Whitely.* Could the woman be Georgie's relative? Perhaps her sister? Or even her mother? With no way of knowing Marjorie's age, any possibility could only be a guess. Then, of course, there was the possibility that the woman wasn't related at all. He wrote down the name on his notepad. Just another thing he'd ask the general manager.

A copy of the preliminary death certificate was attached to the file. The stated cause of death was SIDS. The certificate had been signed by a Doctor Frederick Rolleston and was time-stamped and dated just under a fortnight after Cynthia's delivery. It confirmed that two babies had died from SIDS less than a two weeks apart. *Surely that was unusual?* He needed to find out.

His call connected and he waited for Deborah Healy to answer. It was picked up by her assistant and he quickly identified himself and asked if he could speak with the general manager.

"I'm sorry, Detective. She's on another call. Can I take a message and have her phone you back?"

Cam swallowed his impatience. After leaving his contact details, he ended the call and then returned to Danielle's notes. A few minutes later, the phone at his elbow rang and he snatched up the receiver. "Detective Sergeant Dawson. Can I help you?"

"Detective, it's Deborah Healy. I'm returning your call."

"Ms Healy. Thanks for getting back to me so quickly. I appreciate it."

"No problem. What can I do for you?" The general manager's tone was all business.

"I've been looking over the file you sent over. The one belonging to Danielle Jamison. I was wondering if you could tell me how many babies die at your hospital each year."

"Thankfully, not many, Detective. We pride ourselves on the quality of our service. It's very sad about what happened to poor Danielle Jamison's baby. Thank goodness it doesn't happen very often."

"How often?"

"Danielle Jamison's baby was only the second baby to die at this hospital in the past twelve months for sudden and unexplainable reasons. The other infant passed away more than nine months ago."

Cam frowned. "I'm afraid that's not correct, Ms Healy."

"What do you mean?"

"My niece died within hours of her birth a little over a fortnight ago. Your information isn't right."

"Don't be ridiculous! It's hospital policy that I be notified immediately of *all* deaths that occur in our establishment and the sudden death of an infant is no different. You must be mistaken about your niece. Perhaps you have us confused with one of the other city hospitals?"

Cameron's anger stirred. "I'm not mistaken, Ms Healy," he replied coldly. "I collected my sister off Ward Seven the morning after her baby died. You need to check your sources. They're obviously not keeping you up to date."

"I-I see. If you give me a moment, I'll... I'll check one of our databases," the general manager replied shakily. "Perhaps I was away when it happened..."

Cameron heard the sound of keys clicking on a keyboard. A moment later, Deborah spoke again. Cam heard the tension in her voice.

"Ah, here we are. A list of all infant deaths in the hospital over the past year." There was a long pause on the other end of the phone. Cameron frowned.

"Ms Healy? Are you still there?"

"Yes, I-I'm sorry. I was reading through the data. It's... It's a little lengthier than I expected."

Once again, Cameron swallowed his impatience. "How many?"

"According to the latest reports, there were fifteen infant deaths over the past twelve months."

"That's more than one a month."

"Yes," the general manager responded in a shaky voice. "There must be a glitch in our system. I've only been notified about two."

"Is it possible the information has been entered incorrectly? Duplicated, or something like that?"

"I wouldn't have thought so, but something has happened. I'll need to speak with the head of obstetrics. Those statistics can't be right."

A sudden sense of urgency made Cameron's heart beat faster. "Get back to me as soon as possible. I need that information."

"O-of course."

"Two more things: First, what can you tell me about Georgina Whitely? She was the midwife who delivered Danielle Jamison's baby. She was also present at the birth of my late niece."

"Georgie's been with us for seven years. She's an excellent nurse. She was the Nursing Unit Manager of our pediatrics ward until a couple of years ago. She decided to retrain as a midwife and transferred to Ward Seven. She's been there ever since."

Cameron absorbed the information and made a note on his pad. "And what about Marjorie Whitely? Where does she fit in?"

Deborah's voice filled with pride. "Marjorie's one of our finest, most experienced nurses. She's been at this hospital nearly all of her working life. She's delivered more babies than anyone. You won't find yourself in better hands. She's the Nursing Unit Manager of Ward Seven and Georgie Whitely's mother."

Having guessed there might be a connection between the two women, Cameron nodded and wrote Georgie Whitely's name next to Marjorie's and drew a line between them. It was interesting that mother and daughter chose to work together. There were many people who would run in the opposite direction rather than share their workplace with a relative, Cam included. Georgie and her mother must be in that select group of family members who actually enjoyed working in close proximity.

"Is there anything else, Detective?"

The general manager's sharp question

distracted him from his thoughts. He gave her a hasty reply. "Not at this time, Ms Healy, but rest assured, if I have any more questions, I'll be in touch."

The phone line disconnected in Cameron's ear and he slowly replaced the receiver. Checking his email, he found a message from the switchboard operator informing him that Georgie had called while he'd been on the phone. She'd received his message and had made an appointment at the spa for her and his sister two days hence.

He thought about coming face to face with the sexy nurse once again and his pulse leaped in response, even as his head dictated he proceed with caution. She might very well become a person of interest in his investigation. Besides that, he'd learned early that the people who were supposed to care for you above all others were often the same people who let you down.

Over the decade since he'd left home, he'd guarded his emotions closely and his heart even closer. Though he'd dated casually, he'd taken care not to let any entanglement develop into a serious relationship. Life was so much easier that way.

But with Georgie, things were different. He wanted to get to know her. He wanted to open up. For the first time in his adult life, he wanted to take a chance. It was risky and it could all end in a painful mess, but there was nothing he could do about it. Georgie's name might have been linked to a couple of recent infant deaths, but even that wasn't enough to deter him. Right now, all he could think about was seeing her again and where it might lead...

———

"Tammie! Wake up! It's time to go."

Tammie Sinclair stirred on the gurney that doubled as a bed for the night staff. Blinking away sleep, she stared at her boss through the dimness.

"Come on! Hurry! I need your help." Without waiting for her response, the older woman turned away.

Tammie struggled off the gurney and followed the other nurse into a storage room. A plastic crib stood in the middle of the confined space with a baby asleep inside. "Is it a boy or a girl?" she whispered.

"A boy. Not that it matters."

Tammie came closer and stared down at the newborn. He was perfect in every way. She tamped down on an overwhelming surge of yearning and thought about Wendy. Maybe this time their invitro-fertilization attempt would be successful... She no longer dared to hope.

"What do you need me to do?" she murmured.

CHAPTER 9

Georgie tossed her handbag into one of the staff lockers and closed it. Tucking a loose strand of hair back into her tidy bun, she turned and surveyed her appearance in the bathroom mirror. She was about to begin her last shift before two rostered days' off and she could hardly wait. The week had been a trying one with a full ward of desperate and needy mothers, but thankfully no more babies had been lost. The day stretched out in front of her and she began to count the minutes until it would end. The thought of two glorious days off work seemed like heaven, particularly when it meant she'd see Cameron again. A burst of excitement surged through her.

She'd arranged an appointment at a day spa for early the next morning and had told Cameron she'd swing by his apartment at eight to collect his sister. She tried not to get her hopes up that he might still be there at that time of day, but even if he wasn't, she still had to drop Cynthia home. One way or the other, Georgie was determined to make it clear to the hot detective she was interested—and if her efforts came to nothing, she'd move on.

More and more she'd been feeling the pressure to find a special someone and settle down. She wanted marriage and babies and she wasn't blind to the fact that the time was slowly, but surely, wearing down. The irony that the only child she might bear was the one she'd given away sent a surge of desperate pain rushing through her and she steadfastly forced her thoughts in another direction.

"Georgina, may I see you for a moment?"

Georgie spied her mother's reflection in the bathroom mirror and turned to greet her with a smile. "Of course. Good morning, Marjorie."

Her mother smiled back, but it didn't reach her eyes. They left the staff restroom and headed toward Marjorie's office. Georgie glanced at her mother and took a moment to study the woman she'd loved and admired all her life, despite all that they'd been through. She noticed new age lines etched around the corners of her mother's eyes. Fatigue shadowed their dark depths.

Her mother worked too hard. It was as simple as that. Georgie didn't know of any other NUM who worked weekends, and yet her mother often did. She also did night shifts in addition to her morning shifts and did it without a word of complaint. Georgie's Aunt Rosemary worked similarly hard.

When Georgie had asked her mother about it, once, Marjorie had replied that she and her sister had grown up in a time when work was scarce and jobs were highly valued. Going above and beyond what was expected was the norm for their generation. Besides, with chronic staff shortages in the hospital, it was imperative someone fill in when needed. Babies waited for no one and it wasn't fair to the mother or the child if there were inadequate staff-to-patient ratios. So, sometimes her mother and aunt did double shifts, but they seemed to take it in stride.

It was only recently that Georgie had noticed her mother's hair had turned much grayer and her steps were less sprightly than they used to be. Georgie made a mental note to speak to her father about it. They were wealthy people; both of them had inherited sizeable estates from their parents. Although it was admirable that Marjorie wanted to be there for her patients, it wasn't necessary for her to work herself into the ground. If she kept it up, she'd be the one looking for the hospital bed.

Georgie chuckled at the thought of her mother as a patient. No doubt she'd make a terrible one.

"What's so funny?" Marjorie asked, throwing her a sideways look.

Georgie walked through the open doorway of her mom's office and took a seat opposite the crowded desk. "Nothing much. I was just thinking about how hard you and Aunt Rosemary work and what would happen if you ended up as patients in this hospital."

Her mother looked horrified at the thought. "Don't wish that on me, Georgina! I have far too much to do. Besides, who would want to look after me? I'd be the patient from hell!" Marjorie smiled and gave her a wink and Georgie laughed again.

"Exactly!" she said.

Her mom took her place in the chair that stood behind the desk and moved some of the papers out of her way. Her expression grew serious. Georgie frowned and all of a sudden, tension filled the air.

"Wh-what is it, Marjorie?" She barely formed the question. Dread weighed heavy in her veins.

Her mother sighed heavily and Georgie's concern ratcheted up another notch. Her heart thumped hard against her ribs. "Talk to me, Mom," she pleaded. "What's wrong? Is it Dad? Oh, God! Please don't tell me something's happened to Dad!"

"No, Georgina, it's nothing like that. Your dad's fine. At least, he was when I said good-bye to him earlier."

"Then what? Is it Sasha? Or Clare? Or Montana?" she asked, referring to her adult siblings.

"No. As far as I know, your sisters are all okay. It has nothing to do with our family. It's... It's something that happened here, at work."

Georgie's eyebrows flew upwards in surprise, but she couldn't help feeling relieved. If it was work related, she was sure she could handle whatever it was. Her family, now that would be a different matter.

"What is it?" she asked in a calmer voice, her breath coming easier.

Her mother looked up at her and shook her head sadly. "It's about Sandra Briggs."

Georgie frowned. "Sandra? The young girl who gave birth yesterday afternoon?"

"Yes. I'm afraid her baby didn't make it through the night."

Georgie sat straighter in her chair. "You mean, he *died?*"

Marjorie nodded slowly. "Yes. I'm sorry, Georgina."

Georgie shook her head in dismay, trying to come to terms with what her mother said. Sandra had given birth to a healthy baby boy less than fifteen hours earlier. *How could he now be dead?*

"What happened?" she asked, still shocked and confused.

Her mother shuffled a pile of papers on her desk and then shrugged. "We don't know for sure. I suggested putting the baby in the nursery for a few hours so Mom could get some sleep. When I went to check on him, he wasn't breathing. The poor little thing was suffering a severe withdrawal from heroin. It's possible he went into cardiac arrest. By the time I found him, he was cold and unresponsive. There was nothing I could do."

Georgie gasped in shock. "Sandra said she'd been clean for three months! She'd given it up for her baby."

Marjorie gazed at her sympathetically. "Poor, Georgina. You really shouldn't believe anything that comes out of the mouth of a junkie. I thought you would have learned that by now."

"But..." Georgie shook her head helplessly,

unable to believe it was happening again. She'd worked on Ward Seven for two years and not one of her babies had died. Now there had been three over the course of a couple of weeks. Though the deaths couldn't be prevented, it seemed like things were spiraling out of control. Panic surged through her and icy tendrils of fear clutched at her heart. *What was going on? What was happening to the babies she delivered on Ward Seven?* She wished she knew. She looked in desperation at her mother for answers, but found only sad regret and then she remembered something else her mother had said.

"You were here last night? On night shift?" she asked.

Her mother nodded. "Yes, along with Rosemary and Tammie. Someone called in sick at the last minute. It was just as easy for me to come in, rather than to call around to find a replacement."

"So you've been here all night and now you're doing the day shift?"

Marjorie shrugged again. "I'm the head of this ward. I do what needs to be done. Besides, I had to stay back to complete the report on the Briggs baby."

"Mom! You need to go home and sleep! You've already been on your feet all night. Isn't there anyone else you can call to cover for you?"

Her mother brushed away Georgie's concerns and returned her attention to the paperwork that covered her desk. "I'm fine. I'll finish my report while the details are still fresh in my mind. With a bit of luck, I might get to leave early."

Georgie's thoughts snagged on Sandra Briggs and she pressed her lips together on another surge of emotion. Blinking back tears, she nodded. "How is she?"

"Devastated, of course. She has yet to tell her boyfriend. Neither of them have a phone." Marjorie grimaced. "I guess he'll show up here sooner or later."

"He's going to be shattered. He was so thrilled to become a dad. You should have seen his smile when I told him he had a son. It was like I'd handed him the stars." Georgie's voice faded away and once again, she was overwhelmed with sadness and disbelief. "I should go to her," she said numbly, "and see if she wants me there when she tells Wes."

Her mother nodded. "Yes, that might be best."

In a daze, Georgie pushed away from her chair and stumbled toward the door.

"Have security on standby," her mother added. "You just never know how people like that are going to react."

Anger stirred in Georgie's veins. She rounded on her mother. "What do you mean, people like that?"

"Oh, come on, Georgina. We both know they'll be passed out in the gutter, with the drug of their choice rushing through their veins, just as soon as they clear the hospital. I'm just saying the boyfriend might be unpredictable. He might have even celebrated fatherhood by getting high. Who knows? I'm just trying to cover every possibility. You need to be careful around people like that."

Georgie stared at her mother like she was a stranger. Marjorie had said it again: "People like that." As if they were lesser human beings; ones that didn't quite fit. *How had Georgie lived for twenty-nine years and never before seen her mother's prejudice?* It shocked and confused her even more.

But now wasn't the time to deal with it. A young mother needed her. With a heavy heart, Georgie turned away in silence and made her way out onto the ward.

Tammie drew hard on the end of her cigarette and sucked the nicotine deep into her lungs. Holding it there for as long as she could, she eventually exhaled on a smoky blue sigh that hung on the cool afternoon air. Winter had finally arrived.

Her partner, Wendy, frowned from her seat on the balcony. "I wish you'd quit that filthy habit. It isn't good for either of us. We're trying to get pregnant, remember? Smoking's one of the contributing factors to infertility and given that neither of us are in the first blush of youth, we need every advantage we can get."

Tammie stared at the woman she loved above all others and nodded. She stubbed out her cigarette. "You're right, I'm sorry. I'll try harder to quit. I've cut right back, you know. I'm down to half a pack."

She sighed and shook her head. "It's just that I had a shit of a night at work last night and smoking helps me clear my head." She chuckled softly. "It's funny, isn't it? Cigarettes fill my lungs with poisonous chemicals, but they actually make it easier for me to think. How's that for irony?"

"Why didn't you tell me when you came home this morning?"

Tammie moved closer to her lover of five years and pressed a kiss on the top of her head. "You were rushing off to work and to tell you the truth, I didn't feel like talking about it. All I wanted was to lie down and sleep it off."

"What happened?"

"We lost another baby."

"Oh, no! Tammie, you poor thing! Was it SIDS again?"

"Yes, they think so."

"That's so sad," Wendy murmured and reached for Tammie's hand. "I can't imagine how hard it must have been for you. Especially now, when we're trying so hard for a baby of our own."

"Yeah. It's probably the reason it's hit me worse this time."

Wendy shook her head slowly and shot her a sympathetic look. "How many is that?"

Tammie compressed her lips, feeling grim. "Too many. At least ten this year, that I know of."

Wendy frowned. "What do you mean? Do you think there might be others?"

Tammie stared at her lover for a long moment and then exhaled on a heavy sigh. "I don't know," she finally replied. "It's not something we discuss on the ward, even during handovers. As far as I know, only the staff directly involved in each incident are even aware that it happened. Marjorie decided the less we talk about it the better. I guess she's right. It's not something *I* want to dwell on."

Tears glinted in Wendy's eyes. "I feel sorry for those poor mothers. Fancy going through nine months of carrying a child inside you, only to have it die shortly after birth."

"I hate that they get to fall pregnant at all!" Tammie hissed suddenly, as anger flared to life inside her. "Almost all of them are drug addicts or alcoholics. They don't deserve to be mothers! You should see them, Wen. Half of them are still getting high, right there on the ward! Their babies are suffering from withdrawals—twitching and crying and struggling to feed—and all their mothers can think about is their next fix! It's criminal!"

To her horror, hot tears filled her eyes and spilled out over her cheeks. She swiped at them angrily, furious that she'd been brought to that point. She never cried. *Never.* It made her feel useless and weak.

Without a word, Wendy stood and put her arms around Tammie, drawing her in close. "*Shh*, babe. It's all right. Don't get upset. It's okay."

Her comforting words only made Tammie cry harder. Her sobs came loud and fast. Tears soaked the front of Wendy's jacket, and still, Tammie couldn't stop the flow.

"But, I...I...I..." she hiccupped, trying to make Wendy understand.

"I know, babe. It's all right. It's been a tough year on us both. Three failed IVF attempts is enough to get anyone down. Coupled with the sudden loss of several infants, it's no wonder you're upset."

Tammie squeezed her eyes shut and accepted Wendy's comfort and support. She wished she could explain properly to her partner about the strange goings-on that occurred on Ward Seven, but she wasn't sure if she had the courage—or if she even knew how to make enough sense of it to talk about it.

After awhile, Tammie pulled back and offered her lover a shaky smile. "I'm sorry. I don't know where that came from. It's not at all like me to fall apart."

Wendy smiled at her tenderly and reached out and brushed the hair out of Tammie's eyes. "Hey, cut yourself some slack. You don't have to be the strong one all the time. We're partners; a team. We have each other's backs, right?"

Tammie nodded. "Right."

Wendy drew in a deep breath. All of a sudden, she looked a little nervous.

"What is it, Wen?"

"This probably isn't a good time, with you feeling so down, but then again, maybe it's the perfect time to give you some news that might cheer you up."

Tammie frowned. "What do you mean?"

"We're pregnant!"

Tammie stared at the woman she loved with all her heart and couldn't believe her ears. "You're... You're pregnant? We're having a baby?"

Wendy laughed and nodded and more tears sparkled in her eyes. "Yes! Isn't it amazing?"

Tammie smiled so wide her cheeks hurt, even though a tiny part of her was disappointed it hadn't happened for her. She forced the thought aside. "It's more than amazing, Wen! It's... It's the best news I've ever heard! How far along are you?"

"Four weeks."

Disbelief, wonder and happiness rushed through Tammie until she thought she might burst. She threw her arms around Wendy and hugged her tight. "Four weeks! How wonderful!"

"It is, isn't it?" Wendy grinned.

"How are you feeling?" Tammie asked, all of a sudden beset with concerns.

"Fine. A little tired, maybe, but otherwise I feel great."

"You need to cut back your hours at work. That law firm can do without you for the next little while. It will do them good to lose you. They might have more appreciation for the number of hours you bill if you're not around all the time."

Wendy chuckled. "Hey, let's not get ahead of ourselves. It's early days yet. Besides, many women work right up until a week or so before the birth."

"Yes, but you're not going to," Tammie said firmly. "We're going to make sure you're as rested and relaxed as you can be. This baby deserves to meet you at your very best. I'll take extra shifts to cover your salary. We'll be fine."

Wendy smiled softly, her delight and excitement at the thought of their baby plain for Tammie to see. "I'm not going to argue with you," she said. "From now on, you're the boss."

"I was always the boss," Tammie grumbled, but followed it with a grin. Finally, they were pregnant! It was a dream come true.

Chapter 10

Cameron stepped out onto his balcony for the third time and checked the street below. The morning sun shone bright and cheerful, mocking his concern. It was a couple of minutes past eight. Georgie was meant to be there by now. It was ridiculous how worked up he was getting over the fact she was a little late.

It was a weekday. People were commuting to work. The traffic was heavy, as it usually was during peak hour. She'd probably been held up. He didn't know where she lived, so he had no idea how far she had to come to reach his condo in Bondi. If she lived on the other side of the harbor, it could take her quite a while.

A red Mazda CX-3 swept around the corner and then slowed, as if the driver was unsure of their directions. Cam wondered if it could be her. A moment later, the driver pulled into the curb directly below him and climbed out. Cam's heart leaped in his chest and a rush of nerves kicked into overdrive.

She wore a bright yellow sundress that was in stark contrast to her nurse's uniform and looked way too flimsy for the brisk June day. It floated around a pair of shapely legs. A matching jacket was draped around her shoulders. Her chestnut-colored hair was loose around her shoulders and made her appear younger than he remembered. Her high heels clacked on the pavement as she headed in the direction of the lobby.

Quickly, he ducked back inside and hurried over to the kitchen counter. A pot of coffee brewed on the stove and a plate of fresh pastries he'd bought from the delicatessen around the corner were piled high on a plate nearby. It was probably overkill. More likely than not, she'd collect Cynthia and leave. She probably wouldn't have time for coffee, or feel inclined to linger. She was only there to help his sister, after all.

He should have left for work already. He was usually at the station by six. He'd asked his boss for a late start so that he'd be home when Georgie arrived. It was stupid the way he was getting all worked up about a girl he barely knew, but the truth was, he couldn't remember ever feeling so drawn to a woman.

He was well aware of the good looks and easy charm he'd been blessed with and he was grateful for these gifts. He'd be lying if he didn't admit they'd smoothed his way somewhat during his path from teenager to adulthood. Women found him attractive and he was flattered by their attention. But he never took it for granted and until now, he'd never craved it.

The speed and depth of his feelings for Georgie were a little scary and he was nervous about messing things up. Until now, he hadn't seen her since their initial meeting at the hospital. He was equal parts nerves and anticipation at the thought of seeing her again.

Without conscious thought, his mind turned to the baby deaths and the apparent high incidence of newborn deaths in the very hospital where she worked. He frowned momentarily. The fact the deaths had happened in her workplace didn't mean she was guilty of any wrongdoing, or that anything untoward had happened. SIDS was an accepted medical diagnosis and as tragic as it was to lose a baby that way, sometimes it happened.

But did it happen that often in other hospitals? That was something he'd have to find out. Right now, he was going to concentrate on the beautiful woman who right now was on her way up to his apartment. As if on cue, the doorbell rang and once again, his heart jumped in his chest. Taking a calming breath, he strode over to open the front door.

She looked even more beautiful up close. The breeze had ruffled her hair, setting it awry, but in a nice way. His gaze zeroed in on her lips, coated in a bright red gloss. Her tongue darted out and then disappeared and heat rushed to his groin. With an effort, he controlled the impulse to take her into his arms and instead, stepped back to allow her to enter.

"Hi," he said and smiled at her, wracking his brain for something clever to say.

"Good morning. I'm sorry I'm late. I got caught up in traffic."

"No problem, it's great to see you again. Come in." She followed him into the apartment and he headed toward the open concept kitchen and living area, his heart beating double time.

"That coffee smells great."

"Would you like some?" he threw over his shoulder.

She glanced at her watch. "Why not? Our appointment's not until nine. Even with this traffic, we should make it in plenty of time."

Cam hid his elation by turning away from her and busying himself getting coffee cups from the cupboard. "How do you take it?" he asked.

"With cream and sugar, please." She hopped up onto one of the bar stools that lined the counter.

He grinned. "The only way to drink coffee, right?"

She smiled back at him. "I would have thought, with you being a police officer and all, you'd drink it black as tar. Isn't that how they do it on TV?"

He chuckled. "Not this cop. I like it sweet and creamy, although it's probably not the healthiest thing to do." He patted his flat stomach.

She gave him a slow once-over that sent blood rushing to his groin. "I don't know. You look like you can handle it. You must work out every day of the week."

The teasing glint in her eyes sent his pulse thrumming in his ears. *Was she flirting with him?* Hell, he wasn't sure, but she was a long way from the solemn, professional nurse he'd struck the first time round. Granted, that situation had called for sobriety, but apart from her initial reaction to him, she hadn't given out many positive vibes.

Right now, he could almost feel the current running between them. The thought that she might be interested in him filled him with excitement and relief. He really liked this woman and looked forward to getting to know her better.

"We're out of shampoo, Cam."

Cynthia stepped into the room, her hair still wet from the shower. Cam hid his disappointment. His time alone with Georgie had just come to an end. Still, he was pleased to see his sister up and about, showered and wearing clean clothes. It was a start.

"Cyn, remember Georgie. You met her while you were at the hospital."

Cam was relieved when Georgie took the initiative and extended her hand. A moment later, Cynthia stepped forward and shook it. "Hi," she said shyly, ducking her head.

"It's lovely to see you again, Cynthia, Georgie replied with a smile. "I hope you're ready for a day filled with pampering. I have us booked in for manicures, pedicures, a facial and a massage."

Cam whistled, impressed. "That ought to do it."

Georgie tossed him a grin and his belly somersaulted and filled with warmth. He knew, in that moment, she was good and kind and generous. She barely knew either of them and yet she'd set up all of this for his sister. It was almost too much.

"I've never been to a spa before," Cynthia admitted softly, a blush still staining her cheeks.

"Well, you're in for the treat of your life!" Georgie exclaimed.

Cam handed Georgie a cup of coffee and she murmured her thanks. Their fingers touched. Cam's belly nosedived from the contact and he wondered if she'd felt it, too. He stared at her, but she'd averted her gaze and he was left to speculate.

"What's for breakfast, Cam?"

He dragged his gaze away from Georgie and focused on his sister. "I bought fresh pastries from the bakery and there's orange juice in the fridge. Help yourself." He moved the plate closer to the women.

Georgie took notice of the assortment on offer and smiled. "Almond croissants! My favorite! Boy, if I'd known about this, I would have saved my cereal for another day."

Cynthia screwed up her face. "Cereal! Yuck!"

"Two Weet-Bix, yoghurt, milk and a few strawberries. It gets me going every day."

Cynthia rolled her eyes, but a smile teased at her lips. "Sounds like a TV commercial."

Cam smiled at Georgie. "Sounds delicious!"

"Yes, but not as delicious as this!" Georgie reached over and selected an almond croissant. Taking a bite, she sighed in delight. "*Mm*, this is heaven!"

Over pastries and coffee, the three of them spent the next few minutes in idle chitchat. Too soon, Georgie glanced at her watch and pushed away from the counter.

"We need to get moving, Cynthia. Are you just about done?"

His sister nodded and wiped her mouth with the back of her hand. "I just need to brush my teeth," she said quickly and headed down the corridor toward the bathroom.

Cam turned to Georgie. A dusting of icing sugar was caught on the tip of her nose. He came toward her and his heart started a slow and steady thump. She stared at him, her eyes wide with anticipation. He stopped less than a foot away and reached out and wiped the white powder off her nose. For an instant, her eyes flared with desire before she quickly looked away.

"You had icing sugar on your nose," he managed, his voice husky with need.

"Thank you," she murmured, her gaze still focused at her feet.

"No, thank *you*."

She looked up and his gut somersaulted once again. Her dark liquid eyes seemed to peer right into his soul. "For what?"

"For this. For Cynthia. I've never seen her so engaged. She's almost like a normal teenager, complaining about the food. I can't thank you enough for doing that, for bringing her back."

Georgie shrugged and looked away. A becoming blush stole across her cheeks. "It's nothing."

Cam took hold of her chin with his fingers and tilted up her head. "It's *everything*."

Georgie smiled. "Let's see how you feel after the day is over. You might end up paying for regular trips to the day spa. I might unleash a monster."

He chuckled. "It would be worth every cent."

Georgie's expression turned serious and she slowly shook her head. "You really are the nicest person I know."

His heart filled with warmth. "Right back at you."

CHAPTER 11

Dear Diary,

It saddens me to know she's taken our actions hard. I'm told she's scared and confused and has begun to question her own ability. I wish I could ease her suffering, but I must sacrifice her peace of mind for the greater good.

From the moment I started down this path, I knew I'd found my destiny. Matron knew me better than I knew myself. Once my eyes were opened to the truth, she knew I would see this was by far the best way to go. So many years, so many babies; so many lives I've touched—and all for the better. Of this, I am certain.

———

Georgie glanced across at Cynthia where she lay face down on a table identical to the one Georgie lay on. They each had a massage therapist working over them, kneading the knots out of their shoulders. It felt like heaven and from the soft groans of appreciation coming from Cynthia's direction, it appeared she was feeling the same.

Earlier, they'd enjoyed manicures and pedicures. Cynthia had exclaimed over the range of bright colors. She'd chosen a hot pink with a glittery sparkle in the polish. Georgie had gone for straight crimson. With their facials yet to come, it would be lunchtime before they finished.

She hadn't asked Cameron what he was up to, but she assumed he was heading to work. He was dressed in a suit and tie, similar to the one he'd worn the first day they'd met. The charcoal suit fabric and pale blue shirt contrasted nicely against his dark hair and olive skin and she couldn't help but notice the way the clothing enhanced his physical appeal. There was no doubt about it: He wore a suit well.

"*Mm*, that feels sooo good," Cynthia murmured.

Georgie turned her head in the girl's direction. "You like it?"

Cynthia lifted her head and grinned. "I've never felt anything so fantastic! Thank you so much for bringing me, Georgie."

Georgie smiled and lay her head back down on the cushion. It made her feel good to know she'd helped distract Cynthia from the tragedy that had befallen her and her baby, even for a little while. Georgie's thoughts shifted to Sandra and Wes and her pleasure dissipated. Somewhere in the city was another young mother making preparations to bury her child. It was heartbreaking to have knowledge of it, let alone have had intimate dealings with the devastated couple.

Even now, Georgie couldn't understand how it had happened. The results from the standard newborn tests were all within normal limits and the baby's withdrawal symptoms had appeared negligible. Sandra's baby wasn't one Georgie had identified as being at high risk of severe withdrawals and yet, Marjorie had indicated that, failing any other explanation and even though they couldn't prove it, this was the likely reason for his death. Yet again, the official cause of death would be listed as SIDS.

The fact that three babies in Georgie's care had died shortly after birth in such a short space of time was very troubling. She'd worked as a midwife for two years. Over that time, as far as she knew, infant deaths were few and far between. In fact, until recently, every one of those babies had died in utero and the parents of the child and the staff were aware of it beforehand.

The mother still had to endure labor and the whole procedure was permeated with sadness and pain. Knowing from the outset the baby was deceased made it beyond difficult for everyone to see through to the end. As desperate as Georgie was for a baby she could raise as her own, she could only hope and pray she never had to experience the tragedy of a labor where the baby was stillborn.

But what had happened lately was different.

Every time one of the babies died, she'd wracked her brain, trying to work out where she'd gone wrong. The deliveries had all been uneventful. The babies had tested fine. And yet, twelve or so hours later, they were dead. She was missing something in her understanding, something crucial, and she didn't have a clue what it was. The knowledge was eating away at her.

After each death, her mom assured her it wasn't anything to do with her. Even her Aunt Rosemary had weighed in with her support. The baby had died and nobody was really sure why. Sometimes it happened. It wasn't anyone's fault. There was nothing anyone could do. Though Georgie wanted to believe their reassurances, in the dark of night, the fear that Georgie had overlooked something important during the birth or even shortly afterwards wouldn't be denied.

It had gotten to the point now, where she was losing confidence in her midwifery skills. She'd worked as a pediatric nurse for five years with only a couple of fatalities. She'd been a midwife less than half that time and in the last three weeks, three babies she'd delivered had died. The fact that she hadn't been on the shift when it had happened didn't count. Somehow, somewhere, she'd failed to recognize a problem and it had cost three babies their lives.

"What's the matter, Georgie? You look sad."

Cynthia's quiet comment penetrated Georgie's depressing thoughts. With an effort, she forced a smile on her face and wished it didn't feel so much like a grimace. "Nothing. I'm fine. How's your massage?"

Cynthia grinned, her expression filled with contentment. "Beyond wonderful. I don't think I've ever felt so relaxed."

"I'm glad and you deserve it. That's the reason for coming to a place like this. I used to come quite a bit, but lately it's hard to find the time."

"It should be compulsory for everyone to experience a day spa once in their life! If I could afford it, I'd come every week!" She grinned with such genuine pleasure, once again Georgie was warmed all the way through.

The spa treatments hadn't come cheap, but as far as she was concerned, they were worth every cent. Before she'd left his condo, Cameron had handed her two, hundred-dollar bills, but she'd refused to accept them. She didn't expect Cameron to understand, but this was *her* treat; her way of apologizing to her patient. It could never make up for the loss of a baby, but it was something.

Afterwards, Georgie took Cynthia to lunch at a restaurant on the boardwalk at Circular Quay. The early winter sun was warm on their faces as they watched the seagulls gathered on the wharf. Cynthia ordered fish and chips and a Diet Coke. Georgie ordered a chicken Caesar salad and a latté. While they waited for their food to arrive, Georgie took a moment to study the girl who sat opposite her.

The dark shadows and haunted look had all but disappeared from Cynthia's eyes and though a faint air of sadness still surrounded her, the pleasure she'd enjoyed that morning seemed to have worked some magic. A spark had returned that had been missing since the death of her little Josephine. Cameron would be relieved.

"How are you coping, living with your brother?" she teased. "I hope he isn't too tough on you. Big brothers are renowned for it!"

A smile played around Cynthia's lips. "Cam's been fantastic. I couldn't ask for a better brother." Her smile faded and she eyed Georgie solemnly. "I… I don't know what I would have done if he hadn't offered to let me stay. Thank you for finding him."

"No thanks are necessary, honey. I could tell you needed some support. Having a baby, especially so young, is tough. I made enquires about your brother's whereabouts even before I knew about…about Josephine's death."

A shadow passed over Cynthia's face and Georgie bit her tongue. *Was it too early to talk to the girl about her loss?* Georgie was an experienced nurse and over the years had counseled many patients, but she wasn't a qualified therapist. Perhaps she'd said too much.

"She was so tiny and so beautiful," Cynthia whispered.

Georgie breathed out a quiet sigh of relief. "Yes, she was." Reaching across the table, Georgie took Cynthia's hand. "Do you want to talk about it?"

"Ava—she's my psychiatrist—keeps telling me to open up. She says the more I talk about

Josephine and accept what happened to her, the sooner I'll find closure. Until then, it's like a constant ache, never going away. But sometimes I'm afraid of closure... That I'll forget her." Tears filled the young girl's eyes.

Georgie's heart stuttered. She tightened her hold on Cynthia's hand and cast around for the right words to ease the teenager's pain. "You'll never forget her, I promise. And Ava's right, honey. Remember Josephine how she was. Celebrate her short life. Remember how much you loved her. It's impossible to understand what happened and nobody has the answer. It was just one of those things."

"But why *my* baby?" Cynthia cried, her sobs now falling in earnest. "Okay, I'm sixteen, homeless and her father's nowhere in sight, but I loved her with everything that I had! I would have loved her until I died!"

Georgie pushed back her chair and went around to Cynthia's side. Cradling the girl against her, she gently stroked Cynthia's blond hair. The young woman continued to cry softly and Georgie murmured mindless words of comfort. She agreed wholeheartedly with Cynthia. *Dammit! It wasn't fair.*

At last, the sobs quieted and slowly Cynthia pulled away. Georgie went back to her place and found a tissue in her handbag and gave it to the girl. A waitress approached a little uncertainly, holding a tray containing their order. Cynthia averted her face and Georgie distracted the waitress by offering her a bright, encouraging smile.

"That looks delicious!" she said.

"I have a chicken Caesar salad and a serving of fish and chips."

"Thank you," Georgie said.

The waitress set the food down on the table and then added, "I'll be right back with the drinks."

Georgie picked up her fork. From the corner of her eye, she saw Cynthia reach for a french fry. Georgie's breath eased out. It was okay. Cynthia was going to be okay.

The waitress returned a moment later with a coffee mug and a can of Diet Coke. "Here we go," she said and put the drinks in front of them. "Will there be anything else?"

Georgie shook her head. "I think we're good, thank you." With a nod and a quick smile, the waitress disappeared.

"How's your fish?" Georgie asked a little while later.

"It's good," Cynthia said quietly and then looked up. Her eyes were red, but she stared at Georgie calmly. "Thank you for not making a big scene. It's embarrassing enough that I blubbered in public. I appreciate that you didn't make a big deal of it."

"Hey, it's no problem. Besides, if you want to cry in public, you go ahead and cry. I won't let anybody stop you."

A tiny smile teased at the corners of Cynthia's lips. "You're pretty cool, for an adult, Georgie."

"You're pretty cool, too, Cynthia. Don't let anyone tell you different."

Cynthia's smile widened and her expression grew sly. "My brother's pretty cool. And good-looking. And he has this amazing car. Some kind of sports car that looks like it came out of a movie where the hot guy gets the girl. He's single, you know."

Heat crept up Georgie's neck but she steadfastly ignored her embarrassment. Laughing, she brushed away Cynthia's comments and reached for her mug.

"What? Don't you think he's good-looking?" Cynthia replied in surprise.

Georgie swallowed a mouthful of coffee and cleared her throat. "I-I guess so. I haven't really thought about it."

Cynthia frowned. "What's there to think about? You've got eyes, haven't you?"

This time, Georgie's cheeks ignited and there was no hiding her embarrassment.

Cynthia pounced. "You *do* think he's hot, don't you? Or else you wouldn't be looking at me like that! I *knew* it!"

Georgie fumbled around for something to say, desperate to change the topic. "Oh, look! A ferry's about to dock. Don't you just love the Sydney ferries? Did you know the first commercial ferry service to cross Sydney Harbour was established in 1861? That's a long time ago."

Cynthia merely shook her head slowly back and forth, a knowing expression on her face. The girl was wiser than her years. "So, are you single?"

Coffee spluttered out of Georgie's mouth and she scrambled for a napkin. "Cynthia! You're not supposed to ask me questions like that! It... It's impolite."

The girl shrugged, unrepentant. A few moments later, she spoke again. "So, are you?"

Georgie took a deep breath to reprimand the teenager again and then gave up. *What did it matter if she responded to the girl's question?* "Yes, Cynthia. I'm single."

Cynthia smiled. "Cool. Are you seeing anyone?"

Georgie's eyes widened at the girl's audacity, but once again, she answered. "No, Cynthia, I'm not seeing anyone."

"Good." The girl popped another french fry into her mouth and chewed slowly. "So, how old are you? 'Cause you act young, but you look kind of old."

This time, Georgie laughed outright. "I'm twenty-nine. To you, I'm sure it sounds ancient."

Cynthia grinned back at her. "Nah. Not really. Cam's twenty-seven and even though he's old, he doesn't seem like it. You know what I mean?"

Georgie nodded. "Oh, yeah. I know what you mean."

"Cam said I can stay with him for as long as I want. He's re-enrolled me in school. I like that he cares enough about me and my education, but I don't want to cramp his style. I mean, he's heading for thirty, right? He should find a girl and get married. Isn't that what people do when they get that old? He won't be able to bring a wife home with me living in the spare room. No woman would want that."

Though she spoke with confidence and bravado, Georgie sensed the fear and uncertainty behind Cynthia's words. Her heart tightened at the thought the young girl wasn't sure how long Cam's support would last, and her uncertainty about the future. She sat forward and tried to find the words to reassure her.

"Your brother loves you. I hardly know him, but I can see how much he cares. He won't ask you to leave and he won't let you leave until you're ready. Until you're old enough to live on your own."

"I've been living on my own for the past two years," Cynthia mumbled, her eyes downcast.

"And I'm guessing Cameron had no idea about that."

Cynthia nodded, but remained silent.

"Cynthia, listen to me. I made enquires about your brother's whereabouts the same afternoon your baby was born. The very next morning, he was there, in the ward, asking for you. Are those the actions of someone who doesn't care, and care deeply?"

"I know he cares, but for how long?"

Georgie stared at Cynthia's bowed head. "Have you spoken to Cameron about this?" she asked softly. The girl continued to stare at her plate and shook her head.

"You need to, honey. You owe him that. Who knows? You might be worrying about this for nothing. He might have no intention of settling down and getting married. Or if he does, that could be years away. People are getting married later and later these days. You might even be living in an apartment of your own by the time your brother makes the decision to marry or commit to a live-in girlfriend."

Cynthia lifted her head and stared at Georgie with hope in her eyes. "Do you really think so? I have nowhere else to go."

"It's possible. I don't know him very well. The best thing to do would be to talk to him about your fears and let him reassure you. I'm certain he will. He loves you. He wants to take care of you, at least until you're old enough to take care of yourself—and are able to."

Cynthia appeared to consider Georgie's words and then nodded slowly in agreement. "I think you're right." She flashed Georgie a relieved smile. "Thanks, Georgie. You're the best!"

They finished their meal and Georgie tried hard not to think about the words of reassurance that had rolled so easily off her tongue. Like she'd told Cynthia, it was very possible Cameron might be one of those guys who wasn't interested in settling down. The thought was as depressing as hell. She swallowed a sigh and finished her coffee. Cynthia chewed on her last french fry.

"What are we doing after lunch?" the young girl asked brightly, her earlier doldrums dissolved or forgotten.

Georgie thought for a moment. She hadn't planned to spend the whole day with the teen, but she was enjoying the young girl's company and she couldn't deny the pleasure she felt at seeing Cynthia's demeanor change from the sad and grieving young mom to a girl who was acting more and more like a normal teenager.

"We could go to the movies," she suggested and was immediately rewarded with a huge smile from Cynthia.

"Yes! I *love* the movies! It's been years since I've seen one!" She pushed back her chair and ran around to Georgie's side and threw her arms around her in an awkward hug. "You really are the best, Georgie!"

Georgie accepted the young girl's praise, pleased that her suggestion had been met with so much enthusiasm. Georgie was a movie-addict. Going to the cinema was her single, most favorite thing to do. It was a rare time when she didn't catch at least one movie a week. Sometimes, she spent an entire day in the movie complex. It was one of the reasons she'd made it to twenty-nine without a serious boyfriend in tow. Her mother frequently bemoaned the fact that she'd never find a suitable partner while she was hiding out in the dark in a movie cinema.

Pushing away from the table, Georgie quickly paid the bill and then linked her arm with Cynthia's. Together, they walked away from the café and up the street in the direction of the train station that would take them to George Street, the hub of the movie cinemas.

———

The phone in Cameron's pocket vibrated against his chest. Tugging it out, he checked the screen and frowned at the display. *No Caller ID.* He answered the call on the third ring.

"Detective Sergeant Dawson; can I help you?"

"Detective, it's Deborah Healy from the Sydney Harbour Hospital."

"Ms Healy. What can I do for you?"

"I'm calling about the figures I quoted you the other day. The ones pertaining to the number of infant deaths in the hospital over the past twelve months."

"I take it you're referring to the fifteen deaths recorded in your database and not the two you had knowledge of. How accurate was your official data?"

"Yes, well, I've had a chance to review all fifteen files." There was a pause. When the general manager spoke again, her tone was grave. "I'm afraid the figures are correct."

Cameron absorbed the news calmly, although he could hear the edge of panic in Deborah Healy's voice. He didn't blame her. He'd never had anything to do with having babies or even turned his mind to how many children were born in his city each year, but the thought that more than one a month died at birth in her hospital, seemed alarming. Most people would expect if they gave birth in a hospital in Australia, going home with a healthy baby was almost a certainty. It was apparent this wasn't the case at the Sydney Harbour Hospital.

"I want you to investigate this, Detective, with all due haste. Every one of those deaths happened on Ward Seven and every one of them had SIDS recorded as the cause of death. It's very clear something's not right. Throw in the fact I was kept in the dark about all but two of these deaths and I'm afraid we have a serious problem."

Deborah's solemn announcement broke into Cameron's thoughts. His gut clenched. If the general manager was asking him to look into the matter, things were definitely off-base. Either that, or she was trying to head off something even worse. He hadn't forgotten that at least two of her once highly respected doctors were now warming their butts in jail—and he was sure she hadn't forgotten, either.

"Who's responsible for keeping you informed?" he asked.

"There's a chain of command, but it starts at the ward level. Any incident involving serious injury or death to a patient must be reported by the NUM of that ward."

Cam grimaced. "How many levels of command before it gets to you? How many people are we talking?"

"Four for each department."

"Not so many. It shouldn't be too hard to work out where the communication broke down."

"You're right and I can assure you I'll be looking into the matter very thoroughly."

Cam heard the steely determination in the general manager's voice and was confident she'd do what she said. After all that had gone down on her watch, she couldn't afford to have the police break another scandal among the staff of the Sydney Harbour Hospital.

"I'll need copies of those records," he said.

"Of course. I'll get them over to you as soon as I can."

"I appreciate your cooperation, Ms Healy. I hope I can continue to rely on your support."

"If we have a rogue staff member or members acting illegally, I want to bring an end to it, right now."

Cameron's heart picked up its pace. "Do you really think that's possible? That an employee has something to do with these deaths?"

Deborah sighed heavily. "I'm not willing to speculate, but know this, Detective: No other hospital in this country would have an infant death rate so high. Coupled with the fact most of these deaths weren't reported to me, it's obvious something's not right. We need to find out what's going on."

"I'll need to speak with some of your staff."

"You have my permission to speak with whomever you want. Just...be discreet. I don't want this getting out before it's absolutely necessary."

Cameron thought of Cynthia and her little baby girl and his gut tightened with dread. Was it possible the child had been *murdered* shortly after she'd been born? And what about Danielle Jamison's baby? Was the premier closer to the truth than any of them had imagined? Had a staff member killed his grandson? Was the Sydney Harbour Hospital hiding another criminal? Cam couldn't bear to think about it.

Thanking Deborah for her cooperation, he

ended the call and leaned back in his chair, stunned at the direction of his thoughts. Hot on their tail, were images of Georgie. The premier had said Georgie Whitely had delivered his grandson. Georgie was also present at Josephine's birth. How many others on the general manager's list had involved the beautiful midwife? Cameron wasn't sure he wanted to know, but he sure as hell would have to find out.

CHAPTER 12

Cam swung into the driveway of his apartment block only moments before Georgie's Mazda came into view. She'd sent him a text earlier, to say she was taking Cynthia to the movies and would drop her home a little after six. Despite the unsettling questions that still filled his mind, Cam wanted to be there when she arrived.

Even if he managed to prove that something illegal had taken place, there was no proof Georgie was involved. It could be something to do with the failure of hospital equipment or technology, or involve any one of the thousands of other staff members who worked at the hospital.

His enquires with the other large hospitals servicing the greater Sydney area confirmed Deborah Healy's surety that none of them would have infant death rates as high as hers. Yet, apart from the fact the hospital's reporting system had broken down, there was still no evidence of wrongdoing.

Pulling into his parking space, he climbed out and waited for the girls to join him. Like she had earlier that morning, Georgie parked her car alongside the curb. The two of them walked toward him, arm in arm, and he was moved to see the genuine smile that turned up Cynthia's lips. He hadn't seen her so animated since before he left the family home a decade ago. Not even weeks of therapy had made her smile that way.

"You two look like you've had a nice day," he said when they reached him.

Cynthia's grin widened. "We had the most *fantastic* day, Cam! We spent the morning at the day spa—look, do you like the color of my nails?" She thrust her hands out in front of her and laughed before continuing. "Then we had lunch at this really posh place down near the harbor. To top it off, Georgie took me to the movies." Cynthia spun on her heel and tugged at Georgie's arm. "How did you know I love going to the movies?"

Georgie smiled softly. "I love going to the movies, too. It was fun. Thank you for coming with me."

Cynthia's eyes widened and she shook her head. "No! I'm the one who's grateful. I'm the one who wants to say thank you. I've had the best day ever!" She flung her arms around Georgie and hugged her. Cam's chest tightened with emotion when Georgie hugged her back.

Careful, he silently warned himself. For all her outward goodness, he hardly knew Georgie Whitely, and until he knew the extent of her involvement, if any, in the mysterious infant deaths, he'd do well to keep his distance. He needed to proceed with caution.

"Well, I guess I'd better get going," Georgie said, interrupting his thoughts.

"No!" his sister protested before he could respond. "Come in! Stay for dinner! Cam cooks a mean barbeque. She turned to him with an expectant look on her face. "Don't you?"

He couldn't find the words to turn her down. "I'm surprised you noticed. You've barely eaten anything I've cooked since you arrived," he muttered.

Cynthia had the grace to look embarrassed. "That's not true!"

Cam softened his words with a smile. "Oh, I think it is."

"Well, that was before. I feel so much better now. In fact, I'm starving. What's on the menu?" She shot him a cheeky smile and Cam couldn't help but laugh.

If he were honest, he didn't really mind that she'd invited Georgie to dinner. It would give him a chance to get to know her a little better and to sound her out about the infant deaths. It would be interesting to observe her reaction to a few questions and remarks.

Cam prided himself on being very perceptive. He had a knack for getting inside a person's head and they didn't even know he was there. It had helped him solve an admirable number of crimes over the years and he was confident his skills would continue to serve him well, even with the added complication of his attraction to his witness. His promise of caution would ensure he'd keep his libido under wraps. He turned to Georgie.

"Would you like to stay for dinner? After spending the day with this brat, it's the least I can do."

"Cam! That's not nice!" Cynthia replied in mock outrage and poked her tongue out at him.

Cam chuckled and Georgie sent him a soft smile. It lit up her brown eyes and sent a rush of blood to his groin. He swallowed a groan and once again determined to keep well away from her. She was dangerous to his peace of mind and until he knew what was going on at her work place, it was best he keep his distance. But that didn't mean they couldn't exchange chitchat over dinner. Did it? All of a sudden, he wasn't quite so certain.

"Are you sure?" she said, nibbling on her lip.

Cam dragged his gaze away from the tempting sight and nodded. It was too late now to retract the invitation.

"Yes, of course," he forced himself to reply. "Come on, let's go inside." He threw his arm around Cynthia's shoulders and the three of them walked toward the front entrance to the building.

———

It was getting late when Cynthia finally stretched her arms above her head and yawned and announced she was going to bed. She kissed

Cam goodnight and then surprised him by kissing Georgie on the cheek.

"Thank you for a wonderful day, Georgie. I'll remember it forever."

Georgie smiled with pleasure. "It was great," she agreed. "We'll have to do it again."

His sister's eyes widened in delight. "*Could* we? You mean it?"

Georgie chuckled. "Yes, of course. But we'll have to wait a few weeks. It will take that long before our nails will need to be redone."

Cynthia shrieked with excitement and threw her arms around Georgie and hugged her. "Oh, Georgie! Thank you! You're the absolute *best!*" Then, throwing them a wave, she skipped down the corridor in the direction of her bedroom.

Cam stared at the woman who sat across from him at the kitchen table. She seemed almost too good to be true. Like a guardian angel sent to heal his sister's pain. *Could an almost-stranger really be that kind to a girl she barely knew? Or was it all an act?* Cam was determined to find out.

"Would you like another coffee?" he asked.

"No, thanks. One's enough." She smiled and pushed back her chair and started collecting the dirty plates.

"I'll do that," Cam protested.

"It's no trouble. Besides, you cooked. I have a rule in my house: The cook never has to clean up!"

Cam chuckled. "I like that rule. Too bad I've lived on my own for so long. Until Cynthia arrived, there was nobody around but me. I cooked, cleaned and did whatever else was required."

Georgie headed toward the kitchen with her hands filled with dirty plates. She threw a grin over her shoulder. "Me, too. If only we'd known there was an easier way."

Cameron's heart leaped at the discovery she lived alone. It boded well for the fact that she might be single. The next instant, reining himself in, he told himself he shouldn't be so interested in her personal life. He had yet to broach the subject of the dead infants and still didn't have a clue how she might react.

They'd shared a pleasant meal around the table talking about their day. Cam had kept the conversation light, unprepared to discuss what had kept him busy throughout the day. He needed to comb through the hospital records and get a better sense of what had happened before he went any further. Still, the mood at the table was comfortable and he'd enjoyed getting to know Georgie better.

"You're really good with your sister. She's lucky she found you." Georgie's quiet words broke into his thoughts.

He stared at her. "I'm not sure that *she* found me. The way I heard it, you were the one who made the enquiries. If it weren't for you, I would never have known she was in the city, let alone in a hospital giving birth." He moved closer to where she was stacking the dishwasher. "I haven't had a chance to thank you."

"There... There's no need to thank me. I was merely doing my job." Her eyelids fluttered rapidly and her flimsy dress moved with each quick intake of breath. Cam was pleased to see she was affected by his nearness.

He'd always enjoyed women and they seemed to enjoy him. There had been a fair number of them, in and out of his life. No doubt a therapist would imagine the fact he'd grown up with a wicked adoptive mother, and a birth mother who hadn't loved him enough to keep him, would have been enough to sour him off female companions for life. But that wasn't the case. It wasn't all women he held a grudge against, just two of them. As far as he was concerned, both of them could burn in hell, along with his cowardly father.

Shaking off his dark thoughts, he gave Georgie a soft smile. "Are all nurses as dedicated as you?"

"I'm not sure you'd call it dedication. Like I said, I was merely doing my job. When I first saw Cynthia, she was already in labor and it was obvious she'd had a rough time. I'm sure I don't need to remind you about her appearance that first day."

Cam remembered the dirty state his sister had been in, even after a shower, and nodded slowly. "I remember."

"When I questioned her about her living arrangements, she told me she moved around a lot and was reluctant to give me specifics. It was obvious she had no fixed place to go. I was concerned for her and her baby and what would happen to them when they were discharged. When she told me she had no family other than a brother who was a police officer in the city, I took the only course of action open to me: I made an effort to locate you."

"And you did." Their gazes caught and held and the silence between them stretched out.

The tension in the air escalated and was only broken when Georgie turned away and focused her attention on stacking the rest of the dirty plates. The cutlery followed and the noise of that precluded further conversation. Cam busied himself by collecting the condiments off the table and storing them away in the pantry.

A few moments later, the cleanup was done and he reached for a bottle of port. "Would you like a glass?"

She shook her head. "I'm driving. I'd better—"

"You didn't have any wine at dinner. One glass won't put you over the limit."

She seemed to think about it and then accepted his offer with a slight smile. "All right. One glass."

He poured the drinks and carried them over to the glass sliding door that led out to the balcony. "Let's have them out here. It shouldn't be too cold, yet."

Georgie followed behind him and he handed her a glass. "You have a great view," she murmured, peering through the dark.

The lights from nearby houses and apartment blocks gently illuminated the night. His balcony overlooked a leafy park favored by morning joggers—him, included. He indicated the wooden deck chairs and they each took a seat. Georgie relaxed in one with a quiet sigh.

"What a week," she murmured and took a sip of port.

Cameron stared over at her and wondered what she was thinking. "It can't be easy, doing what you do. How do you keep it up?"

She smiled softly. "It's my job and I love it. I guess it's as simple as that."

Cameron nodded. He understood how a job could keep someone enthralled, the good times far outweighing the bad. There were many people who wondered how *he* could do what he did for a living, but it was like Georgie said: Policing was his job and he loved it.

"It must be difficult to lose a newborn. How do you cope with that?"

"Yes, it's difficult, all right. Thankfully, it doesn't happen too often."

"How often?"

She gazed at him for a moment, as if trying to work out where his interest lay and then answered. "I've worked as a midwife for two years. During that time, to my knowledge, three babies have died. That's three too many as far as I'm concerned and each and every one of them broke my heart... But I've learned to accept that sometimes bad things happen for no good reason. Is it really our job to question why?"

He stared at her and his heart began to pound. The three deaths she referred to were well below the fifteen the general manager had mentioned, and the GM's figures had been drawn from only the previous twelve months of the twenty-four Georgie had worked there. *Was*

Georgie really unaware of the others, or was she lying?

His mind snagged on something else she'd said: 'Sometimes bad things happen for no good reason. Is it really our job to question why?' *What the hell did she mean? Was she implying she knew more about them, but didn't feel at liberty to say? Was she sending him some sort of cryptic message? Or did she really approach the tragedies with such a fatalistic attitude?*

He groaned under his breath. So many unanswered questions were doing his head in. He prided himself on being able to read people well, and yet from Georgie, he could ascertain nothing. He was still of the opinion that she was a good person with the kindest of hearts, and yet she appeared to accept the deaths of the babies with a sense of fatalism he found a little cold. He had to know more.

"Do you really believe bad things just happen and there's nothing you can do about it?"

Her eyes widened. She stared at him for a long moment and then blinked and looked away. She lifted her glass and sipped at her port and then exhaled on a heavy sigh.

"The truth is," she began quietly, "I *want* to believe those deaths just happened. I have no choice. If I believe otherwise, I'll drive myself mad with guilt. I birthed each of those three babies. I should have noticed there was something wrong, something that would cause them to stop breathing before the next day was done."

She shook her head and stared at the floor, her

voice a low monotone. "I did the usual checks. Not one of those babies showed any signs there was something wrong."

"And yet there was."

She looked up at him and his breath caught at the pain in her eyes. Slowly, she nodded.

"Yes, there was. There *had* to be. Nothing else makes sense."

Cameron's heart thumped at the raw emotion on her face. Any doubt he'd been harboring that she was involved in wrongful deaths—if there even *were* wrongful deaths—was swept away like the cool breeze that blew in from Bondi Beach.

"My mother's tried to reassure me that it wasn't my fault, but even with all of her years' experience on a labor ward, it's so difficult to believe her. They were *my* babies. I was responsible for ensuring they would be all right. How can their deaths be anything but my fault?"

Her voice broke and tears welled up in her eyes. Without hesitation, Cam pushed away from his chair and went to her. His only thought was to ease the suffering in her eyes. He'd never be able to believe she was capable of deliberately ending a baby's life. She simply cared too much.

Taking her hand, he gently pulled her upright and enfolded her in his arms. She collapsed against him and cried softly into his shirt. Cam stroked her hair and down her back and murmured words of comfort in her ear. Her devastation tore at him. He'd always shied away from emotion, keeping himself removed, but listening to her forlorn weeping was a difficult thing to do.

At last, her crying eased to the occasional hiccup and sob and he set her gently away from him. Swiping at the dampness on her cheeks with the pad of his thumb, he stared down at her ravaged face. Even in the dimness of the evening, he could see her eyes were swollen and red. Her nose dripped. Her lip still wobbled.

To him, she was still beautiful.

Powerless to stop himself, he slowly dipped his head and captured her lips. Barely touching, he grazed her mouth and heard her indrawn breath. He pulled away and stared at her, sure that the desire that pounded through his veins was clear to see.

Her eyes grew round and then flared with an answering need. She stepped into him, closing the distance between them and her arms went around his neck. Needing no further encouragement, Cameron pressed her to him and kissed her like there was no tomorrow. And for that moment, it seemed the truth.

She tasted warm and sweet and heady, like the port she'd recently consumed. With a groan, his tongue swept over hers and danced inside her mouth. She matched his passion, kiss for kiss, until his body raged with fire. Somewhere, in the back of his mind, a tiny voice urged caution.

They were outside on his balcony. It was no place to make love. Inside, his young sister slept in one of the spare rooms. Now was not the time to have their passion get out of control, no matter how much he wanted it to. Knowing it was the only thing he could do, he eased away from her and loosened her arms from around his neck.

"Hey, sweetheart, we need to stop. We need to slow things down."

She stared up at him, her eyes dark with need and confusion. She blinked once and then blinked again. Slowly, reason appeared in her eyes. Almost immediately, a blush raced across her cheeks. She stepped away from him, like she'd been burned.

"I'm sorry. Oh, my goodness! I don't know what came over me! I'm sorry, Cameron. My God, I barely know you. I don't normally do this; fall to pieces and then kiss men I barely know. Please, can we just forget it ever happened?"

Cameron pressed a finger against her lips in an effort to silence her increasingly frantic speech. "Georgie, it's okay. Stop apologizing. I was a willing participant. In fact, I initiated it, remember?"

She blushed again and turned away. He almost smiled at her discomfort, enjoying the thought that his kiss had left her so frazzled, but he held himself back, knowing she wouldn't take kindly to his mirth.

"I-I should be going," she stammered and opened the sliding door.

He followed her inside, understanding her need to flee. Things had moved fast. His head was spinning, too. It was probably best for both of them that they call it a night.

She gathered her handbag from where she'd left it on a small table by the front door and then turned to him. "Thank you for dinner. It was lovely."

"It's the least I could do after what you did for Cynthia. She had a fantastic time and I know the excursion's done wonders for her state of mind. She looks so much better already. I can't thank you enough."

"It's fine. I was happy to do it for her. It won't go anywhere toward making up for the loss of her baby, but it's all I could think of to do."

Cam frowned. "I hope you're not blaming yourself for what happened to Josephine?"

Georgie shrugged and turned away. "Of course I'm blaming myself. What else would you expect me to do?"

Cam drew in a deep breath and exhaled slowly. "I'm sorry you feel that way. I'm sure Cynthia doesn't blame you."

"That might be so, but I... I can't help it."

"Sometimes bad things just happen, right? Isn't that what you said? Get this: I'm adopted. My birth mother didn't care for me enough to want to keep me. She handed me over for strangers to raise, and hell, they did a terrible job. But I don't blame myself." He stared at her long and hard and then shrugged. "Sometimes bad things just happen."

She held his gaze. It gave him no satisfaction to notice the color had leached from her cheeks. Her eyes were huge in her pale face, wide and uncertain and clouded with fear.

Fear? What the hell did she have to be afraid of? No, he must have been mistaken.

"I-I have to go," she stammered, averting her face.

He frowned in confusion, but silently turned away. He undid the security lock and opened the front door. She made a move to leave. Halfway through the doorway, she turned and shot him a sad smile. "Thanks again for dinner. Cynthia's right. You do a mean barbeque."

And with that, she was gone.

Chapter 13

Dear Diary,

Every now and then, usually deep in the night, I wonder if I've made the right decision; if I've chosen the right path. It happens most often when one of the women stare at me with their sad, haunted eyes, mourning the loss of their child. It is then, I find it hard to sleep and I am plagued by uncertainty.

Most of the time, of course, I'm content with my choices and not even a thunderstorm raging outside my window can wake me. So many mothers battling crippling addictions. They have no place raising a child.

A child needs love and security, comforts only money can bring. These women are destitute, living off the streets, with no further thought but their next fix.

Yes, all things considered, I've made the right decision. Of that, I'm...mostly certain...

———

Georgie pressed the stethoscope against the chest of the tiny baby who lay in the hospital crib. She counted his heartbeats. With his pulse still fast and erratic and his body jerking spasmodically—even in his sleep—the poor little thing continued to show signs he was suffering acute withdrawal from methamphetamines. His mom was passed out in her bed, sleeping off her own enforced meth withdrawal. She'd barely spent twenty minutes with her son over the course of Georgie's eight-hour shift.

Her heart broke at the thought of the baby who was, as yet, oblivious to the hardships he'd be forced to endure from the moment he and his mom left the safety and security of the post-natal ward. The likelihood of developmental delays and learning difficulties and the fact his mother lived on the streets and seemed totally uninterested in seeking help or improving her circumstances—for either her, or her son—all pointed to a bleak future. Georgie had already put in a call to FACS, but as yet, she hadn't seen a staff member on the ward. It was the same old, depressing story.

Usually, when she pondered the hopelessness of it all, it got her down, but today, nothing could take the glow off her memories of the evening she'd spent with Cam. Except the part where he'd talked about his adoptive parents and birth mother.

It was obvious from the anger and bitterness in his voice that he had major issues regarding his adoption. The knowledge unsettled her. He thought his birth mother didn't care enough about him to keep him. Is that how *her* son felt about the mother he'd never met?

Until then, the night had been like something out of a fairytale. Their conversation around the dinner table had been warm and spontaneous, with none of the uncomfortable silences she usually experienced when she dined with a man she barely knew.

Granted, Cynthia had been present for most of the time, but Cam's little sister had seemed content to sit and eat and listen to the conversation flow around her and had only made the occasional contribution. It was Cam who made it easy. He had a natural grace and charm that Georgie had initially mistaken for arrogance. The fact that he was sinfully good-looking only added to his appeal. He was solicitous of his sister and asked questions about Georgie's work. He appeared genuinely interested in her responses. And afterwards, out on the balcony, they'd kissed.

And what a kiss! At the memory of his lips on hers, heat crept up Georgie's neck. Never in her twenty-nine years had she been kissed so...thoroughly. He kissed like a man who knew what he was doing and who sought to give as much pleasure as he received. It was only when he'd called a halt to their increasingly heated embrace that she'd been embarrassed at her uninhibited response.

Not that he seemed to mind. She was sure he was as attracted to her as she was to him. If it weren't for the adoption issue, she'd be skipping over the clouds. She thought again of how he'd spoken about the fact he was adopted and dread settled heavily in her stomach.

Would the fact that she'd put her baby up for adoption at seventeen be a deal breaker? Would he judge her as harshly as he judged his birth mother? When he said he'd been put up for adoption because his birth mother didn't care, she'd wanted to shout out in protest. It might not have been like that. It hadn't been that way for her.

She'd wanted her son like she wanted to keep breathing. Signing the adoption papers had been like severing a limb. She'd died a thousand deaths and her heart was always heavy. There hadn't been a day pass since when she didn't think about him and hope that he was safe and happy.

But her relationship with Cam—if she could even call it that—was so fresh and new and fragile, she didn't know if it was strong enough to put to the test. She liked him. She really liked him. And now she was terrified a decision she'd made in her past would tear them apart, before they'd even had a chance.

No, the best thing to do would be to stay quiet. There was no need for him to know, at least, for now. Her past was her past. The decision she'd made as a teenager could stay hidden, deep inside her heart.

If her relationship with Cam deepened into something more substantial, something more permanent, then perhaps she'd take the risk and share it with him. If they cared enough about each other for her to share her innermost secrets, then she could only hope he would love her enough to understand.

After all, his little sister had also made some difficult choices in her life, but from the love and concern he showered on her, it appeared Cam neither judged her, nor laid blame. She could only hope he'd be as merciful if, and when, it came to her.

She remembered how she'd left him, in a rush to get away. She'd spent all of her second day off in her apartment, rehashing the night and dredging up memories of the past. She should call him and apologize for her hasty departure and thank him again for his hospitality.

She also hadn't had a chance to talk to him about Cynthia's fears and insecurities. Georgie was sure he'd want to know. She was just as certain he'd offer the teen all the reassurances Georgie had already mentioned to her. Whatever else Cameron Dawson was, he was good and kind and compassionate, at least when it came to his sister.

Removing the stethoscope from her ears, she made a notation on the baby's hospital chart and then hung it back on the crib. It was almost time for her break. She'd grab a coffee and head outside into the wintery sunshine. The morning had been cool when she'd arrived at work, but by now it ought to be perfect. Even in winter, the temperature in the heart of Sydney remained pleasantly mild. Most June days saw the mercury climb to at least sixty-two degrees. There was no better time to make a call to the man she just couldn't get out of her mind.

With coffee in hand, Georgie found a spot on the grass out the front of the hospital. Several other nurses lay sprawled on the ground chatting with each other or texting or talking on their phones. She tugged her cell from her pocket and dialed Cameron's number. It was answered on the second ring.

"Good morning," he greeted her and she could hear the smile in his husky voice.

Her heart skipped a beat. "Good morning," she replied, all of a sudden feeling unaccountably shy.

"How are you?"

"I-I'm great," she stammered and then cursed the blush that burned her cheeks. She felt like a tongue-tied teenager greeting the guy she'd been crushing on all year. With an effort, she slowed her breathing and forced the nerves aside.

"I... I just wanted to call and apologize for leaving so abruptly the other night. I had a lovely evening. I... I don't know what got into me."

"It's fine, Georgie," he replied, his voice soft and caring. "It's my fault. I shouldn't have mentioned my past. I could tell my attitude alarmed you, and I'm sorry. It's been a sore point for me for as long as I can remember, but it's my bad. I shouldn't have dragged you into it. No wonder you ran."

"I didn't run," she protested gently. "Besides, I'd like to hear more about your past, about the real Cameron Dawson. We all have a past—me, included. Sometimes it's good to show your vulnerable side." She thought about the way she'd blubbered all over him and added, "Like I did."

"I'm honored that you trusted me enough to do so."

The gentleness in his voice sounded so genuine, she couldn't help but believe he meant it. *How had she stumbled across this wonderful man?* A man who seemed to share her interest, if his heated kisses were anything to go by.

"Th-thank you," she stammered, suddenly overwhelmed by a wave of emotion. "You're very kind."

"I'm not sure kindness has anything to do with it. I'm just being honest."

She smiled and her heart sang with joy. *Could he get any more perfect?* There must be something wrong with him that she hadn't yet discovered. There had to be some reason a man like Cameron Dawson was still single. Nobody was as good and kind as he was without some hidden flaws. It just wasn't possible.

"How's Cynthia?" she asked, remembering the other reason for her call.

"She's great. Better than I've ever seen her. I can't thank you enough for what you've done for her."

Georgie brushed off the praise. "It was nothing. Besides, I had a good time, too. Who wouldn't want to spend the day getting pampered?"

Cam laughed. "Me, I guess. Maybe it's a girl thing?"

Georgie chuckled and then her smile faded. "Cynthia's a little concerned you might ask her to leave if you start a relationship with a woman," she said quietly.

It was only after the words were out of her mouth that Georgie thought about how that might sound. *Did he think she was angling for a relationship? That she wanted to move things between them so fast?* A fresh wave of heat burned her cheeks. She hurried to explain.

"I-I don't mean you and me... That is, that we might... Oh, God..."

His gentle laughter did nothing to ease her embarrassment. "You're making this harder than it needs to be, Georgie. I understand what you're trying to say. Somehow or other, you were able to get Cynthia to confide in you about her feelings and she told you about her insecurities. Is that right?"

"Yes," Georgie replied, relieved he was taking it in the manner she meant.

"I admire you for getting her to open up to you and I'm grateful for it. She raised the subject with me this morning over breakfast, so your revelation doesn't come as a complete surprise."

Georgie was filled with satisfaction, pleased that Cynthia had taken Georgie's words of advice to heart. "She did?"

"Yes, I was going to call you and thank you, but I hadn't found the time."

"What did she say?"

"Pretty much what you just did, only your name came up in the conversation as the relevant third party. I think she suspects there might be something between us."

Georgie's heart beat a little faster. She tightened her grip on her phone. *There was something between them? Had Cameron just admitted it?* She couldn't believe how much she wanted it to be true.

"Cynthia was plain about her feelings," Cam continued. "She wanted to know where she stood; what would happen to her if I moved a girlfriend into my apartment."

"W-what did you tell her?"

"That it didn't matter who I was dating; she'll always have a home with me for as long as she needs it." His tone lowered to a husky drawl. "I told her I was sure you'd understand."

A swarm of butterflies took up residence in Georgie's stomach and her pulse kicked up another gear. She couldn't believe they were talking about having a relationship; that he'd begun to think of her in that way—the same way she'd begun to think of him.

After leaving his condo, she'd spent the rest of the night dreaming about what it would be like to spend every spare moment with him, claiming him as her own. The fantasies had been overshadowed by her concern about his attitude toward adoption and she'd been kept sleepless for the past two nights. She'd woken tired and restless, yet eager to see him again.

From what he'd just said, he was as keen about her as she was about him, but she needed to be certain. She was way past the age of playing games and the last thing she wanted to do was embarrass herself by presuming feelings that might not be there. She cleared her throat of a bout of nerves. "Just so we're clear on this, you... You like me, right?"

"I thought I made that clear when I kissed you the other night?"

Georgie blushed once again at the memory, but managed to reply. "Yes, well I guess you did. It was a very nice kiss."

"*Nice?*" he asked, his voice tinged with laughter.

Georgie smiled into her phone. "Okay, it was a little more than nice. It was...amazing."

"Yeah," he agreed softly, "it was."

Silence fell between them, like they were both remembering the explosiveness of their first kiss. Georgie couldn't help but wonder what it would be like to take things further.

"I want to kiss you again," Cameron murmured.

"Me, too," she admitted breathlessly.

"Where are you?"

"At work. How about you?"

"Same."

"What time do you finish?"

"Six. How about you?"

"I'm supposed to get out of here at four. If I'm in the middle of assisting a labor, I'll sometimes stay later, but today I'm working on the post-natal ward, so I should get away on time."

"We might be able to get together, maybe grab a bite to eat."

Georgie's heart skipped a beat. "Are you asking me out?"

There was another brief pause and then Cam said, "Is that all right?"

Excitement and anticipation swirled through Georgie's belly. An image of her infant son materialized before her, but she steadfastly pushed it away. She forced a grin. "You bet."

"Great. I'll call you when I get done here and we'll work something out. Is that okay?"

"Yes, of course. I'll wait to hear from you."

Cam cleared his throat. "I... I was wondering if I could ask you something work-related?"

"Sure."

"Do you remember when I asked you about the number of babies that have died on your ward during the last twelve months?"

Georgie frowned slightly, bemused at his change of topic. "Yes."

"I've been going over the hospital records. The actual number is fifteen."

Shock rendered her momentarily speechless. "*Fifteen!* No, there's no way that can be right."

"That's exactly what Deborah Healy said at first, but the records verify the fifteen."

Georgie's thoughts spun madly. She'd worked on Ward Seven the past two years. Surely she'd know if there were more deaths than the ones she'd been directly affected by. The nurses had a handover before the start of every shift. Something like the unexpected death of a newborn would be mentioned as a priority... Wouldn't it?

She thought back to the three dead infants she

knew of and tried to remember whether any reference to them had been made in front of the other staff. She realized that only the death of Cynthia Dawson's baby had been mentioned by her mother at the handover. For the babies of Danielle Jamison and Sandra Briggs, Marjorie had spoken to her in the privacy of her mother's office. Was it possible so many more babies could have died on the ward without her knowledge or the knowledge of some of the other nurses? She refused to believe it.

"The records must be wrong," she replied adamantly. "I know of only three. I... I was involved in the delivery of all three. It's not something I'll ever forget. You need to go back to the general manager and get her to check those records out. There must be some explanation for the mistake."

"That's the thing, Georgie," Cameron replied, his voice now scarily somber, "I don't think there has been a mistake."

Georgie stared dazedly at the beautiful day that surrounded her and was oblivious to the warm sun on her face. Cameron sounded so certain... *But how could that be right?* She needed to talk to her mother. Marjorie had been in charge of the ward for many years. She'd know the true numbers. She might also know why the hospital records were wrong. Georgie would go to her right away and seek an explanation. If anyone knew how to set her mind at ease, it was her mother.

"I-I have to go, Cameron. My break's nearly over."

"Okay. I guess I'll call you later."

If he was puzzled by her abrupt farewell, Georgie didn't care. She had to speak to her mother and get this sorted out, once and for all.

With that, she finished what was left of her coffee and tossed the Styrofoam cup into the trash. Brushing off her skirts, she headed back to the ward. She was halfway back when another thought raised its head: Cameron was a detective. Why was he looking at the hospital records? Though she had nothing to fear, she shivered with a sudden premonition that her life was about to be turned on its end—and not in the way she imagined.

CHAPTER 14

Cameron stared at the files piled high on his desk and sighed. He was certain Georgie's shock at the number of babies who had died on her ward over the past year was genuine and that certainty only emphasized the GM's suspicion that the lines of communication had broken down.

The three most recent deaths were the ones Georgie had referred to and she'd been the midwife on duty during the births, though the files showed she'd not been on duty when the infants died. According to the hospital notes on each patient, autopsies had been offered, but none of the mothers had taken up the opportunity to possibly get answers into the cause of their babies' deaths. His sister included.

Cynthia's file had been among the most recent baby deaths that had occurred on Ward Seven. Georgie's report of the labor was much as she'd said: The labor was uneventful. Cynthia delivered a healthy baby girl. There were no abnormalities detected on the tests conducted on the baby straight after her birth. The report was eerily similar to the one he'd read in Danielle Jamison's file.

The later report, prepared by Marjorie Whitely in her capacity as the Nursing Unit Manager, stated that at 0200 hours, the baby was found in her crib, cold and unresponsive. CPR was administered, but the baby couldn't be revived. The mother had been informed and was understandably devastated. An autopsy was offered, but declined. It was Marjorie Whitely's opinion that the baby died from complications arising from the mother's long-term, illicit drug use.

The line caught Cam's attention and he frowned. *Cynthia hadn't done drugs...* How could the NUM have gotten it so wrong? He flipped over a few pages and found a copy of the hospital's death certificate which gave SIDS as the cause of death. It had been signed by a Doctor Frederick Rolleston, who had a string of letters after his name.

Had Marjorie Whitely merely presumed Cynthia's baby died from the side effects of her mother's drug habit, without ever giving the matter serious consideration? Was it because the majority of patients who gave birth on Ward Seven were drug addicts that she'd jumped to the most obvious conclusion? Was that all it was? A mistake made in the early hours of the morning when no other evidence of the cause of death was forthcoming?

To Cam, it sounded sloppy at best. He couldn't help but think of the premier's accusations. Could there be something more sinister at play? Could there be a murderer on Ward Seven? Or alternatively, could someone be stealing babies and selling them?

The very thought was ludicrous, but once it had formed, Cam found it impossible to dislodge it from his brain. With an impatient curse under his breath, he flipped through the remaining files.

The twelve other files contained much the same information. The major difference was that Georgie wasn't the midwife present at the delivery. Out of the twelve, four deliveries had been assisted by a nurse by the name of Jennifer Proctor. Another three had been delivered by Nurse Olive Bardon. The remaining five listed Julia Flowers as the midwife.

Interestingly, the night nurses on duty at the time the babies died were smaller in number. Cam accepted that in most professions where shift work was necessary, there were a certain type of staff who preferred to work nights. The staff on Ward Seven appeared to be no different. In almost all of the cases where babies had died unexpectedly, two names consistently appeared: Rosemary Lawson and Tammie Sinclair.

In itself, it wasn't necessarily alarming. Staff who preferred to work night shifts tended to work only those shifts. It wasn't unusual in itself to find the same two names showing up on almost all of the reports. The women worked permanent nights. The babies had all died in the early hours of the morning. But, he needed to find out more about the nurses. He needed to interview them and get a sense of them; find out what they had to say.

Cameron thought about Georgie and not for the first time wondered if it were wise for him to get involved with a woman who could very well be a witness in his investigation. At this point in time, he wasn't sure if there would be an investigation, but his gut was telling him something was definitely off. Just like his gut instinct told him to believe Georgie had nothing to do with it— whatever *it* was.

What he knew with certainty was that he didn't want to lose her. In all of his twenty-seven years and countless women during that time, he'd never felt like he did with her. The mood between them was so relaxed and comfortable, like they'd known each other for years. She was sweet and kind and smart and beautiful. And when they kissed... *Whoa!* The passion had been instant and explosive. He couldn't wait to kiss her again...and more.

With a sigh, Cam went to close Cynthia's file. Josephine's death certificate stared back at him. On a hunch, he checked the other files for death certificates and discovered that, though the names and dates were different, they'd all been signed by Doctor Frederick Rolleston and like Josephine's certificate, the cause of death for each of them was the same: Undetermined. Probable cause SIDS.

Cam frowned. The same doctor had been on duty each and every time. The likelihood of that happening seemed highly improbable. Surely a hospital as large and busy as Sydney Harbour had a number of obstetricians employed? And yet one man had certified every single one of the unexplained infant deaths.

Staring at the papers in front of him, Cam's heart thumped. Dread trickled like icy tentacles through his veins. Something strange was happening on Ward Seven of the Sydney Harbour Hospital. He was sure of it. The only things he wasn't certain of was who was involved...and why.

Chapter 15

Georgie returned to the ward with her heart beating fast, intent on finding her mother and demanding some answers, but one of the other nurses informed her Marjorie had left for a meeting. Disappointed, Georgie did her best to keep her mind off Cameron's bombshell by spending extra time with the babies in her care.

Most of them had been born weeks before they were due. Premature birth was another common side effect of illicit drug use during pregnancy. Some of the preemie babies had difficulties feeding and that left both mother and baby tired and irritable. One tiny infant, Nathan, was particularly upset. Georgie glanced at his mom who lay groaning in her sleep, the recent track marks up her arms, clear for all to see.

Bending over the crib, Georgie lifted Nathan out of his bed and cuddled him close. A surge of protectiveness rushed through her and for a few seconds, she was transported back to the night, twelve years earlier, when for the tiniest amount of time, she'd held her newborn son against her chest. The feeling almost overwhelmed her and she closed her eyes against the pain. Blinking furiously, she forced back hot tears.

The baby continued to fuss and squirm and she switched positions. Lifting him over her shoulder, she patted him on the back. Swaddled tightly for security and warmth, she jiggled him gently up and down and murmured wordless sounds of comfort. Scanning his chart, she noted he was due for a bottle. No wonder he was irritable. With Nathan in her arms, she headed for the milk room.

The bottles were all labeled with the name of each baby's mother and Georgie took care to check each label closely. Although all of the bottle-fed babies were given the same kind of formula, each infant had their own bottle. Locating Nathan's, she put it into the microwave and quickly warmed it. She took a seat in one of the comfortable recliners in the back of the room and coaxed Nathan with the teat.

The baby continued to fuss, even though his mouth opened and closed in a desperate effort to grasp the teat. Patiently, Georgie used her finger to ease the teat past his lips. When he finally sucked it into his mouth and hungrily began to feed, she was filled with a fierce surge of satisfaction. Relaxing against the recliner, she closed her eyes and let the baby take his fill.

The bottle was almost empty when Nathan finally pulled away. A tiny bubble of milk remained on his rosebud lips. His eyes drifted closed and within moments, he'd fallen soundly asleep. Wriggling to the edge of the recliner, Georgie stood and went over to the change table that had been conveniently set up in one corner of the room.

Careful, so as not to wake him, she changed Nathan's diaper and then swaddled him with a wrap once again. Babies suffering from withdrawal needed the comfort and security of being held close and tight and the swaddling served this purpose well, especially if Mom wasn't well enough or interested in cuddling. Georgie put the sleeping baby over her shoulder and was gratified when he let out a little burp. Almost immediately, his eyes closed once again in sleep. She smiled and her heart filled with joy.

For years, she'd resisted her mother's urging to train as a midwife. Georgie was content to nurse sick children. A part of her was afraid about how she'd react watching other women give birth. The absolute joy of welcoming a baby into the world; the indescribable hours of wondrous discovery and bonding, surrounded by a halo of love. They were things Georgie had been cheated of and she was sure she wouldn't be able to cope watching them happen for others.

Her mother kept telling her she was wrong, that working in a maternity ward was exactly what she needed. When Marjorie intimated that Georgie was afraid of becoming a midwife, Georgie at last found the courage to apply for the course and prove her mother wrong. And she hadn't regretted her decision.

While it was heartbreaking to witness yet another drug-addicted woman give birth,

Georgie loved being surrounded by babies. Each and every one of them was a special gift from God and she couldn't help but feel guilty over her decision to give her son away.

Working on Ward Seven became her penance and eased the turmoil in her soul. Over time, she came to love the hours she spent there. She strove hard to ease the suffering of the newborns and offered unconditional support and compassion to their moms. She gave it her everything and took from it comfort and satisfaction, knowing she'd done all she could to help.

She turned and headed toward the exit with the sleeping baby snug in her arms. The door to the milk room opened and Marjorie stood before her. At the sight of her mother, Georgie's heart skipped a beat.

"Here you are, Georgina. Julia told me you were looking for me."

Georgie's heart picked up its pace. Now that the moment of confrontation was upon her, she wasn't sure she had the courage to give voice to the questions that burned inside. A sense of foreboding told her she wasn't going to like the answers. She stared at her mother with a steady gaze and knew she didn't have a choice. Her mother was in charge of Ward Seven. She had to know what was going on.

"Yes, I... I needed to ask you some questions."

Her mom looked at her long and hard and Georgie did her best not to squirm. It felt like Marjorie could see right through her to the questions she dreaded to ask.

Or maybe Georgie was imagining the tightness around her mother's lips? Maybe there was a perfectly reasonable explanation about why fifteen babies had died on Ward Seven shortly after delivery and why it was that Georgie was only aware of three. There was only one way to know for sure. With her courage in both hands, she took a deep breath and plunged in.

"Why didn't you tell me about all the other babies that have died in the past year? Each time a baby of mine died, we talked about it, including the most recent death. Why haven't you ever said anything about the other twelve?"

Marjorie's expression didn't alter. Instead, she closed the distance between them. Taking Georgie by the elbow, she led her over to the recliner Georgie had so recently vacated and then took a seat opposite.

"Who do you have there?" her mother asked quietly, indicating the baby in Georgie's arms.

"Nathan Reynolds."

"Dolley Reynolds' baby?"

"Yes."

"How's he doing?"

"Good, now. He's been fussing all day, but I've finally managed to get him to take almost all of a bottle and he's gone right off to sleep."

Marjorie nodded and smiled. "You're a natural, Georgina. Perhaps now it's time to give thought to having one or two of your own?"

Georgie tensed. "I had a baby, Mom. You forced me to give him up. Don't tell me you've forgotten?"

Her mother tut tutted. "You're so dramatic, Georgina! Of course I haven't forgotten. As to forcing you..." She laughed, but the humor failed to reach her eyes. Instead, her gaze hardened. She stared at her daughter.

"Do you have any idea what your life would have been like if I'd let you raise that child? You were barely *seventeen!* You hadn't even finished high school! How do you think you would have managed it? And as for college—as if that would have ever happened if you'd had a child to support—there would be no nursing degree, no degree of any kind! You'd be little better than some of the patients who drag themselves in here!"

Georgie's face flushed with anger. She clenched her jaw tight. Nathan stirred against her and she was sure he could feel her tension. "That's not fair, Mom. I would have found a way. You and Dad would have helped me. He was your grandson, after all."

Marjorie scoffed. "Ha! Don't bet on it! Your father was horrified you were pregnant. If you'd kept the child, he would have cut off any financial support and cleared out your trust fund. There would have been no help from that quarter."

Georgie gasped in shock, staring at her mother. She couldn't believe what she was hearing. She'd come seeking the truth about the babies on Ward Seven. Instead, her life was unraveling before her eyes.

"It was fortunate things didn't come to that," her mother continued in a conversational tone.

"You saw sense before I was forced to make enlighten you about your father's attitude, but don't be mistaken, that threat was imminent and very real. I knew your father. I knew he'd follow through and you'd be forced to support yourself and your baby on your own. Your life as you knew it would be over and you'd never achieve your dreams. I didn't want that for you. I loved you too much to let you make that choice."

Georgie shook her head in disbelief. "*Love?* Is that what you call it?"

"It's exactly what I call it. I loved you then and I love you now, just like I love your sisters. You're my children. I'll love you until I die."

"Exactly." Georgie stared at her mother with a narrowed gaze and she could tell by the sudden widening of her mother's eyes the moment Marjorie understood. Georgie might have been given only moments with her newborn son, but she'd love him for the rest of her life.

"I... I don't know what you want me to say, Georgina."

For the first time, Georgie saw fear and uncertainty flood her mother's face. Her voice, usually strong and authoritative, had weakened to something much less.

"I want you to admit that my son existed; that he still exists. I want you to acknowledge that maybe, just maybe I would have been able to raise him on my own. I want you to admit that you should have given me the chance to prove I could be a mom...and I want you to say you're sorry that you never gave me the chance."

Her mother shook her head slowly back and forth, her forehead creased in a frown. "We can't undo the past, Georgina."

Georgie sighed heavily. "No, but neither can I pretend it never happened. I had a baby, Mom! I loved him with everything that I had. Not a day goes by when I don't think of him and wonder how he is. A piece of me was stolen from me the day those papers were signed. I can't pretend any longer that I've moved on, that I'm happy about what you did."

A sudden wave of anger stained Marjorie's cheeks. She sat forward in her chair. "What *I* did? You ungrateful wretch! I did it all for *you!* I don't need to re-explain the reasons why. All I can hope is that one day you'll look back and accept I did what I thought was best."

Georgie stared at her mom and realized that no matter what Georgie said, her mother would never understand. As far as Marjorie was concerned, being a teenaged Mom was tantamount to bringing your life to an end. It was clear Georgie would never convince her otherwise.

With another sigh, she adjusted the baby in her arms and made a move to leave. She was halfway across the room when she remembered her mom hadn't answered her initial question. The nerves rushed back again. She stopped and turned and stared at her mother again. "You haven't answered my question."

Marjorie lowered her gaze to her hands which were now clenched in her lap. It was a long moment before she looked up. "Which one?"

Georgie's gaze didn't waver. "You know which one."

"We get so many mothers through these doors, Georgina. Every day, every week, every month, every year. An endless procession of wannabes and not so wannabes—young girls and women who have no idea how to care for a baby. And the few who actually want to learn what it takes to be a mother leave here with no support, no framework with which to succeed. They come in, pregnant and wasted on drugs and their innocent babies suffer." Her voice turned harsher.

"They give birth to these children who are born addicted to drugs or alcohol or both and even though these innocent babies will come through the withdrawal and will rid their system of the drugs, the permanent damage their mother's lifestyle has caused will never go away. They'll struggle for the rest of their lives: in school, in social situations. They'll struggle to control their anger; they'll struggle to fit in. More often than not, they'll grow up to be addicts like their mothers and the vicious cycle starts all over again."

Her mother's color was high and her breath came fast. Her voice had risen, along with her anger. Georgie frowned in concern, her earlier upset forgotten. "Mom, are you all right?"

"Of course I'm all right," Marjorie snapped. "It's just that I get so worked up about the wrongness of it all. Not one of these women are fit and proper mothers. They should never be allowed to fall pregnant, let alone give birth."

Georgie remained silent, although she had some sympathy for her mother's position. Every day, the nurses of Ward Seven dealt with the effects of babies born to drug-addicted mothers. It wasn't a nice sight, but the staff didn't have the right to play God.

"It's not for us to say who should be allowed to be a mother and who shouldn't," she finally murmured. "Some of these girls want to do the very best they can by their babies. When they hold their newborn in their arms, it's like the reality of having a child finally sets in. They want to do more to be worthy, get clean and offer their baby a better chance at life."

"It's too bad they didn't think like that the moment they fell pregnant. It would have been a whole lot better for their babies if they'd done more to get clean while they were pregnant than waiting until afterwards, when the poor child's left with lifelong disabilities."

The bitterness in Marjorie's voice took Georgie by surprise. She understood the anguish that came with the reality of working with drug-addicted babies, but she'd never felt bitter toward their mothers. If anything, she felt sorry for the often young girls who gave birth to the children on Ward Seven. Georgie couldn't help but wonder about the adults in these girls' lives and where they'd let them down, and why.

If what her mother had just revealed was true, Georgie could have also found herself as a teenager with a newborn, all alone. She still couldn't believe her father had voiced such an ultimatum, even to her mom, and she was grateful she hadn't known about it at the time. She didn't want to think what choice she would have made under those circumstances. As it was, her mother had managed to convince her on her own, to give the baby up.

"Some of these girls have had a pretty tough life, Mom. It's not our place to judge," she said quietly, patting Nathan rhythmically on the back.

"Don't give me excuses! I can't abide them," her mother retorted. "We're all given choices in this life. Some of us take the easy way out, that's all it is."

Georgie frowned, a little disconcerted at her mother's unforgiving attitude and she couldn't help but wonder how many of Marjorie's words were directed at her own flesh and blood. "That's a little harsh, don't you think?" she said.

"No, I don't. We're lucky to live in this country. Free education, free healthcare; low unemployment and opportunities galore. As far as I'm concerned, there's no excuse to turn to alcohol and drugs. It's a coward's way out. To bring an innocent child into the mix is an abomination and one I'll never condone. If we are to allow these girls to give birth, they should never be permitted to keep them." Once again, Marjorie's breath came fast and her face was flushed a dark red.

Georgie stared at her mother like she was a stranger. All of a sudden, she was transported back in time and was listening to the tirade that spewed forth from her mother's lips as she spoke to Georgie about her baby.

But it wasn't Georgie her mother was talking about now. It was the women in their care. Georgie had no idea Marjorie felt so strongly about them. Now that she did, she felt confused and more than a little alarmed.

In an effort to rationalize her mother's strong words, Georgie reminded herself how hard her mom had been working lately, pulling extra shifts. Perhaps Marjorie's cold stance on the drug-addicted mothers was merely a response to being tired and overworked. Everyone could get irrational when they were sleep deprived. Besides, it wasn't like this was really personal—Georgie had never turned to drugs.

Nathan stirred for a second time against her shoulder and she hurried to reassure him it was safe to return to sleep. Tossing her mom a troubled look, she gave a brief nod of farewell and quietly left the room.

CHAPTER 16

"Hi, Daddy. Thanks for making time to see me."

Georgie leaned across the table of the hospital cafeteria and forced herself to give her father a peck on the cheek. Up until her mother's recent revelations, Georgie would have told anyone she and her father were close. After hearing how strongly he'd been against her keeping her baby, she no longer knew what to think. *What kind of loving parent could force their child to make such a choice?*

The fact that her mother had convinced her to give up her baby, had driven a lifelong wedge between them. Georgie loved and admired her mother for many things, but her feelings weren't without reservation. She'd been hurt irreparably by her mother's actions and even though most of the time she accepted Marjorier had been acting in her best interests, it still didn't eradicate the pain. Now, she discovered her father had been just as adamant that she give her child away. It was an awful jolt to her equilibrium and it would take some time to come to terms with what she'd learned.

Her gaze moved over him. He was well into his sixties, but his tall bearing and athletic physique defied his years. His thick white hair lent him an air of authority and sophistication. Now, his blue eyes twinkled at her in delight. It was obvious he hadn't yet spoken to her mother.

"I always have time for my first born," he smiled. He slid a mug of coffee and a chocolate éclair toward her. "I took the liberty of ordering for you."

"You shouldn't have. It's way past lunch. I shouldn't be eating anything."

He eyed her slim figure and shook his head. "It looks to me like you don't eat enough."

"I eat plenty," Georgie murmured. Before her recent conversation with her mother, she would have been touched at the obvious signs that he cared. Now, she just wanted to get the meeting over with. As if reading her mind, her father reached for his coffee and then said, "What is it you wanted to see me about, honey?"

Georgie looked down at her hands where they were twisted in her lap. She wasn't ready to reveal to him that she was now aware of his true feelings about her baby. She'd had enough emotional upheaval for the day.

Until the recent conversation with her mother, although she'd always sensed her father's approval of her decision to give her son up for adoption, he'd never come right out and expressed his opinion on the subject. She needed time alone to come to terms with the fact that he wasn't as unconditionally supportive and loving as she'd thought.

But now wasn't the time or the place. She'd sought him out to talk to him about her concerns about her mother. Knowing there was nothing to do but come right out with it, she took a deep breath and blurted out, "I'm worried about Mom. I think she's working far too hard. Do you think you could convince her to take some time off?"

"Why? What happened?"

"Nothing happened as such, it's just something she said. I'm worried that she's losing a little of her patience and compassion and you know how important those things are in our line of work."

He shook his head. "Oh, I know, all right. I don't know how the two of you do it, caring for those people day in, day out."

"Daddy!" Georgie exclaimed, surprised at his tone of voice. "They're patients who need our help, like every other patient in this hospital. You ought to know."

"Of course I do, Georgie," he hurried to reassure her, patting her hand. "I didn't mean it like that."

She stared at him. Once upon a time she would have believed him without question. Now she sought out the truth of his statement in his eyes. He looked away. With a sigh, she picked up her coffee mug and took a sip. It was hot and creamy and sweet, just as she liked it. Pushing aside her disquiet, she sighed in satisfaction. "Thanks for the coffee."

"You're welcome. It isn't every day I receive an invitation to afternoon tea from my daughter."

"It wasn't exactly an invitation to afternoon tea," Georgie grimaced. "I wanted to talk to you about Mom."

"Yes, that's right. You think she's working too hard."

"It's not just that. Earlier today, we had a conversation about the mothers on our ward. Mom made it clear that she felt no sympathy for their plight. She became quite upset about the whole thing and even implied the women shouldn't be allowed to have children or if they do, to keep them."

Her father's eyebrows rose in surprise, but he remained silent. His lack of response alarmed her, but then made an awful kind of sense. It reinforced what her mother had told her. He was just as judgemental as his wife.

For all of Georgie's life, her father had been her rock. It was unsettling to discover her faith in him had been grossly misplaced. Still, she needed reassurance; needed to know her mother wasn't a lost cause.

"Why would she work on a ward like that if she really felt that way? It doesn't make sense. I must have misunderstood," she added a little desperately, waiting for her father to agree.

He shook his head slowly back and forth. "Perhaps she simply cares too much? Did you ever think of it like that? Sometimes when you really care what happens to someone, if it doesn't work out so well, it can leave you feeling disappointed, like somehow they've let you down, like it's their fault things didn't work out the way you'd hoped." He reached over and brushed a stray piece of hair out of her eyes and Georgie couldn't help but wonder if his words were directed at her.

"Your mom's a remarkable woman, Georgie and she's devoted her life to the women and babies who come onto her ward. It might be that, over the years, she's distanced herself a little from them emotionally for her own sake. Perhaps that's the only way she can cope. But don't ever think she doesn't care, honey. Like I said, I think her problem is that she simply cares too much."

Georgie stared out of the large bay window that took up most of one wall of her living room and thought again about her mother. Her shift had ended hours ago and the night had settled in, but despite her father's reassurances, concern still weighed heavily in her heart. Marjorie had seemed so adamant that their patients shouldn't be allowed to be mothers. The longer Georgie thought about it, the more she was convinced her mother had meant every word that she'd said—and that knowledge scared her to death.

With her legs curled up beneath her on the couch, she took another sip of her third vodka and lime, and sighed. Just when the future seemed so full of exciting possibilities in the form of one very sexy detective, life had thrown her a curve ball.

She hadn't heard from Cameron since his call earlier that day and their promised date had yet to materialize. She could only assume he'd been caught up at work. To make matters worse, she'd been so taken aback over her mother's attitude and the revelations about her dad, she'd forgotten Marjorie hadn't answered her question about the disconcertingly high number of newborns who had apparently died on their ward.

Had her mom become so sidetracked by her feelings about the down-and-out mothers that she'd simply forgotten to address Georgie's question, or had she employed deliberate evasive action?

The second possibility settled heavily in Georgie's heart and filled her belly with unease. She'd hoped her father would calm her fears, but his explanation seemed oversimplified and after what her mother had revealed, she'd never quite trust his judgement again.

The fact was, Georgie probably cared too much, too. It broke her heart to watch tiny babies suffer, through no fault of their own, but that didn't mean she looked upon their mothers with contempt. If anything, she admired the women for going ahead with the pregnancy. This day and age, termination clinics were readily available. Years ago, the choice of an abortion had also been open to her.

Now, she wished she'd pushed her mom for the answer. That way, she wouldn't be feeling so antsy, as if something were wrong. Her mom's comments about their patients wouldn't have hit such a nerve if she wasn't already on edge about Cameron's information.

She contemplated calling him. After all, they had been going to meet after work. At the very least, she could talk to him about her mom and get some objective feedback. She reached for her phone where it sat on the coffee table in front of her. As she dialed his number, her heartbeat picked up speed.

"Hello?"

The deep timbre of his voice washed over her, sending a rush of nerves to her throat. She licked her dry lips and answered. "Hi, Cameron. It's Georgie."

"Hey. I was just thinking about you."

The way he drawled the words in that sexy voice sent a shiver of desire coursing through her. Her nipples tightened in response. "Really?" she managed.

"Yes. I'm sorry I didn't get back to you. I got called out on a job and didn't return to the office until late. I was filthy after coming into contact with a few of the less desirable inhabitants of our fine city and I came straight home to shower. Now I'm standing out on my balcony all alone, contemplating life. Cynthia's gone to bed. I've been looking at the empty deck chair for the past thirty minutes and I can't help remembering when you were here."

His voice dropped to a husky murmur and as the memory of that evening crashed over her, heat suffused her body. Their kiss had been amazing and she'd been left yearning for more. She couldn't help but wonder what would happen if and when they finally found themselves alone in his condo.

When he'd pulled away, she understood it was probably for Cynthia's sake. Cam was responsible enough to want to set a good example for his young sister and sleeping with a woman he barely knew didn't quite cut it. Georgie ought to be grateful for his restraint—and she was—but her body still ached for his touch.

"Would you like to come over?" The words were out before she could stop them and she blushed at her forwardness, but refused to take them back. Cameron's hesitation lasted less than a second.

"Yes."

CHAPTER 17

Cameron knocked on the door to Georgie's condo and waited for it to open. Wiping his sweaty hands on his Levis, he drew in a deep breath and eased it out. He wasn't sure why he was so nervous. He felt like a teenager around the girl he'd had a crush on all summer—a girl who'd finally noticed him. And not just noticed him, but who had invited him around...

The door opened and she stood before him, beautiful in a plain pink T-shirt and jeans that clung to her curves. Her soft smile lit up her eyes and his heart somersaulted.

"Hi," she said.

"Hi."

They stood staring at one another for a long moment and then Georgie blinked and said, "Come in."

Cam nodded and smiled inwardly at the becoming blush that stained her cheeks. At least he wasn't the only one feeling nervous. She stood back to allow him to enter and he followed her down a short corridor that opened up onto an older-style, open concept kitchen and dining area. The room was tastefully decorated with simple but expensive pieces of furniture. High ceilings and decorative architraves added to the room's old-world charm. A large bay window looked out on the city, framing the view perfectly.

"You have a nice place," he said.

"Thank you. The building's a little dated for some, but I like it."

"How long have you lived here?"

She frowned in thought. "It must be nearly seven years. I moved here not long after I finished college."

Surprise shot through him. Not many college students could afford the mortgage on a place like this.

"I dipped into my trust fund," she said, as if reading his mind.

She'd surprised him again, although he should have cottoned onto it earlier. The cultured accent and air of refinement should have clued him in from the start: Her family had money. Their backgrounds were poles apart. His family had been barely able to get by, scratching to exist, from week to week—and Georgie had a trust fund.

Some men might take issue with the fact the girl they were dating had grown up wanting for nothing, but Cam wasn't one of them. His self-esteem was healthy enough that he didn't think less of himself for having grown up without. As far as he was concerned, it was what you did after you left home that mattered.

Kids were powerless, with no choice but to suffer whatever situation they were born into, but as adults, their options were only limited by how hard they were willing to work. Anyone could get a college degree if they were smart and prepared to study hard. With a good-paying job, it was possible to rise above lowly beginnings and make a mark on the world. Conversely, just because a person had money, didn't mean they were clever—or hard working. There were plenty of young people born rich who squandered it all before they turned thirty.

After being kicked out of home, Cameron had been determined never to be poor again. Poverty made things more difficult than they had to be. It was as simple as that. He studied hard for his final exams and was accepted into the police force. From there, he'd worked himself up the ladder. There was an undeniable sense of pride and accomplishment in knowing he'd done it all on his own.

"Would you like a drink?"

Georgie's question broke into his thoughts and he blinked away the ghosts of his past. "Thanks, a drink would be great."

She moved over to a small bar that stood in the corner of the room. "I have Budweiser and Coors in the fridge and bottles of scotch, rum and vodka on the shelf. Or you can have a glass of wine."

He cocked an eyebrow. "Red or white?"

"Either."

"So many options," he teased and was rewarded with an embarrassed smile.

"I'm sorry. I guess I was raised to be a good hostess, always able to anticipate the needs of my guests. After having it drilled into me for so many years by my mother, it's a hard habit to break."

"Hey, I'm not complaining. I love having so many choices."

"So, what will it be?"

"I'll have a Bud, thanks."

She bent down and pulled a beer from the bar fridge and handed it to him. He twisted off the cap and took a mouthful. The beer was icy cold and slid down his throat. "*Mm*, that's good."

On the bar was a glass filled with ice and clear liquid. A wedge of fresh lime was stuck to the side of the glass. Georgie picked it up and brought it to her lips.

Vodka…or maybe gin. "What's your poison?" he asked, curious.

"Vodka and lime. It's my weakness," she grinned.

She took another sip from her drink and he watched the movement of her throat as she swallowed. A smattering of freckles he hadn't noticed before dotted the smooth skin of her neck. Everything about her fascinated him. His head might be urging him to stay away, but the rest of him wanted none of that.

From the moment she'd issued her invitation, he'd had a hard-on. On the way over to her apartment, he'd fantasized how she'd taste and smell and feel and it had been all he could do to keep his attention on the road. Now here he was, in her apartment, with no chance of being discovered or interrupted by his little sister. He wanted so much to take the woman before him in his arms and kiss her senseless and the effort of holding himself back was agony.

"Have you eaten?" she asked, moving over toward the three-seater leather couch opposite the bay window.

"Yes," he murmured, tracking her every move. "Have you?"

She shook her head. "No, but I'm not hungry." She threw the words over her shoulder and then curled up on the sofa and tucked her feet underneath her. For the first time, he noticed they were bare. The intimacy of it struck him full force and once again, he was filled with the need to touch her. He walked toward her, his gaze fixed on hers.

Sitting down close beside her, he reached across and gently tugged the drink out of her hand. Her eyes widened in surprise. A small table stood next to the couch and he placed both drinks on it before turning to her once again. Slowly, he reached out and took her chin between his fingers.

He heard her small intake of breath a moment before his lips found hers. Forcing himself to take it slowly, he barely grazed the surface. She sighed softly and leaned into him. Fire scorched a path through his veins and centered in his groin. He groaned.

With a sigh of acquiescence, her arms came up around his neck. He crushed her to him, delighting in the feel of her full, soft breasts pressed against his chest. Her lips opened under his and his tongue stole into her mouth.

Her mouth was cool and delicious. She tasted of the tartness of her drink. He kissed her with mindless need. His hand cupped her breast and he found her taut nipple and caressed it with the pad of his thumb.

She moaned against his mouth and moved closer. He angled her head to deepen the kiss and tasted her over and over again. The blood pulsed through his ears and through his cock until he was desperate to bury himself inside her, but still he held back, wanting to be sure they were heading in the same direction.

"I want you," he murmured, his voice husky and thick with need.

She opened her eyes and stared up at him with an expression of desire. A pulse beat madly in the side of her neck. Her lips parted and she offered him an unsteady smile. "I want you, too."

"Are you sure?"

"Yes."

Passion ignited inside him and he drew her back in his arms. Half-lifting her, he settled her in his lap. The exquisite feel of her jean-clad ass on his erection was blissful torture and when she wriggled to get herself more comfortable, he couldn't contain another groan. With her arms still clasped around his neck, she leaned over and whispered in his ear.

"How about we move to the bedroom?"

"Sounds good to me," he growled. Coming upright, with her in his arms, he cradled her against his chest and headed in the direction she indicated.

The polished wooden floorboards creaked every now and then beneath his boots. Vaguely, he noticed the walls were lined with art works, mostly modern pieces he didn't recognize, but they added a splash of color and style to the hallway.

"Second on the right," she murmured and flicked his ear with her tongue.

His heart pounded and once again, the blood rushed through him. He burned to feel her beneath him, naked and wild and yearning, welcoming him into her heat. The door to her bedroom stood open and he strode in and deposited her gently on the bed. The king-sized, white wooden headboard was decorated with a mountain of soft pink and white pillows. Pushing them aside, he followed her down and covered her body with his.

"Your boots," she squeaked.

He looked down and noticed the lacy white bedspread. It was embroidered in tiny pink flowers and looked like it cost a fortune. Reluctantly, he rolled away from her and tugged off his boots. They landed with a thump on the bare floor.

Not wasting another second, he reached for her.

———————

Georgie burned with need from the inside out.

She'd never felt like this before and it filled her with both excitement and disbelief. She'd read her fair share of steamy romance novels and had giggled at the sex scenes where the heroine was almost breathless with desire and the man was built like a God. Cameron still had all his clothes on, but from the feel of his taut chest muscles and thick erection pressed against her, she was sure he wouldn't disappoint.

From the moment he'd arrived at her doorstep, she'd been humming inside with anticipation. It had taken him an hour to get there and the wait had been almost unbearable. She'd had plenty of time to reconsider and it was sweet that he still insisted on making sure she was agreeable about having sex. He was a gentleman through and through and she still couldn't quite believe he was here, in her bed, kissing her like he couldn't get enough.

She tugged at his T-shirt, pulling it free from his jeans, and pushed it up over his chest, impatient to touch his skin. He assisted her by lifting it over his head and tossing it to the floor. His pectorals bulged, covered with dark hair. She ran her fingers across his chest and flicked her nails over the small nubs of his nipples. His breath caught and she smiled, enjoying the heady feeling of being able to turn him on. He murmured something against her mouth and then his hands were at her hips.

"Your turn," he mumbled and pushed her shirt up and over her head. His hands went straight to the clasp of her bra and a moment later, her breasts sprang free. She slipped her arms out of the underwire bra and dropped it over the side of the bed and then turned to him and threaded her fingers around his neck.

Drawing his head down to hers, she kissed him thoroughly, taking her time to tease and taste. She nibbled at the corners of his mouth and then swiped her tongue across his lips. He submitted to her attentions for a moment and then rolled over so that she lay flat on her back.

He smiled down at her. "That's better."

With most of his weight on his elbows, he lay on top of her. With their chests bare, he teased her nipples with his chest hair. Through the thickness of his jeans, his erection pressed into her and she yearned to be skin to skin. Moving restlessly beneath him, she voiced her desires.

"Take off your jeans."

His eyes flared brighter and he quickly acceded to her request. Sitting back on his haunches, he unbuttoned his Levis and slid down the zip. Shucking the jeans down his hips with his underwear in tow, within moments he was naked. Georgie took her time and looked her fill.

Cameron's cock stood out from a dark nest of hair. Thick and hard, there was no doubt it more than lived up to its earlier promise. Heat rushed through her and centered in her core. She squirmed beneath him. Without conscious thought, she licked her lips.

As if the motion propelled him into action, he bent forward and reached for the button on her jeans. With his gaze fixed on hers, he undid the zipper and slowly eased her Levis down over her hips. She lifted her bottom to assist him. He returned to lie on top of her and her senses kicked into gear, registering several things at once: His firm skin was warm and supple. The hair on his legs tickled. She breathed in the spicy, exotic scent of his cologne. She flicked her tongue across his lips and tasted mint.

His cock lay hard against her belly. She yearned to feel it inside her. Reaching up, she pulled his head down for a kiss so thorough, it made no secret of her longing. When at last they pulled apart, gasping for breath, Cameron stared down at her, his eyes shadowed with desire.

Bending his head, he nuzzled her breasts and then took one of her nipples in his mouth. She gasped at the feel of him suckling her and a surge of need echoed deep within her core. When he moved over to her other breast, her heart pounded in anticipation.

"You're so beautiful," he murmured and then reached down and fondled the soft curls between her legs. A moment later, his fingers slid through her slick folds and stroked. Mindless pleasure coursed through her. She gripped his shoulders.

"Do you like that?" he whispered.

She was almost beyond coherent speech. "*Mm*, very much."

His fingers continued their magic until she couldn't stand another moment of the sweet torture.

"Please," she gasped. "I need to feel you inside me."

Cam growled low in his throat and reached over the side of the bed for his jeans. Finding his wallet, he pulled out a condom and quickly sheathed his cock. A moment later, he positioned himself between her legs. His cock probed at her entrance.

Her legs fell open in encouragement and she stared at him, hoping he recognized her need. Slowly, he eased into her and she gasped again at the feel of him stretching her deep within. He stroked in and out and she clung to him, her nails digging into his back.

Over and over, he thrust into her, picking up force and speed. Desire reached fever pitch inside her and she clung to him. When she reached her peak, she cried out in ecstasy and relief. Her inner muscles clenched around him, leaving her weak, but fulfilled. Gradually, her breathing slowed and she offered him a smile.

"Good?" he asked.

"More than good."

His expression filled with satisfaction and then a baser emotion took control. His strokes became longer and faster and soon he tensed and then groaned in heartfelt relief. For a long moment, he lay still on top of her, his breath coming fast and harsh in her ear. Finally, she squirmed underneath him and he immediately lifted his weight.

"I'm sorry. I'm way too heavy for you." He rolled to his side, taking her with him.

She reached up and pressed a finger to his lips, shushing him. "Don't apologize. I love the way you feel."

He smiled down at her tenderly and then pressed a soft kiss against her mouth. "You feel pretty darn good, too."

It was a long while later that they began to talk, sharing stories about their childhood. He told her about his dysfunctional family and his revelations didn't come as a surprise. Cynthia had already told her the reasons she'd run away from home at fourteen. The thought of what her mother had done... It still filled Georgie with anger and despair.

Knowing Cameron had relied on no one but himself to get to where he was only increased her respect and admiration for him. He hadn't been born with a silver spoon in his mouth, like she had, and yet he'd risen above his disadvantaged background and had achieved much to be proud of in his life.

"Have you ever been back home?" she asked, tracing idly through his chest hair with her finger.

He tensed and then blew out his breath on a heavy sigh. "No. My parents lost any right to have me call them that the day they asked me to leave. They'll never be parents to me again."

"Have you ever talked to your dad about it?" she ventured, hating the thought of their estrangement. Even though she'd been hurt over her mother's recent revelations, her parents were still an important part of her life. She couldn't imagine not having them around.

Anger stirred in Cameron's eyes. "I haven't seen or spoken to either of them since it happened and I'm never going to. They're gone forever, as far as I'm concerned. I've cut them out of my life. I don't need to go back. Those memories are burned into my brain. They help to remind me how far I've come and help me to work harder and strive for even greater accomplishments. I'll never feel powerless again."

"Is that why you entered the police force? Were you attracted by their authority and power?"

He shrugged and some of the tension in his body eased. "Maybe. I've never really thought about it. From the time I was about seventeen, I wanted to be a cop. We had a recruitment officer visit school that year and he inspired me to join. He talked about mateship and teamwork and fighting the fight against evil. I guess it appealed to me. Who doesn't want to slay dragons?"

His anger disappeared under a smile so tender and warm it nearly took her breath away. She brushed a piece of hair off his forehead and then pressed her lips to the spot. His arm tightened around her.

"Do you ever think about your birth mother?"

The moment the words were out of her mouth, she wanted to take them back. Cam's expression hardened and an unfamiliar coldness entered his eyes. Georgie shivered.

"I feel nothing but contempt for that woman."

A shaft of pain stabbed through her, but she forced herself to continue. She needed to know whether there was any chance he'd understand

and feel even a little compassion toward the woman who'd given him life.

"She could have chosen to have an abortion. Then you wouldn't be here. Did you ever think of that?" she asked quietly.

Cam's frown darkened. "I prefer not to think about her at all."

"There might have been good reasons why she gave you up."

His bark of laughter contained no humor. "Yeah, like she didn't want me, didn't love me. She probably didn't even know my dad. The space for the father on my birth certificate is blank."

The bitterness in his eyes sent icy dread flooding through her veins. Her soul filled with despair. She could never hope to pierce the hurt and pain that had grown, thick and hard, like scar tissue over his heart. She bit back a sob. One thing was clearer than ever: She could never tell him about her son.

He turned on his side and brought her with him. Pressing her close against him, he kissed her softly on the mouth. "Let's not talk about me anymore. I'd prefer to hear about you."

Georgie forced a smile. "What would you like to know?"

Cam winked. "Anything. Everything. Like... What made you choose nursing?"

She drew in a deep breath and eased it out on a soft sigh before settling down against him. "Would you believe, when I was a young girl, I dreamed of being an artist," she began.

"I grew up in the Blue Mountains and there were plenty of creative people up there. But with a mother working her way up through the nursing ranks for the best part of forty years and a father who was a well-known obstetrician, I guess a career in some kind of medical field was always in the cards."

Cam looked at her in surprise. "Your dad's a doctor?"

"Yes. He works at the Sydney Harbour Hospital. We like to keep it in the family," she chuckled.

"What's his name?"

"Well, I said he was well-known, but I'm guessing you've never heard of him. After all, he's in the business of delivering babies and I imagine you haven't had anything to do with that."

His answering smile was there, but it didn't reach his eyes. Georgie wondered at his sudden change in mood. *God, she hoped she hadn't read him wrong.* What if he had a wife, or even a girlfriend—and children? She should have asked more questions, if not of him, then Cynthia. Then she remembered Cynthia had told her he was single and she relaxed against him again.

"You still haven't told me your father's name."

She wondered briefly at his insistence and then shrugged it off. "His name is Doctor Frederick Rolleston."

Cameron's face paled and his expression went blank. She stared at him, wondering at his strange reaction.

"Don't tell me you *have* heard of him?" she

teased in an effort to lighten the sudden tension in the air.

His answering smile looked forced. "No, I don't think so."

———

Cam's mind whirred in a kaleidoscope of shock and disbelief. Doctor Frederick Rolleston was Georgie's father. Cam would bet his condo on the fact the good doctor was the same one who'd signed off on the suspect death certificates. It was an unusual surname and one he'd committed to memory. Despite the warmth in the room and the heat emanating off Georgie's naked skin, he shivered.

"Cold?" she asked and reached for the covers. Tenderly, she tucked them around his shoulders. Still, an icy block of dread and foreboding sat heavily against his chest.

He hadn't thought it particularly odd that Marjorie Whitely had completed every one of the final nursing reports. After all, she was the head of the ward. It stood to reason that something as serious as the sudden death of a newborn would be brought to the attention of the most senior staff. What was less believable was that Marjorie's husband had been at work during each and every one of the deaths.

If Cam recalled correctly, the death certificates had been completed within hours of each baby's death. *Surely there was a roster?* The likelihood of

Doctor Rolleston being on duty each and every time was coincidental beyond belief—and if there was one thing eight years in the police force had taught Cam, it was not to trust in coincidences. One thing he knew, he couldn't stay in Georgie's bed a moment longer.

Pushing back the covers, he swung his legs over the side and began to dress. From the corner of his eye, he saw her raise herself up on one elbow, a look of hurt and confusion on her face.

"Where are you going?"

Forcing himself to look at her, he gave her a tight smile. "I'm sorry, I just remembered I have some statements to go over before I head into work tomorrow. I'd also rather not leave Cynthia alone overnight, if I can help it. She's still just a kid and I—"

"It's fine. I understand," Georgie interrupted. "You've promised to look out for her. You need to go and make sure she's safe."

Guilt surged through Cam at the look of kindness and compassion on Georgie's face. Whatever might be happening with her parents, one thing was certain: He didn't deserve the likes of Georgie Whitely.

Forcing another smile, he leaned over and pecked her on the cheek. "Thank you. I appreciate it. I'll call you."

And with that, he collected the rest of his things and left.

CHAPTER 18

Cam stared at the files before him. The sick feeling in his gut just wouldn't go away. He'd left Georgie in her bed the night before and he still felt bad about giving her the lame excuse he had to get home to Cynthia, but he couldn't bear to tell her what he'd been thinking and until he had proof that her parents were involved in something untoward, he wouldn't breathe a word.

It was obvious from the way she spoke about them that she loved and admired them. He wouldn't disillusion her unless he had to. Not everyone had to have their world come crashing down. If it were possible, he'd keep hers intact.

As soon as he'd arrived at work that morning, he'd checked the files again. Just as he remembered, the death certificates were signed by Doctor Frederick Rolleston with a date and time stamp on each one, indicating they were completed not long after each baby was formally declared dead.

Cameron tugged his keyboard toward him and typed in Rolleston's name. Clicking on Google images, he was immediately rewarded with several photos of a distinguished-looking man sporting a thick crop of white hair and a wide smile. He was a man who, even in his photos, exuded confidence. Cam saw a little of Georgie around the mouth and nose and his heart clenched. One of the photos showed Rolleston with his arm around a woman who looked to be around his age. Stylishly dressed and with her hair perfectly coiffed, Cam guessed the sophisticated woman was Georgie's mother. Another quick search confirmed it.

Cam scrolled through the pages of hits the name Frederick Rolleston had brought up. Opening one link after the other, and scanning their contents he was impressed with the man's social conscience. According to several reputable sources, a decade earlier Rolleston had set up a charity for the benefit of single mothers unable to cope. He raised several million dollars every year in aid of it.

It was a worthy cause and one that Cam wholeheartedly approved. No doubt there were thousands of young girls like Cynthia and not all of them had older brothers in a position to take them in. His sister was one of the lucky ones and he was sure she knew it.

Only that morning, as he was heading out the door, she'd asked him if he'd come with her to spread Josephine's ashes. The fact that she was moving forward and dealing with the past warmed Cam all the way through. He knew Georgie had a lot to do with it and he was filled with tenderness and gratitude that left him conflicted because of his suspicions about her father.

He thought of the conversation he'd had with Georgie the night before about his birth mother and his gut clenched reflexively. He hadn't meant to display his anger, but the very thought of cutting the woman a little slack for giving him up made him furious.

It was easy for Georgie to play devil's advocate and wonder at his birth mother's possible motives. She didn't know what it was like to lie in bed, night after night, feeling lonely and unloved and wondering why the hell your own mother didn't love you enough to keep you. He couldn't count the number of nights when he was a kid that he'd cried himself to sleep...until one night, after yet another bout of endless questioning and tears, he'd determined to forget about her, cut her from his life and his heart, just like she'd cut him from hers.

From that night, he'd been better; had forced himself to come to terms with his sad beginnings and put them behind him, forever. He focused on the here and now; he focused on the future. He didn't believe in looking back. And then his parents had kicked him out and he was back at the start again: alone, unloved and unwanted. If it hadn't been for the kindness and generosity of his best mate's parents, he'd have found himself out on the street...like Cynthia.

He couldn't help but wonder how that had come to pass. What had happened that she found herself homeless and alone at the age of fourteen? He hated to think life for his little sister under their parents' roof might have become as intolerable as it had been for him.

She hadn't talked about their parents or how she'd come to be living on the streets. Until recently, her mental state had seemed so fragile, he hadn't dared ask. But now that she appeared to be improving, he probably owed it to both of them to find out. For all he knew, she might even be missing them.

It was different for Georgie. She'd obviously grown up in a house where everyone loved each other and support and loyalty was a given. He could tell by the way she spoke about her family that she'd had a decent childhood and he was happy for her, but it didn't mean he had to reconcile with his own parents, or, as she seemed to suggest, feel kindly toward the woman who'd given him life. He couldn't help but wonder how Georgie would feel about her father after all this, if his suspicions were confirmed.

The thought made him frown. Rolleston's name kept jumping out at him on the screen. On impulse, he keyed the name Marjorie Whitely into a new search and another listing caught his eye: *City of Sydney Adoption Agency*. With his heart beating faster, he clicked on the link and waited for the page to load. It opened to the home page.

Scanning the welcome message, Cam clicked

on the tab labeled "About Us" and a moment later, stared in disbelief. Professional portraits of the company's founding directors stared back at him. Though at least one of the pictures had been taken some time ago and had been airbrushed to maximum effect, there was no mistaking Marjorie Whitely's smiling image.

The second photo was of a woman he didn't recognize, although there was something about her that looked familiar. He read through the blurb which described the establishment of the agency by two sisters: Marjorie Whitely and Rosemary Lawson.

Cam's heart pounded against his ribcage and the blood roared in his ears. Rosemary Lawson had been referenced in the hospital notes. She was the nurse who'd been on duty at the time the majority of the infants had died. No wonder she'd appeared familiar. *She was Marjorie Whitely's sister.*

Georgie's aunt and mother were the directors of a corporation that owned and operated an adoption agency. Fifteen newborns had died at the hospital where both of the directors worked. The ramifications and possibilities hit him in the head with the force of a sledgehammer.

It wasn't about murder, at all. The premier was right. The babies were being stolen and then adopted out through the agency, no doubt for a sizeable sum.

The deaths must have been falsified by none other than Georgie's father. *But what about the funeral services?* Cam had attended upon the crematorium himself. He'd helped Cynthia choose a coffin. They had Josephine's ashes in an urn. *Didn't they?*

A piercing headache made itself known in the space behind his eyes. He groaned from the pain and hunted around for some paracetamol. Digging a couple of tablets out of the bottle in the top drawer of his desk he swallowed them dry and continued to stare at the screen. He rubbed at his eyes.

Was he leaping to ridiculous conclusions, with little or no proof? He'd been working too hard. He was sleep deprived. It had been way past late when he'd stopped tossing in his bed, thinking about Georgie and her family—and his. Even now, hours later, his eyes still felt gritty and tired.

Yes, that had to be it. His fatigue had made him delusional. Nobody in the twenty-first century went around stealing babies and falsifying their deaths. It was something out of the dark ages. Or the sixties and seventies, at least. A lot of years had passed since then.

Society's views had changed with regard to single women and their ability to raise children on their own. People no longer frowned on them or whispered about them behind their backs. They lived their lives openly, without fear of being ostracized or censured. Yes, times had certainly changed from half a century ago—and for the better.

There could be other explanations for the high rate of newborn deaths and with that thought, he squashed the faint flare of hope that his baby niece might still be alive. If he went down the path of suspecting Georgie's family, he'd have to include the funeral directors in the abhorrent scheme and that was simply way too far-fetched. As if two hospital employees could convince a third party to pretend he had a body in the coffin. It was ridiculous, by anyone's standards, to contemplate the possibility for even another second.

Still, he could always put his questions to Georgie's relatives when he interviewed the hospital staff. He'd arranged with Deborah Healy to have the relevant people available to meet with him later that afternoon. He'd ask them about the adoption agency and gage their reaction. Hopefully he'd get the answers he needed. Then he'd know once and for all.

Until he could obliterate the bizarre notion from his mind, he'd never get a moment's rest and that meant every minute he spent with Georgie would also be affected. That was beyond acceptable. He cherished their time together and didn't want a second of it tarnished by the ugly cloud of suspicion that now filled his head. Once and for all, he wanted to satisfy himself that Georgie's family wasn't involved.

Needing to hear her voice, he reached for his phone and then pulled up short. He wasn't going to be able to warn her about the forthcoming interviews and it wouldn't be fair to speak with her beforehand and pretend all was well when who knew what might come out during his meeting with the staff. He was hoping the interviews would put an end to his ridiculous speculations, but what if they didn't? *What if they implicated her family members rather than exonerated them? He might have to interview her, too.*

Common sense told him it would be best to stay away from Georgie Whitely, at least until he'd spoken to the staff. Hopefully, after today, he'd have a better understanding about what—if anything—had happened to end the lives of fifteen babies so unexpectedly.

Deborah Healy stared down at the sheet of paper in her hands and tried to still her trembling. The words were bold and succinct. She'd been summoned before the hospital board for a formal interview with regard to increasing concerns the members of the board had over her management of the hospital.

When Detective Sergeant Dawson phoned and requested she make available for interview certain staff members who worked on Ward Seven, she knew she had to bring it to the attention of the board before it turned into a major police investigation. She'd waited too long on the previous two cases and the results had been disastrous.

The board had summoned her within the hour after Doctor Alistair Wolfe's high profile arrest outside the Glebe Morgue. A stern censuring had followed and an overt threat of disciplinary proceedings had been made in the event her leadership skills were found wanting again.

At the time, she'd been grateful to be let off with a warning and had been determined not to let anything like what had happened with Doctor Wolfe occur again. But it looked more and more like she'd failed again and she had no one else to blame.

The fact that her husband was terminally ill with a rare form of liver cancer was of no one's concern. She should have been strong enough to keep the pressures and fears she had on the home front well away from her thoughts while she was at work. But the truth was, she couldn't.

Hours disappeared every day. She found herself staring blindly out her office window, thinking about Alan and wishing with all her heart that there was something she could do to stop the inevitable greed of the disease that slowly consumed him.

She could no longer concentrate on the many issues, large and small, that came before her every day. She fell behind in her work. Calls often went unanswered. But instead of taking time or walking away, she'd clung to her job and the sanity it offered, like a drowning person clings to their rescuer.

When the detective had first contacted her about his concerns regarding baby deaths on Ward Seven, she hadn't given it serious thought. As far as she knew, there was nothing untoward about their statistics and until the premier had insisted on meeting with her about his daughter, she hadn't been aware of any complaints.

But it quickly became clear something was wrong. She'd checked the data twice. Regardless of the fact the infant death rates on that ward were far too high, she should have been notified and she was almost certain that she hadn't.

As promised, she'd quietly done her own investigation into the reasons why she hadn't been told. She'd spoken to Marjorie Whitely and was secretly dismayed when the woman insisted she'd reported the deaths to her superior, who Marjorie believed in turn had passed them on. Deborah suddenly couldn't prevent the awful thought that perhaps she *had* been notified and she hadn't paid any attention.

Was it really possible for her to have received that many reports on infant deaths and not remember them? It had been a terrible year and she'd had so much on her mind. Could she have simply overlooked them? It terrified her to know that she couldn't be sure she hadn't.

And now she had to face the board and come up with answers to their questions—and she had no doubt there would be plenty of questions. It was obvious there was something dreadfully wrong on Ward Seven.

She'd wanted to head it off at the pass, before it became the explosive, media-grabbing issue she'd experienced in the past. It was why she'd called the detective and insisted he investigate. It was why she'd informed the board of his pending interviews.

If she had any hope of holding her job, she had to convince the board members she was still the one in charge and the one who still knew exactly what went on in the hospital she'd served for so long. The board might be dubious about her claims, but at least if she was upfront about the potential criminal investigation, they might see their way to being a little more lenient.

With one hand, she screwed the paper into a ball and tossed it toward the trash can that stood beside her desk. She needed a drink, but she was at work and nothing like that would be forthcoming. She hadn't yet succumbed to the temptation of hiding a bottle of scotch in her bottom drawer.

No, she had to stand up and face the board, cold stone sober, and leave them feeling confident that she had a steady hand on the wheel. Drawing in a shaky breath, she smoothed back her hair, straightened her shoulders and headed back to her desk. It was time to get to work.

CHAPTER 19

Cam glanced across at the woman who sat across from him in the temporary interview room that had been made available by the general manager. She'd given her name as Tammie Sinclair and confirmed that she worked permanent night shifts as a nurse on Ward Seven.

While her short, spiky hairstyle did nothing to add to her femininity, the scattering of freckles across her nose and cheeks softened her face and made her appear younger than her stated thirty-six years.

He moved the pile of papers on the desk in front of him and she jumped, as if startled. The interview had started six minutes earlier and she hadn't yet brought herself to look him in the eye. He was curious to discover the reason behind her nervousness.

He'd already interviewed most of the other nursing staff, including Marjorie Whitely. None of them had exhibited signs of agitation. The NUM had remained steely in his presence, answering questions with the briefest of replies. She'd been cooperative, but far from helpful. At one point, she'd asked if she was under arrest. Cam admitted that she wasn't. A moment later, she brought the interview to an abrupt end.

But something was up with Tammie Sinclair and Cam was determined to find out what. He got straight to the point.

"There have been an unusually high number of babies die on your ward. What can you tell me about them?"

The woman squirmed in her chair. She looked at the floor; around the room and then stared down at her hands where they were clenched tightly in her lap.

Cam held his gaze steady. "Ms Sinclair? Did you hear what I said?"

"Y-yes, I heard you."

"Fifteen newborns have died on your ward in the past twelve months. We haven't even begun to look back any further. You were on duty when ten of the fifteen passed away. There must be something you can tell me."

Do… Do I need a lawyer?"

Cam tensed and his heart skipped a beat a moment before adrenaline rushed through his veins. With his heart thumping, he answered her question with one of his own. "I don't know. Do you?"

The nurse stared at him. He could almost see her mind turning over the possibilities, weighing her options. And then her shoulders slumped and she groaned aloud on a heavy sigh.

"I don't know what's going on in the ward, but something's not right."

Cam sat forward. "Why do you say that?"

"I've worked as a midwife for ten years. I've never worked on a ward with an infant mortality rate so high."

"What can you tell me about the babies who died in your care?"

Her eyes flashed. "I didn't do anything! I swear! Yes, I was on duty those times, but I never had anything to do with their deaths. It was Rosemary who found them. I only found out about it afterwards. I... I didn't even see them."

"When you say Rosemary, you mean Rosemary Lawson, right?"

"Yes."

"You expect me to believe that ten babies died on your shift and it was Rosemary who found them, every single time? That sounds a little too convenient."

"It's the truth!" Tammie protested, her freckles standing out in stark contrast to her ashen face.

"I find it hard to believe you worked the same shift as Rosemary and yet apparently you didn't see anything. Where were you, Tammie?"

The woman lowered her eyes and a red flush crept up her neck. "I was... I was asleep."

Cam frowned in astonishment. "Asleep? What the hell is that supposed to mean?"

Tammie's embarrassment grew. "I've had some...difficulties at home. I haven't been sleeping well. I've been coming to work exhausted. Rosemary's been kind enough to let me rest whenever we're quiet."

"So you mean to tell me you go to work and if the ward isn't busy, you go off someplace and sleep. Is that correct?"

The nurse kept her gaze lowered to the desk, but nodded. Cam shook his head in disbelief and swore under his breath.

"Rosemary woke me to tell me when a baby was found dead. She always offered to be the one to inform the mother. I... I was relieved she was willing to take on that responsibility. I can't imagine how difficult it must be."

"And what about the babies? You said you never saw them. Did Rosemary take care of them, too?"

"It sounds farfetched, but yes, she did. She told me she'd already called the doctor who'd pronounced the baby dead and then arranged for the body to be transported to the morgue."

"And all this went on while you were asleep? You must have slept away half a shift at a time!"

Tammie shrugged, but refused to look him in the face. "Sometimes I did."

Cam shook his head again. "Unbelievable."

"There was only one time I saw a baby," Tammie said quietly and Cam stilled.

"I woke in the early hours of the morning and went looking for Rosemary. I couldn't find her. And then I heard the sound of a baby crying. I remember thinking how strange it was."

"You work on a post-natal ward. Why would the sound of a crying baby be strange?"

Tammie stared at him. Her blue eyes were huge and round. "You don't understand, Detective. The baby's cries were coming from behind the door of a storeroom. It's a room where we keep old furniture, pillows and other odds and ends. There should never have been a baby in there."

Cam stared back at her and once again, his heart began to pound. "Go on."

"I... I opened the door, convinced I had to be wrong, but inside the storeroom was a baby in its crib, crying."

"What did you do?"

"Nothing."

Cam frowned. "Nothing?"

"Rosemary came up behind me, startling me. When I questioned her about the infant, she brushed my concerns away. She told me it was Marie Fallow's baby. He was suffering such acute withdrawals, she just couldn't get him quiet. Rosemary had removed him to the storeroom so that his crying wouldn't disturb the other patients and their babies."

"Was that standard procedure?"

"No! I'd never heard of it being done."

"Was the baby returned to his mother?"

"I assume so. Rosemary told me she'd deal with him and sent me on my way."

Cam absorbed the information and scribbled down some notes. Rosemary Lawson had some explaining to do.

"That wasn't the strangest thing, though, Detective."

Cam looked up and frowned at the nurse. "No?"

"No. The strangest thing was when Rosemary told me it was Marie Fallow's baby. I'd caught a glimpse of the little boy a moment before Rosemary arrived. He was wearing a blue-and-white knitted bonnet. I'd seen that bonnet on another baby earlier in my shift and it wasn't on the head of Marie Fallow's son."

Cam stilled. Every nerve ending stood on end. "Who was the other baby?"

"The bonnet belonged to Danielle Jamison's son."

Cam swallowed a gasp and did his best to get his heart rate back under control. "Are you sure?" he managed.

"Yes. I overheard Danielle telling the patient in the bed next to her that her mother had knitted it especially. A gift for their first grandson."

"When did this happen?" Cam demanded.

Tammie took her time in answering. Cam tried to contain his impatience. At last, she lifted her head and met his gaze. "It happened hours after she'd informed me that the Jamison baby had died."

Cam closed his eyes against the rush of adrenaline that poured right through his veins. *It was Rosemary Lawson.* It had to be. What other reason did she have to lie about the baby's identity? But he needed to find hard evidence. Right now, he had nothing but the tale of some strange behavior from a work colleague and a gut feeling that Rosemary was responsible. He needed more. It was a good thing she was next on his interview list.

Rosemary Lawson looked enough like Marjorie Whitely that it was obvious they were related. But that was where the similarities ended. Unlike her sister, Rosemary couldn't be more obliging. Though younger than Marjorie by a couple of years, her face bore increased signs of aging. From the course of tight wrinkles around her eyes and mouth, Cam guessed she was a smoker and a sun worshipper—or had been in the past—but even those wrinkles didn't take away from her charm.

She smiled at him and introduced herself with a firm handshake and immediately asked him about his day. She tut tutted over him like a kindly grandmother when he admitted he'd slept late and skipped breakfast. If he hadn't already spoken to Tammie Sinclair, he might have found it difficult to believe she could be involved in anything evil, let alone the murder or abduction of newborns.

Then again, he had yet to find any hard evidence that pointed toward her guilt and he hadn't been a detective for so many years without learning you couldn't always believe what you heard. The fact was, Rosemary Lawson was the nurse on duty on almost all of the nights when the babies had met their death. Guilty or not, she was an important link in the chain and he would treat her accordingly.

"Thank you for seeing me, Ms Lawson. I appreciate you coming in early. I understand you're rostered on night duty tonight?"

Rosemary smiled. "Yes, I do permanent nights, but when I heard why you wanted to see me, I was more than happy to give up a few hours' sleep. Those poor, poor babies..." She shook her head slowly back and forth and tears glinted in her eyes. "I just wish there was something I could have done."

Cam was surprised that she got straight to the point. "What can you tell me about them?"

She remained silent for a moment and then let out a heavy sigh. "There was nothing unusual about any of those babies. That's why it's so hard to accept. They were perfect little human beings, every one of them. There was no indication that they wouldn't make it through the night. It just happened, without warning, without explanation." She glanced up at him and then looked away. "It sounds hard to believe, but that's the way it was."

"You found them."

"Yes."

She answered without hesitation and without a sign of nervousness. Cam noted her response on the legal pad in front of him. So far, her evidence corresponded with Tammie Sinclair's.

"There's at least one other nurse on duty with you, isn't there?" he asked.

"Yes."

"I believe a lot of the time it was a nurse by the name of Tammie Sinclair, is that right?"

"Yes, Tammie also works permanent nights."

"I'm curious," Cam said in a conversational tone. "How is it that you were the one to find the babies every single time?"

"Detective, I've been nursing all of my adult life. During the night shift, I'm the most experienced nurse on the ward. I probably shouldn't, but I tend to let the younger ones rest while they can, particularly Tammie. She and her partner have had a rough time of it. They've gone through three failed IVF attempts. Tammie's been on an emotional rollercoaster for the best part of a year. She often arrives at work exhausted, unable to sleep from the stress. I've tried to cut her some slack."

"She's trying to get pregnant?"

Rosemary grimaced. "Both of them are."

Cam frowned in confusion. "I don't understand."

Rosemary rolled her eyes. "She's a lesbian. Her and her partner figured they'd double their chances if they both underwent the treatment. It's why it's cost them so much. They've spent all their savings. They have nothing left."

Cam recalled Tammie making a reference to some difficulties on the home front. He guessed she'd been referring to this. Still, Rosemary allowing her colleague to sleep on the job seemed way too noble for anyone to contemplate, especially when it had been going on for so long. No one could be that kind hearted, could they?

Cam held her gaze. "That's very kind of you to allow her to sleep while you're overseeing the ward. Not everyone would be so generous, regardless of the circumstances. Are you sure there isn't any other reason why you're so charitable toward Tammie?"

"No, Detective. Believe it or not, some of us do good deeds for the sake of it and to help out another colleague. I don't mind doing it for her in the slightest. Besides, you never know when we're going to get busy. Babies are like that. They often come without warning. It's best for the staff to rest when they can." She paused. "I guess the odds were in my favor for being the one to find those infants. I was often the only one awake."

Cam nodded and made another notation. Her explanation was supported by the statements given by the other night shift nurses he'd interviewed, including Tammie Sinclair. It was time to increase the pressure.

"Do you know how many babies have died on your ward in the past twelve months?"

"I'm not sure. A few."

"More than a few. Try, fifteen. And out of those fifteen, twelve of them occurred during your shift."

Rosemary looked surprise. "Wow, that's a lot. I didn't realize it was so high."

"Tammie Sinclair also thought it was high. In fact, she's of the opinion that there is something untoward about all those deaths. What do you think?" Cam stared at her.

Rosemary frowned. "I don't know what you want me to say."

"I interviewed Tammie a little earlier. She told me about a baby she found in a storeroom. You identified the baby as belonging to a certain patient, but Tammie's adamant the infant's mother was somebody else—a baby who she'd been told by you had already died. What do you say to that?"

Rosemary stared back at him and slowly shook her head. "Poor, poor Tammie. I had no idea her mental health had deteriorated to such an extent. She's obviously delusional. Why would I have a newborn in a storage room? And one that was apparently already dead. The very idea is ludicrous."

"Are you saying Tammie was lying?"

"I'm saying she's mistaken."

Cam held her gaze. "It isn't true?"

"Not in the slightest."

"Why would she say something like that?"

"I don't know, Detective. I'm guessing she's sicker than I thought."

"Why hasn't she been relieved of her duties?"

Rosemary sighed. "I feel sorry for her. She needs the money. She's exhausted her sick leave and holiday entitlements with the IVF treatments. If she takes any more time off, it will be without pay."

Cam absorbed the information. So, Tammie Sinclair needed money. It was strong motive to sell babies on the black market, if that was what was happening. He made another note on the legal pad.

"My sister's baby died on your shift nearly three weeks ago," he said, changing tack.

Rosemary gasped, looking genuinely distraught. She lifted a hand to her mouth. "Oh, no! I'm so sorry!"

Cam compressed his lips and nodded, silently accepting her condolences. "It's been tough, especially for my sister. She was given a business card by one of the nurses after her baby had died. It was a card that had the contact details of the *Peaceful Passing Funeral Parlor and Crematorium*. What can you tell me about it?"

"Oh, those. That's my boss' idea."

"You mean Marjorie Whitely. Your sister, right?"

"Yes, she's the NUM—the Nursing Unit Manager," she added.

"Thank you, I'm aware of what it means."

Rosemary stared at him a moment and then shrugged. "Marjorie thought having the business cards available might ease the burden of dealing with the sudden death, even a little. Grieving over a lost baby, even thinking about arranging a funeral and all it entails, is very difficult and is sometimes beyond our moms. It was Marjorie's suggestion that we try and help them any way we can, including pointing them in the direction of a reputable funeral home."

While Rosemary's explanation made sense, Cam was disconcerted to discover the idea had originated from Marjorie Whitely. When he'd put the same question to the NUM, she'd refused to answer. He couldn't help but wonder what she had to hide.

Could she have an illegal arrangement with the funeral director? Was that the reason she urged her grieving patients to use that particular service and was so reticent to talk about it? Or was he completely off the mark? Once again, he didn't know and it irritated the hell out of him. What he did know was that he needed to pay a visit to the *Peaceful Passing Funeral Parlor and Crematorium*.

"Will that be all, Detective?"

Cam forced his attention back to the nurse. "Almost. I have one more question: You and your sister established an adoption agency some years ago, right?"

A wide smile broke out across Rosemary's face. "Oh, Detective! Are you looking to lend your support to our charity? We're always open to donations."

A blush stole across Cam's cheeks. "No, I...um... I wanted to know more about the agency. You started it with your sister, didn't you? The two of you are directors."

"Yes. Marjorie and I have always worked as midwives. In the early years, we came across many girls who, for one reason or the other, found themselves unable to care for and raise their newborns. We grew up in the country and there were limited facilities and resources that catered to girls who found themselves in trouble. We decided to open up an adoption agency to help facilitate matters."

She glanced up at him. He scrawled a few notes and then nodded for her to continue.

"Marjorie and I already knew the girls. It was a small hospital. One or the other of us was usually on the ward. The girls trusted us to take care of their babies. We kept it private; we made it easier for them to give up their unwanted children."

Cam stared at her and felt like he was suffocating. *Had his birth mother been one of those girls?* Relying on the discretion of kindly midwives to help her problem disappear? Did she even have a second thought for the baby she was giving up? He squeezed his eyes shut tight against the pain. He couldn't bear to think about it.

"Are… Are you all right, Detective?"

With an effort, he opened his eyes and found Rosemary staring at him with an expression of concern. He forced a smile.

"Yes, I'm… I'm fine. It's been a long day." He glanced at his watch. "I think we're done."

Cam stood and Rosemary pushed away from her chair. "It was nice meeting you, Detective. You look tired. You go home and get some rest."

Cam nodded. "I will. Thank you for your time." With that, he showed her out of the room.

When the door closed behind her, Cam returned to his seat. With a heavy sigh, he leaned his elbows on the makeshift desk and rested his head in his hands. Despite several hours of interviews, he'd made very little progress. The whole process had raised more questions than answers.

There was the curious reaction of Marjorie Whitely, but what did it mean? He'd been sure Tammie Sinclair was sincere and yet she'd been very nervous. Not only did she need money, Rosemary Lawson had accused the nurse of being delusional. None of the other nurses had provided him with anything useful. The only nurse he hadn't interviewed was Georgie.

He was comfortable with his decision not to speak with her formally. Though she'd been involved with some of the deliveries, she wasn't on duty when any of the babies had died. She couldn't possibly be a part of it—whatever "it" was. At the moment, he had no hard evidence connecting anyone to a crime.

Besides, he was sure he knew her well enough to know she'd never be involved in something as heinous as the murder of a baby and even if the premier's accusations of baby stealing were closer to the mark, Cam didn't believe she was capable of that, either.

He groaned, feeling hopeless. It was like he was going round and round in circles. He'd talk to the owner of the funeral parlor in the morning. Perhaps he could clear things up. It was worth a try.

In the meantime, he'd ask one of the junior detectives to dig further into the activities of the City of Sydney Adoption Agency. Rosemary had spoken about the agency almost as if their use of it had been contained to the past. It would be interesting to know just how recently the last adoption had taken place.

CHAPTER 20

Cam entered the modest front room of the Peaceful Passing Funeral Parlor and Crematorium and waited for someone to appear. The décor was much as he remembered when he'd come there with his sister to make arrangements.

Dark velvet drapes blocked out a lot of the morning light that shafted in through the single window and shrouded most of the room in shadows. A cheap, imitation leather sofa and two matching armchairs almost filled the small space. A pine coffee table covered in a scattering of dated fashion magazines was the only other piece of furniture.

Cameron glanced at his watch, impatient to ask his questions and be gone. The whole place was deathly silent and he couldn't help but remember the last time he'd been there. Cynthia had been a wreck, sobbing uncontrollably. He was surprised that she'd even remembered the coffin with the gold and white bows. The niggling thought that baby Josephine might not have died as his sister had been told, just wouldn't go away. That was part of the reason he was here, at the funeral home. He wanted answers.

A door further down the corridor opened and closed and footsteps sounded, moving in his direction. He breathed a sigh of relief. At least someone was in residence. A moment later, a white-haired, elderly man, sporting a hideous comb-over, filled the open doorway to the room. It was the same man Cameron and Cynthia had met with to arrange Josephine's cremation.

"Can I help you?" The man stared at him with narrowed eyes, showing no signs of recognition.

Cam got to his feet. "I'm Detective Sergeant Cameron Dawson. Are you the owner here?"

Fear flashed across the man's face. Though it wasn't unusual for people to feel threatened to have a detective in their midst, even if they'd done nothing wrong, Cam filed it away.

"Y-yes. Bernard Lawson's my name."

Cam stepped closer and shook the man's hand. Too late, he remembered the last time he'd done it: Bernard's hand had been cold and clammy, reminding Cam too much of the man's undesirable occupation.

"What are you doing here?" Bernard muttered.

"I'd like to ask you a few questions. Do you work as the undertaker?"

The man nodded. "Undertaker, embalmer, receptionist and anything else that needs doing."

"I take it you work alone?"

"Yes."

"No employees?"

Bernard shook his head. "I like it that way. It's not like I'm too busy to cope. You're the first person to come in today."

Cam contemplated what the man had said and found it a little peculiar. If he was the preferred funeral director for the Sydney Harbour Hospital, Cam would have expected the man to be rushed off his feet.

"I understand you get referrals from the Sydney Harbour Hospital. I was hoping you could tell me about the newborns you've had through here."

Bernard's expression turned wary. "It's a sad thing, burying babies. It's not meant to happen like that. I feel for those poor mothers. They'll grieve until the day they die."

Cameron couldn't help but think of Cynthia. "How many babies have you prepared for burial during the past twelve months?"

The man pursed his lips and appeared to think about it. "Ten or twelve? Maybe a few more. I don't know, Detective. I don't keep count. It's not something I like to dwell on."

"No, of course not. Do you keep records on them?"

"Yes, but I'm so behind on the paperwork and my filing system's way out of date. I wouldn't know where to put my hands on anything."

Yet, he seemed to have no trouble locating his invoice book. Cameron recalled the bill he'd received in the mail within a week of Josephine's cremation. He'd paid with a check that had been presented to his bank the very next day.

"Will there be anything else, Detective? I must get back to what I was doing."

Cameron stared at him. Given that the man had told him he wasn't run off his feet, Cam wondered at Bernard's impatience to get away, but he had no evidence to contradict the undertaker's answers.

"Do you take referrals from other hospitals?"

"No. My arrangement is exclusively with the Sydney Harbour hospital."

"Whose idea was it?"

The undertaker frowned. "Whose idea was what?"

"The referrals. The business cards. Did you approach the hospital or did they approach you?"

The man thought for a while. "I can't rightly remember, Detective. The arrangement's been in place for so long, I've forgotten how it came about."

Cam stared at him for a long moment, trying to gage the man's sincerity. Bernard held his gaze. Cam was the first to look away. With nothing further to ask, he thanked him for his time and left.

Outside, Cam stood on the pavement and thought about their conversation. He'd gained very little from his visit, apart from more or less confirming the number of deceased newborns. The man had no employees, so there was no one else to question. Though Bernard was kind of weird, there was no law against that. Cam supposed anyone who chose to work with the dead would have to be a little unusual.

With a sigh, he jammed his hands in his pockets and turned toward the squad car parked a short distance down the street. From the corner of his eye, he spied a brand new shiny, black Porsche Cayenne in the driveway of the funeral home.

He came to a halt and stared at the vehicle. The car was worth close to two hundred thousand dollars. It was so at odds with its owner and the building it was parked beside, Cam was taken aback. Taking note of the license plate, he went back to his vehicle and ran it through the computer. It was registered to Bernard Lawson.

How the hell could the undertaker afford a car like that when he hadn't seen a customer all day? Cam shook his head and cursed under his breath. Just another thing to puzzle over.

Frustrated and out of sorts over his lack of progress, Cam returned to the station. Checking through his emails, he found a message from Georgie and was immediately flooded with guilt. He hadn't spoken to her since he'd left her bed. She must be wondering what the hell had happened.

With a sigh, he reached for the phone and dialed her number. She answered on the second ring, sounding breathless. He couldn't prevent the soft smile that came to his lips.

"Hello, you," she breathed.

"Good morning to you, too."

"It *is* a good morning, isn't it?" she said.

He remembered their night of passion and his body tightened in response. "The best," he agreed, hoping like hell he wasn't about to put a lie to his words.

"I thought you might have called me yesterday. Is everything okay?" He heard the uncertainty in her voice and hated himself.

"Yes, of course. I've just been busy. Work's getting out of control."

"I understand." There was a pause and then she said, "So, are you calling about anything in particular, or did you just want to say hello?"

"I miss you. I wish I didn't have to leave you the other night. It was lonely in my bed."

She sighed over the other end of the phone and he could tell she was pleased. "I wish you could have stayed, too, but I understand about Cynthia. You didn't want to leave her alone all night." She paused again and then added softly, "I miss you, too."

"Are you at work?" he asked.

"Yes."

"What time do you finish?"

"Same time as yesterday, but I'm in the labor ward today and birthing Moms don't always keep to a schedule. Why?"

"I thought we might try to get together again. Maybe we could go out for dinner? There's a great little Italian restaurant not far from where I live."

"It sounds great," she replied. "I'll let you know how my day develops."

"Great."

"There's a rumor going around that you were interviewing some of the night staff yesterday."

Cam bit back a curse. He kept his voice as casual as hers. "Yes."

"Can I ask why?"

"I'm not at liberty to discuss an ongoing investigation. Let's just say you have nothing to worry about."

"Good."

Cam winced. The relief in her voice was palpable. Feigning a pressing appointment, he quickly brought the call to an end and tried to ignore the rush of guilt that flooded his veins.

Shit. Now what? He couldn't very well tell her he was investigating members of her family. It would be unprofessional at best and might even compromise his case. The justification for keeping quiet didn't make him feel any better. He wished he could fast forward to the time when the whole thing was behind him and he could concentrate on getting to know her even better. One thing he did know, he was falling for her, fast.

"Cameron, you got a minute?"

Cam looked up and spied one of the junior detectives. "Sure, Felix. What can I do for you?"

"I've finished with the research on that adoption agency. I've printed out a few things. I have them here, if you want them."

Cam took the sheaf of papers from the younger man's outstretched hand. "Thanks, Felix. Good job."

The man blushed under Cameron's praise. "No problem, Cam. I'm always happy to help out. Let me know if you need anything else."

"Will do."

Cam glanced through the papers. The first page gave details of the directors and told him the adoption agency had been established in the early seventies. The next few pages listed real estate owned by one or both directors. Cam noted several impressive addresses: Darling Point and Edgecliff were exclusive eastern suburbs locations; Seaforth boasted multi-million dollar mansions on the waterfront, north of the harbor; Leura was a sought-after area situated in the Blue Mountains, a couple of hours west of Sydney.

Felix had also printed out two pages of testimonials given by past clients of the agency. Cam scanned them. Every one of them was phrased in glowing terms and several mentioned Marjorie Whitely and Rosemary Lawson by name, thanking them for their kindness, compassion and professionalism. To some of their clients, the women were the closest thing to a saint.

Though none of the testimonials bore an exact date, the month and the year were given at the end of each one. Cam flipped the page over and noticed the last testimonial was dated three months ago. Several others had been written over the course of the present year.

He frowned and cast his memory back to his interview with Rosemary. Even though she'd joked about taking donations, from the way she'd spoken, he'd assumed the agency had been used mostly in the past, when single Moms with no one to turn to had offered their babies for adoption. He'd even assumed his own mother had fallen into that category.

But the testimonials seemed to paint a different picture. In fact, all of the testimonials on the pages Felix had provided had been made in the past two years. It was obvious the agency was well and truly still in business.

And then another memory struck him like a blow. His heart beat so hard it felt like it was going to explode right through his chest. He couldn't believe he hadn't made the connection earlier.

Lawson was the surname of the funeral director he'd spoken to. Okay, the name wasn't exactly uncommon, but it could be the missing link that provided him with the evidence he needed to prove something was horribly wrong and Georgie Whitely's family were right in the middle of it.

With adrenaline pumping through his veins, he pulled his keyboard toward him and opened the page to a search engine. He typed in Bernard Lawson's name and then added the words: Peaceful Passing Funeral Parlor and Crematorium. Almost immediately, he was rewarded with several hits. Scrolling through them, his eye snagged on an article from the social pages of one of the city's daily papers.

Cam clicked on the article and waited impatiently for it to open. When it did, he was confronted by a large photo of Bernard Lawson and his "lovely wife, Rosemary." *And there it was.* The connection. No wonder Rosemary had done her best to cast suspicion on Tammie Sinclair. It all clicked into place.

Rosemary Lawson and her sister were midwives who also owned an adoption agency. By her own admission, Rosemary agreed she and Marjorie had assisted young mothers in giving up their babies for adoption, now, and in the past.

Rosemary had been on duty when twelve of the fifteen babies had died on Ward Seven. Rosemary's sister was the head of the ward and prepared the final report. Coincidentally, the death certificates had been certified by none other than Marjorie's husband.

Even more interesting was the fact Rosemary Lawson was married to an undertaker. The very same undertaker who was recommended to grieving patients by none other than Marjorie—at least, that's what Rosemary said.

Cam could do nothing but shake his head back and forth in utter disbelief. The tangled web pulled tighter and tighter. He was stunned at the extent of the deceit. He had one more call to make.

With a sense of urgency, he dragged the phone toward him and punched in the numbers for Deborah Healy. His impatience eased slightly when the phone was answered on the second ring and the general manager's receptionist confirmed her boss was in. Cam tapped his fingers on the desk while he waited for Deborah to take the call. A moment later, she came on the line.

"Detective Dawson, what can I do for you? I take it you received the files."

Foregoing preliminaries, he got straight to the point. "What can you tell me about the business cards?" he rasped.

"Business cards?"

"Yes, the ones belonging to Bernard Lawson, advertising the Peaceful Passing Funeral Parlor and Crematorium. They're handed out by Ward Seven staff to patients in need of the service. I assumed it was part of a broader hospital policy and that Lawson's funeral home was a preferred service provider."

"Not at all. I don't know anything about our staff handing out business cards. We take pains not to favor any of the funeral homes in the area. It's not our place to recommend one over the other."

She sounded so genuine and confused, Cam believed her. Perhaps the treachery was limited to the senior members of the Whitely and Lawson families? At least he could be grateful it hadn't infiltrated the highest levels of the hospital's hierarchy. That was a headache he definitely didn't need. It was bad enough that senior members of the medical and nursing staff appeared to be guilty of something abhorrent. He couldn't help but wonder what Georgie knew about it.

After thanking the general manager for her time and giving her a somber assurance that she'd be the first to know any details and if an arrest was imminent, he ended the call. Pushing away from his desk, he strode into his boss' office.

Detective Superintendent Holt Denman looked up from the paperwork spread across his desk. "You look like a man on a mission, Cam. What can I do for you?"

Cam sank into the vacant chair opposite Holt's

desk and sighed heavily. Holt's eyebrows rose.

"That bad, hey?"

Cam nodded grimly. "Worse."

Holt's expression turned serious and he sat forward in his chair. "Does it have anything to do with the premier because that man's been driving me nuts wanting to know about the progress of the investigation."

Cam compressed his lips into a thin line. "Kind of. And I can't help but wonder if my sister's baby is also involved." Cam couldn't prevent the tiny spark of hope his words ignited deep down inside him.

Holt's face grew even more somber. "Talk to me."

When Cam finally finished relaying the events of the past few hours, Holt sat still and silent for a long moment, his lips pursed in thought.

"Let me get this straight," he said. "Over the past twelve months, fifteen newborns on Ward Seven at the Sydney Harbour Hospital have died suddenly and without explanation. The midwife who found them is the sister of the Nursing Unit Manager, who wrote the final reports. The death certificates were signed by the same doctor, who also happens to be related to the nurses." He stared at Cameron. "Am I right so far?"

"Yes, sir."

"But it gets better. The midwife and NUM own an adoption agency and one of the nurses is married to a funeral director." His eyebrow quirked, but there wasn't a hint of amusement on his face. "How am I doing?"

The evidence sounded even more damning coming from someone else. Cam's lips tightened. "All true."

Holt stared off into the distance and tapped a pen against his desk. The sound grated against Cameron's nerves, but he waited his boss out. He understood Holt's quietly unspoken shock. It was a lot for anyone to take in.

"I take it the premier's grandson is part of these fifteen?"

"Yes."

"He accused the staff of the hospital of either murdering or stealing the child. Do you think his accusation has credence?"

"To tell you the truth, at the time I agreed to look into his claim merely in an effort to placate him, but over the past week, it's become obvious something evil is going on. The only evidence I have is circumstantial, but we need to keep looking into this."

"Do you think it's possible these staff members are making false statements to the mothers, claiming their babies have died, when in fact they haven't? Is that what you're implying?"

Cam stared at his boss and his heart thumped. Though he hadn't wanted to admit it, the awful suspicion had been floating along in his subconscious for some time. A long moment later, he nodded. "Yes."

"And you think these same staff members are removing the children in secret and then trafficking them through the adoption agency."

Once again, Cam held his boss' serious gaze. "Yes."

"How reliable is your eye witness?"

Cam shrugged. "She's a midwife who was on duty when most of the babies died. Although she was nervous, she came across as rather convincing."

Holt nodded thoughtfully. "Where does the undertaker fit in?"

"It's my theory that he's been in on it from the start. He's fed information from the nurses about the supposedly deceased baby and meets with the grieving mother. Almost all of them have no fixed abode and no family and many of them have significant histories of drug and alcohol abuse. They're easy prey for people with evil in their hearts. The funeral director goes through the motions of preparing the child for burial or cremation, but in fact, a body never appears."

Holt nodded again, his expression grim. "By then, the baby is long gone, presumably on its way to being adopted to persons unknown who are oblivious to the child's origins."

"As an obstetrician, Doctor Rolleston has the wherewithal to procure new birth certificates containing false information. It would be a simple matter for the nurses to complete the paperwork required to register the birth and have it signed off by him. Or perhaps they even use genuine information, including the babies' real details. The biological mother is hardly going to find out. As far as she's concerned, the baby died shortly after birth."

Holt let out a low whistle and slowly shook his head. "Fuck."

Cam stared at him solemnly. "You can say that again."

With a heavy sigh, Holt scrubbed his hands through his closely cropped hair. When he looked up, his eyes were bleak. "Leave it with me, Cam. I need some time to think. Given the people involved, we need to tread carefully. When the premier gets wind of this, he'll go ballistic. We don't need him fronting the media, tainting our jury pool. If what you say is true, these people need to be put away for a very long time."

"I'll need a subpoena to get hold of the adoption agency records."

"Agreed. File it with the courthouse as soon as you can. We need to move on this."

After completing the necessary paperwork, Cam headed out the door. With a bit of persuasion, he might even have copies of the agency's adoption records on his desk before the day was over.

CHAPTER 21

Dear Diary,

I'm in a quandary and I hate that I feel like this. My uncertainty is interrupting my usually peaceful sleep. The thing is, I'm not so sure we're still acting in everyone's best interests. For years, I was convinced we were on the right path and God was on our side.

But today, I heard from a man whose sister fell victim to our plot. She wasn't alone, as we imagined. It was obvious her brother cared for her and would have cared for her child. And then there was the premier's grandson...

It used to be so easy. Even Marjorie agreed. The two of us were on the same page. For so many years, we worked as one with a common goal and all was good and well. So many babies we saved from lives of misery and hell! But has it been appreciated? I'm not sure we'll ever know.

———————

Cam stared at the writing on the page in front of him until it blurred and his heart thumped hard in his chest. Hundreds of files, recording every adoption that had occurred in the City of Sydney Adoption Agency, graced every surface of the squad room. He didn't know what had snagged his attention about this particular file, but he could only guess it had something to do with the name GEORGINA WHITELY that had been written in bold black print across the front of it.

A fresh wave of disbelief, shock and anger surged inside his veins. Georgie had given a baby up for adoption when she was seventeen and she'd never mentioned it. Even when they'd talked about his past.

His anger morphed into fury. It must have been deliberate. Nobody forgot something like that. She had to know it was a deal breaker. How could she have betrayed him like that? Had she cared for him at all? The sweet kisses, the tender smiles. *Had it all been a farce?*

Cam wanted to shout out his denial, but the words died in his mouth. When it came down to it, what did he *really* know about her? His gut told him she was kind, caring and compassionate, but what if his instincts were wrong? *What if he'd let his judgement get clouded by his attraction? Could she be as despicable as his birth mother?* The thought was too much to bear.

He was supposed to be meeting her for dinner. They'd spoken about it earlier in the day. It felt like a lifetime ago. He didn't know how he was going to look at her and then, just as quickly, he couldn't wait to confront her and watch her wriggle and squirm.

Would she proclaim her innocence, try and convince him there'd been a mistake? Or would she confess all, knowing the game was up? It was impossible to tell. The woman he thought he knew well enough to fall for, had proved beyond a doubt he didn't know her at all.

———————

Georgie heard her phone beep, indicating a new text message. Pulling it out of the pocket of her uniform, she glanced down at the screen and smiled. It was from Cam. She hadn't heard from him since he'd called that morning.

Can u get away on time?

She chuckled at his eagerness and her heart beat a little faster. The thought that they might end the night in each other's arms filled her with excitement and anticipation. Quickly, she sent off a response.

So far, so good. Should b out of here by 4.

Meet me @ Bar Luca in Phillip Street. I'll b there by 5.

Georgie knew the bar well. It was down the Circular Quay end of Phillip Street and was frequented by youngish professionals. The contemporary, elegant style suited her and the food was first rate.

Sounds good. I'll do my best 2 get there on time.

C u there.

Georgie frowned at his abruptness, but sent him a thumbs up emoji and then added two smiley faces in reply. She couldn't wait to see him.

In the end, it was closer to five-thirty when she stepped across the threshold of Bar Luca. A last-minute admission of a heavily pregnant nineteen-year-old meant that Georgie hadn't left on time. Now, she fought her way past the crowds of suited professionals and looked around for Cam. Feeling a little out of place in her uniform, she was grateful when, a moment later, she spotted him tucked away in a private corner of the room.

He was dressed in a tailored navy-blue suit and a matching blue-and-white polka dot tie. The color looked good on him. Then again, with his tall, fit physique, she was sure there was nothing he couldn't wear well. She caught his eye and he acknowledged her with a nod. Reaching him, she leaned over to kiss him and was surprised and embarrassed when he pulled away.

The last time she'd seen him was the night they'd spent in her apartment and she couldn't help but wonder at his cool reaction. His behavior was odd and confusing. *What had happened between his last text and now?* After all, he'd been the one to issue the invitation. Refusing to play games, she gathered her courage and asked him.

"What's the matter?"

He averted his gaze and for the first time, she noticed the tension in his face. His lips were compressed and his expression was grim. He looked nothing like the carefree, laughing, sexy man she'd recently farewelled from her bedroom. Icy foreboding trickled through her veins and set like concrete in her stomach. With her fists now clenched, she repeated her question. This time, he looked at her and she almost gasped at the fury behind his eyes.

"You tell me," he said coldly.

She shook her head back and forth, at a loss to fathom what had caused his change in attitude. "I don't know what you're talking about."

"Try again, honey. I'm not falling for your sweet act again."

Anger stirred inside her. She didn't have a clue what he was getting at, but he wasn't going to speak to her like that.

"You should know by now I'm not the kind of girl who plays games, Cameron. Either come right out and tell me whatever it is that's got you so hot and bothered, or forget about it. It seems obvious to me you've already made up your mind." She pushed back from the table and went to turn away. His arm snaked out and grabbed her elbow, halting her in her tracks.

"Let go of me," she said through gritted teeth.

"Not until you answer my questions."

They eyeballed each other. Georgie's chest rose and fell, keeping pace with her racing heart. "I don't know what you're talking about."

His gaze narrowed. "Let's start with the baby you put up for adoption."

She gasped in shock, aghast. The icy dread in her stomach morphed into a ball of fire that burned itself up her chest and across her face. "H-how did you find out?"

His lips twisted into a bitter smile. "At least you're not going to deny it."

Dazed, Georgie tried to get her bearings, stunned that Cam had discovered her secret. She risked a glance in his direction. The hurt and pain on his face tore her heart in two.

"I… I wanted to tell you. I did. I just—"

"Never got around to it, right? Not even when we were talking about it, when I was baring my heart and soul. No, not even then."

She closed her eyes against another wave of pain. She never meant for him to find out like this. How *did* he find out? She suddenly realized he hadn't answered her question.

"Who told you?" she asked quietly.

"Nobody. It was written there in black and white. Among the files owned by the City of Sydney Adoption Agency."

She stared at him in confusion. She'd never known the name of the agency that facilitated her son's adoption. Her mother had handled all the details. Cam stared back at her with a cynical look in his eyes.

"Don't tell me you've never heard of it, because I won't believe you."

Georgie held his gaze, determined to make him see the truth. "I've never heard of it."

"Bullshit," he shouted. "It's owned by your aunt and your mother. Don't tell me you don't know anything about it."

Another wave of shock rendered her speechless. The crowd around them disappeared. She fought back a wave of dizziness.

"Sit down, before you fall over," Cam growled and pushed her into a seat.

Georgie drew in a shaky breath and stared at him. *Could he be telling her the truth?* Did Aunt Rosemary and her mother own an adoption agency? And if so, could her mother have *profited* from facilitating the adoption of her own grandson? The thought was repulsive.

"How do you know about the agency?" she rasped.

His expression hardened. "You don't need to know."

Desperation welled inside her. "Please, I really do."

He stared at her for another long moment. His nonchalant shrug belied the tension in his face.

"After you told me about your father, I got curious. I searched his name on the Internet. Then I added your mom's and hey, presto! I got a hit on the agency. A simple company search gave me the rest."

The foreboding in Georgie's belly seemed to grow and expand, snatching away her breath, but she forced herself to ask the question. "Why would you be curious about my father? You'd never heard of him before I mentioned his name." He held her gaze.

"I lied."

This time, anger ignited, lightning fast and red hot. Her jaw was clenched so tightly she could hardly speak. "Answer the question: Why were you curious about my father?"

Cameron stared at her steadily. "We haven't finished discussing the fact you failed to tell me about the baby you adopted out when you were seventeen."

"*Tell me!*"

"Your father's name was on all fifteen of the death certificates issued for the babies who'd died on Ward Seven over the past year. I have reason to believe those very same babies didn't die at all. They were stolen by your mother and your aunt and offered for adoption."

Georgie gasped in shock at his incredible accusation and then began to cough. Her chest was so tight, she couldn't breathe. It felt like she was combusting from the inside out.

Cam was at her side in an instant, his earlier anger now replaced with concern. "Slow it down, Georgie. Breathe. In and out. Big breaths. In and out. That's better." When she was calmer, he regained his seat.

Finally able to speak again, she lifted her gaze to his. "How... How could you even think something so ridiculous! What you're suggesting... It's beyond repugnant. My mother? My aunt? My father? Stealing *babies!* There's absolutely no way in the world! You're mad! The very idea is completely and utterly distasteful!"

"I've failed to mention your uncle's also involved."

He shook his head back and forth and threw her a humorless smile. "I have to hand it to them, they've got it all worked out. Women of dubious backgrounds come onto the ward to give birth. Shortly after the baby's delivered, your aunt brings the sad news to the new Mom that the baby has died.

"Somehow, the infant is spirited away and offered up for adoption. I haven't yet looked into the agency's financial records, but no doubt the adoption takes place for a hefty fee. Your mother completes the reports; your father signs the death certificate and in the meantime, arranges to register the newborn's birth. A birth certificate is issued and you have all you need to effect an adoption."

Georgie reeled from one relentless blow to the next. The heat of her anger gave way to an icy coldness that filled her from head to toe. She began to tremble uncontrollably.

"No! No! No! You have it all wrong!" she gasped weakly. "I don't believe it! It's not true! It *can't* be! Do you have any evidence?"

Cam stared at her without flinching. "Yes."

With a horrified gasp, Georgie snatched up her handbag and turned blindly into the crowd. Ignoring Cameron's shout, she plowed through the press of bodies. She pushed past a man holding a tray of drinks and gritted her teeth when he lost his balance and the drinks spilled everywhere.

He cursed and frowned at her, but she didn't pause and couldn't even summon the wherewithal to offer an apology. All she could think of was getting out of there and finding her mom and dad. They would reassure her of Cameron's ridiculousness. They would calm her fears.

They'd always been able to do that, from the time she was a little girl. Apart from her teenage pregnancy, she couldn't remember the number of times she'd gone to one or the other of them and received comfort and understanding when life threw an unexpected obstacle in her way. This was no different.

The seriousness of Cameron's allegations was completely off the scale and despite his claim that he had proof, she was sure her parents could explain that away and her world would once again right on its axis. Until then, she couldn't be around Cameron another second. No matter how much her heart rebelled against it, there could be nothing between them until this nonsense was sorted out.

Bursting through the double entry doors that led outside to the street, she pushed blindly through the crowd. Panting hard, she gulped in air and filled her lungs in an effort to slow down her racing heart. People passed by her on the pavement, but she remained oblivious to their curious stares. In a daze, she started walking, barely aware of where she was going. She flagged down a taxi and at the last minute, remembered she'd driven into the city from work.

Lowering her arm, she turned away and hurried in the direction of the parking station, clinging to the fact that soon she'd have the truth from her parents. Then she prayed she could set about repairing the damage her secret baby had done to her relationship with Cameron. He'd been furious that she'd kept it from him. She only hoped he'd come to understand.

CHAPTER 22

Cam stared into the darkness from where he stood out on his balcony and cursed aloud. He'd left the bar straight after Georgie and the image of her devastated face kept coming back to haunt him. She'd endured one shock after the other, not the least his discovery of her secret.

The knowledge that she'd kept it from him still angered him—after all they'd shared. She knew how he felt about adoption and yet, she hadn't said a word.

A shaft of guilt pricked his conscience and he winced. He wondered just when she would have found the courage and opportunity to bring it to his attention. He'd made it clear how he felt about his birth mother. His attitude hadn't exactly invited confidences of that nature.

What could she have said? *Oh, it's sad to hear how much you hate your birth mother, but guess what? I gave my baby up for adoption, too.*

He remembered how she'd tried to offer up

various scenarios that might have explained his birth mother's actions and how he'd shot every one of them down. He hadn't wanted to listen to any reasoning. He'd despised the woman for too long. Now, he couldn't help but wonder about Georgie's reasons.

She'd never struck him as heartless and self-centered. In fact, just the opposite. The kindness and compassion she'd shown Cynthia was only one example. His sister had ceased to be Georgie's responsibility from the moment Cynthia had been discharged and yet, Georgie had come to his aid when he'd called for help and was instrumental in his sister's ongoing emotional recovery.

And yet, she'd given her baby away... All of a sudden he wanted to know why.

If he'd held any doubt whether or not she was aware of the evil wrongdoings at the hospital, they'd dissolved the moment he'd voiced his suspicions. Her reaction was one of shock and sheer horror. Nobody was that good an actor. It was clear she was oblivious to what her family had been up to.

He frowned at the memory of his outburst. He'd spoken without thinking. He shouldn't have said anything at all. Though he was fairly sure she wouldn't tip off his suspects, he couldn't be certain. A couple of days earlier, he would have answered with a resounding yes, but his recent discoveries proved he didn't know her as well as he thought. The knowledge worried him.

The problem was, he still didn't have any

tangible proof that the babies had been stolen. He hadn't yet found any adoption records that pointed to the babies involved in his investigation. But it was early days. There were hundreds of records.

There was also the possibility of exhuming the bodies of those babies who hadn't been cremated. It would only take one to know the truth. He was sure it was only a matter of time before he'd uncover enough evidence to make an arrest.

His thoughts returned to Georgie and the way she'd rushed from the bar, so pale and distraught. He worried for her safety, but it would also be wise to remind her that aiding and abetting criminals was an offense. Warning her not to speak with her family about the ongoing investigation wouldn't do anything to repair the damage between them, but it had to be done. It was his stupid ass on the line. He couldn't take the risk. Tugging out his phone, he sent her a text.

R u OK? Don't talk 2 anyone. Call me. Please.

He waited for a few minutes and then cursed again. His phone remained frustratingly silent. Striding to the low table that stood between the matching deck chairs where he and Georgie had sat and flirted a lifetime ago, he picked up the half empty bottle of beer he'd left there and swallowed the rest of its contents. The beer tasted yeasty and was cold on the back of his throat—but it wasn't alcohol he wanted.

He wanted Georgie. He wanted her to answer her phone; to call him or text him and tell him she was fine. He wanted to go back to when they were two young single people attracted to each other and not frightened to admit it. He wanted life to be simple and not have the prospect of a personal, complicated investigation getting in the way of what could possibly be the real thing.

He wished he could talk to the woman who'd quietly stolen his heart. He wanted to reassure himself she'd arrived home safely and he wanted to apologize. He was ready to hear her explanation, if she'd give him one.

He checked his phone again to make sure he hadn't mistakenly switched it to silent mode, but the device remained stubbornly quiet. He composed another text.

I understand ur upset, but please just let me know ur OK. Call me.

He sent the text and hoped this time she'd respond. At least then he'd be able to go to bed and try and get some sleep before working out a battle plan for the morning. It wasn't late, but he was beat. It had been a difficult few days and the next few promised to be even worse.

Georgie heard her phone beep for the second time, but paid it no heed. She swung her Mazda into the driveway of the palatial Darling Point home where her parents now lived alone. She climbed out and locked the door behind her, all the while swiping angrily at the stupid tears that continued to scorch a path of devastation down her cheeks. She'd been crying since she'd run out of the bar, leaving Cameron to stare after her.

She'd sat across from him and listened to his words, but it had taken some time for her to accept the awful truth. Now, as she looked back over her time on Ward Seven, she wondered why she hadn't suspected or even noticed.

She'd been told about the deaths of the three babies she'd helped deliver and it hadn't occurred to her to ask if there had been others. *Would her mother have told her the truth?* She didn't know. She squeezed her eyes shut as tightly as she could manage and fought off the shaft of pain that forced its way into her heart.

According to Cam, twelve other babies had "died" over the course of the past year and her mother and aunt were likely responsible. She didn't want to believe either woman capable of such evil, but Cam's explanation made an awful kind of sense. It also explained her mother's strident and judgemental attitude toward the patients in their care.

The fact that Georgie had been oblivious to the possibility of their evil deeds was unforgivable. She should have asked more questions, demanded to see the bodies. Instead, she'd blindly accepted her mother's explanation.

Another shaft of pain nearly bent her over and she gasped from the agony of it. She thought of the other nurses on the ward and could only assume they were just as clueless as she had been.

Cameron had put it all together. She didn't know how, but he'd said he had the proof. He had no reason to lie to her. She had to accept that what he'd told her was the truth. All except the part about her father's involvement.

Even with her mother's recent revelations about his insistence that she give her baby up for adoption, she refused to believe he had any culpability for the evil that had occurred on Ward Seven. He might have signed the death certificates, but it didn't mean he knew what his wife and sister-in-law were up to.

Finally, reaching the heavy double front doors that led into her parents' home, Georgie drew in a ragged breath and keyed in the security code. She heard the corresponding click. Putting her shoulder to the wooden panel, she pushed open the doors and stepped inside the marbled foyer.

Twenty-foot ceilings and wide open spaces greeted her. Custom-made hall tables and silk-embroidered chaises lined both sides of the entryway. Walls covered in priceless artworks that normally gave her pause left no impact this time. She headed straight for her father's den, calling out to him as she went.

"Dad! Where are you? It's Georgie. Dad! I need to talk to you!"

She rounded the corner and slid open the pair of carved wooden doors that closed off the room where her father spent most of his leisure time. Her heart pounded against her ribs. The room had been furnished with dark, masculine pieces that reminded Georgie of a gentleman's smoking room from centuries ago. In desperation, she looked around for him.

Several leather armchairs stood across from the occasional two-seater and were positioned to encourage conversation. Crowded floor-to-ceiling bookshelves lined one wall. An ornate sandstone fireplace took up most of another. An enormous window framed the magnificent city view and added to the opulence of the room. Amidst all of the luxury, Georgie spied her mother standing by the window. She came to a sudden halt.

Marjorie stood with her back to her, nursing a glass of scotch. She turned slowly and Georgie gasped. The look on her mother's face was terrifying.

"Whatever are you carrying on about Georgina? You'll disturb the entire neighborhood."

Her mother's tone was so mild and soft, Georgie was taken aback. It was so at odds with the coldness in her eyes, she couldn't help but shiver. A frisson of fear slid down her spine, but she told herself not to be silly. This was her mother, a woman she loved and who loved her in return.

"I-I was looking for Dad," she stammered.

"Your father isn't here. He's been called into the hospital. Apparently, some undeserving, drug-addicted wretch requires his services during a long and difficult delivery."

The rancor in Marjorie's voice and the bitterness in her eyes shocked Georgie to the core. *How had it taken her so long to become aware of how much her mother despised the patients they worked with?* Like the news of stolen babies, it seemed inconceivable that she'd spent two years on Ward Seven and until recently, had never noticed. If she hadn't caught a glimpse of this other side to her mother the last time they'd been together, she'd never have believed Cameron's accusations.

Now, in the privacy of her home, Marjorie appeared to have dropped all pretenses of caring one iota for the desperate women in their care and in that moment it was obvious to Georgie: The woman she had admired and respected and loved could very well be guilty of the crime. The knowledge horrified her and her hand flew up to her mouth to hold in a distraught gasp.

"It's true, isn't it?" she cried, coming toward her mother.

Marjorie just stared at her with pity in her eyes. "Poor Georgina. Always the last to know. We had such high hopes for you, but alas, you've let us down."

Tears streamed down Georgie's cheeks as she listened to her mother's words. Marjorie hadn't even tried to deny it. "Those babies didn't die, did they? You were all in on it. You, or Aunt Rosemary would break the sad news to the distraught mothers and then spirit the babies away. You set up an adoption agency to make things easier and got rid of the infants that way. I assume you paid Uncle Bernard handsomely to go along with it and to pretend he'd taken possession of the bodies."

Her mother nodded. "Of course. How else do you think we got him to agree? That lazy, no-good undertaker didn't have a penny to his name until we came along. Your aunt purposefully sought him out. She knew he'd be good for business."

Georgie gasped. "How long has this been going on?"

"I think we facilitated our first adoption toward the end of nineteen seventy-three. Rosemary and I were young nurses. Rosemary was approached by Matron. It was all Matron's idea. Rosemary was initially taken aback, but once Matron explained her reasons, my sister was fully supportive. It didn't take her long to convince me it was the right thing to do. I'm curious though, how did you know about the agency?"

"Cameron Dawson told me."

"Ah, the detective. Cynthia's brother. You made mention of the existence of a brother the day she delivered, but if I'd known he was a police officer, we would have let her baby be."

Anger ignited in Georgie. "So, you took Josephine, too. Just like Cam thought. I... I just don't believe it!" She rounded on her mother, her fury finding its feet. "How *could* you? How could you *steal* their babies?"

Marjorie's laughter rang out in the room and her expression turned ugly. "Those women are a blight on our society! Single, without means of support and often teenagers, destroying their lives with alcohol and drugs. They don't deserve to be mothers! A child is a precious gift from God! It deserves only the best love and attention. How can those women give a child what it needs? Surely you must agree!"

"I don't, but even if I did, it doesn't give you the right to steal their babies and give them to someone else!" Georgie shouted, fresh tears streaming down her face. "I assume that's what you're doing."

Her mother's lips twisted up in a sick imitation of a grin. "Well, you're almost right; all except the giving away part. There's nothing free about adoption. There are people who'll pay a fortune for a baby of their own, even one going through a heroin withdrawal."

With a wave of her arm around the room, she continued. "How do you think we got this place? Not to mention the top private school, ballet lessons, sax, flute, clarinet and piano lessons, overseas holidays, 5-star restaurants and hotels. You and your siblings have wanted for nothing and there's plenty more where that came from. You'll get your fair share, don't worry."

Georgie stood there, too horrified to speak. She'd always assumed her parents' wealth came from legitimate means. To discover she'd been raised with money from the sale of stolen babies... It was too much.

Bile rose up from Georgie's stomach and she thought she was going to be sick. She stumbled around the room before collapsing on one of the leather couches. Tugging out her phone, she spied Cameron's messages and frantically sent him a text. She couldn't stay there another minute, but she was in no fit state to drive. The way she felt, she could cause an accident and that was the last thing on earth she needed.

Her mother came toward her, the scotch glass no longer in her hand. Her narrowed gaze was fixed on Georgie's phone. In a flash, Marjorie snatched the phone right out of Georgie's hand and scrolled through her messages. When she turned back to stare at her daughter, her eyes were like shards of black ice.

"You shouldn't have done that, Georgina. I wanted to keep this between us."

"You're insane! Cam already knows! How do you think—?"

"Ha! That young detective knows nothing! You don't think we've done this for more than forty years without learning to cover our tracks. He'll dig around and ask his questions, but in the end, he'll come up with squat! Certainly not enough to press charges. The four of us are much cleverer than that."

Blithely, she typed in something on Georgie's phone. A moment later, the *swish* of a text message being sent could be heard in the silence. She tossed the phone back to her daughter.

Georgie stared at her mother, dazed and confused by her shocking revelations. "The *four* of you? You mean, Daddy? No! I won't believe he's part of this!"

Her mother laughed without humor. "Believe what you want, Georgina. It means nothing to me."

Georgie's anger stirred at the contempt in her mother's voice. Her head still spun with confusion. She stared at her mother, trying to understand. "You and Rosemary were both young nurses forty years ago. You couldn't have left school very far behind you. How? Why? I... I don't understand."

"And you don't need to. Let's just say, the history lesson's over. It's time we made a move before that boyfriend gets concerned."

Georgie's eyes widened in surprise and Marjorie snorted. "Oh, yes, I read the messages about getting together for dinner and the rest. I'm not stupid."

"On your feet," another voice ordered.

In some distant part of her frantic mind, Georgie recognized her aunt's voice. Swiveling on the couch, she spied Rosemary who held a wicked-looking handgun. It was pointed straight at Georgie.

Georgie stared at it in shock and terror. "What...?"

"We're going for a little ride, you and your mother and I. Up to the cottage in the mountains. I'm sure you remember it. Such a pretty spot. Now, get up."

Prodding her with the barrel of the gun, Rosemary forced Georgie to her feet. Georgie's heart thumped so hard, she could barely breathe. Panic clutched at her belly and fear tangled her feet. Tears poured down her cheeks. In desperation, she turned to her mother.

"Why, Mom? *Why?*" Sobbing, she stumbled over the corner of a rug.

"No more questions," her mother snapped. "You know too much already. Now, get moving and watch where you're going. Walk to the front door. We'll take your car."

"You're not going to get away with this!" Georgie cried out, hating the fear and panic in her voice.

"*Move!*" Rosemary screamed, threatening her with the waving gun.

Georgie studied her aunt's face, contorted with anger. A crazed light gleamed in her eyes. Georgie gasped on another sob, this one laden with fear. She no longer recognized the woman she'd known her entire life. Her mom appeared equally foreign.

With no other choice, she turned and made her way out of her father's den, across the wide expanse of Italian marble and back to the heavy front doors. Pulling them open, she stumbled down the steps and walked over to her car. Rosemary stood behind her with the gun inches from Georgie's head. Her mother waited not far away.

"Get in. And don't try anything stupid, or you'll be dead," Rosemary warned.

Georgie gasped, but both women ignored her cry of fear. With trembling limbs, Georgie managed to slide in behind the wheel. All she could do was pray that Cameron had received her message. With the gun at the ready, Rosemary climbed into the seat opposite. Marjorie took a seat in the back.

"W-where are we going?" Georgie stammered.

"We're heading west, like I told you," Rosemary growled. "To the cottage in the Blue Mountains."

Georgie put the car into reverse and backed out of the cobblestone driveway. Checking for traffic, she eased the Mazda into the street.

Rosemary held the gun with a steady hand, pointed in Georgie's direction. It was all Georgie could do to stay on the road.

"It's a shame it had to come to this," Marjorie stated matter-of-factly from behind Georgie. "But I guess this is the only way."

Fresh fear raced through Georgie's veins, but she kept her attention steadfastly focused on the road. "What do you mean?"

Rosemary shrugged nonchalantly. "You'll see."

"But the police—"

"Will never find you," her aunt added. "While we were inside, I got your mother to send a text from your phone to hers. You're meeting her in the city to catch a late-night movie. Just the two of you. Some quality mother-daughter time. She'll be suitably confused and uncertain when she attends the police station in the morning to file a missing person's report. By the time they get off their asses to look for you, any trace of you will be long gone. It will be like you didn't exist."

The calmness in her aunt's voice sent shivers down Georgie's spine. In desperation, she half-turned toward her mother. "Mom, please... You can't—"

"Shut up!" Rosemary screamed and pushed the gun within inches of Georgie's face. Once again, Georgie's frantic thoughts turned to Cam.

As if he could tell she was thinking about him, her phone rang. Tugging it out of her pocket, she glanced at the screen. It was him.

"Don't answer it!" her aunt shouted, waving the gun at Georgie's head. "Give that phone to me."

With great reluctance, Georgie handed it over and listened with a heavy heart as the phone continued to ring. After what seemed a lifetime, the call went through to voicemail and a moment later, a beep indicated Cam had left a message. Rosemary put the phone up to her ear. In the silence, Georgie could hear the deep timbre of his voice.

"Ha!" her aunt scoffed when the message had come to an end. "How sweet! He's worried about you. He wants you to call him back." With the gun still pointed in Georgie's direction, Rosemary quickly sent off another text. "There, that should do it."

Dread welled up in Georgie's belly. "What did you tell him?"

Her aunt smiled. "Let's just say I hope you're not expecting your boyfriend to come to your rescue any time soon."

Georgie clenched her teeth so hard they ached. "What did you tell him?"

"Just that you were meeting your mother in the city. You're going to the movies, remember?" The look of wide-eyed innocence on her aunt's face turned the blood in Georgie's veins to ice.

Rosemary had it all worked out. Cameron would no doubt accept her text at face value, even if it did leave him a little confused. The text she'd sent to him earlier from her mother's house had only contained five words: *I need help. Please call.*

CHAPTER 23

Dear Diary,

Matron was forever telling me to always have a Plan B. 'You never know when you're going to need it,' she'd say. I'd say, she was right. But then, she was right about everything.

Cameron stared down at his phone in confusion. *What the hell was Georgie on about?* One moment he received a text that sounded desperate, even fearful and half an hour later, she told him she was going to the movies with her mother. It was odd. Going to the movies at that time of night was strange enough, but going with her mother after all he and Georgie had discussed at Bar Luca was downright weird. The last person Georgie ought to want to be hanging with was her mother.

Cam looked at the screen again and couldn't rid himself of the feeling something wasn't right. After the first text, he'd tried to phone her, but his call had rung out and then gone through to voicemail. He'd left a message, expressing his concern and asking her to call him back, but all he'd gotten was the second text.

Striding down the corridor, he found Cynthia lying across her bed, engrossed in a book. It warmed him to know she took pleasure from such simple, ordinary things.

"Hey, how are you doing?" he asked.

She put her finger on the page to hold her place and looked up and smiled. "I'm fine. What's the matter?"

He hastened to reassure her. "Nothing. At least, I don't think so. I received a strange text from Georgie. It's got me a little on edge."

Cynthia frowned and sat up, tucking her feet beneath her. "Is she all right?"

"I think so. I'll be happier after I hear from her."

"You really like her, don't you?"

Recalling their earlier conversation about her fears that she'd be asked to leave, Cam came further into the room and perched on the side of her bed. "Yeah, I do, but it doesn't change things between us. You'll always be my little sister and you'll always have a home with me, no matter what female companions come in and out of my life."

The tension around her mouth eased. She smiled softly. "Do you really mean that?"

"Yes," he said, reaching out to give her a hug. "I really do."

They sat in silence for a little while and then Cynthia said, "I like Georgie."

Cam pressed a kiss against her hair. "I like her, too." He hesitated and then remembered something else he and Georgie had discussed.

"I'd like to know what happened at home that forced you out onto the streets. Would you talk to me about it?" He'd voiced his question gently, making sure she knew it was all right if she didn't, but he was quietly relieved when she sighed softly and replied.

"Life didn't get any better after you left. Mom no longer had you around to scream at and blame for everything, so she turned her attention to me."

Cam was immediately filled with outrage. "You were a little kid! Barely five years old! What kind of person picks on a child?"

Cynthia's lips twisted into a grimace. "A bully. You remember what she was like. She was never happy. I couldn't do anything right. It got worse over the years, right up until the day I left."

"So Dad didn't throw you out?"

"No, not like you, but he did nothing to make me stay. I told him I couldn't keep living there, being a punching bag for his crazy wife. He just shrugged and looked a little forlorn and then watched me walk out of his life."

The anger that always smoldered right below the surface whenever Cam thought of their dad sprang to life. "What a coward! I'd hoped he'd grown some balls over the time since I'd left."

Cynthia shrugged sadly and shook her head. "I guess not."

The memory of that awful day and the pain he'd endured when his father had ordered him to leave, hit him in a wave so hard it could have happened yesterday. "I'll never forgive them," Cam rasped.

Cynthia scooted closer to him and laid her hand on his arm. "Don't say things like that, Cam. A grudge like that will eat you up inside. One day you'll realize you're so full of hate, there isn't room for anything else. You don't want to end up like that. There'd be nothing left for anyone, including me and Georgie."

Cam stared at her in confusion. "Don't tell me you're not angry at them?

"Of course I'm angry! Or at least, I was. I spent the best part of the first year I lived on the streets, being angry at them. Then I met Albert and he made me see things clearer. Some people aren't strong enough to stand up against a bully. Dad was weak like that. It was easier to give into Mom's demands than to stand up to her." Her voice lowered to a whisper and tears glinted in her eyes. "It was easier for him to let us go."

"Why the hell did they bother to adopt when it was obvious they didn't like kids?"

Cynthia looked up at him earnestly. "Dad loved us. I'm sure he did."

"Just not enough."

Cam wanted to rant and rave against the injustice of it, but something in the quiet acceptance and forgiveness in his little sister's demeanor stopped him. Here she was, still a child and yet she had more understanding and kindness inside her than he could ever hope to have. Her compassion shamed him into silence.

Tightening his arms around her, he hugged her for a long time. "I love you, Cyn," he whispered.

"I love you, too, Cam."

He pressed a kiss against her hair and squeezed her again. Then, remembering Georgie's conflicting texts, he gently set Cynthia aside. "I need to make some calls."

"About Georgie?"

"Yes. I'm a little more worried about her than I said. I'll be out in the kitchen if you need me."

"Okay." Cynthia threw him a soft smile and then returned to her book.

Cam strode back down the hallway. His sister's attitude had been a revelation and one he needed to ponder, but right now, thinking of Georgie, he was filled with a sense of unease and growing urgency. Apart from the fact he needed to make sure she hadn't spoken to anyone about his investigation, she'd been distressed when she'd left him and he needed to know she was okay. It didn't make sense that she was in the mood to go to the movies—with her mother no less. Tugging out his phone, he dialed the station and was relieved when one of his colleagues picked up.

Rohan Coleridge was a detective with years of experience under his belt. He was just the man Cam needed to talk to.

"Rohan, it's Cam. I need you to do me a favor."

"Sure. Fire away."

"I want you to check a cell phone signal. I need to know what tower it's bouncing off."

There was a hesitation on the other end of the phone. Cameron bit back his impatience and added, "It's my…girlfriend. I'm worried about her. She sent me a couple of texts that have weirded me out. I just want to check to ensure she's where she says she is."

"From anyone else but you, Cam, that might sound a little creepy."

"It's legitimate, Rohan. I swear."

Rohan sighed. "Yeah, okay. What's the number?"

Cam supplied Rohan with the information.

"Do you know her phone carrier?"

"No, but let's start with Telstra."

"Give me five. I'll call you back."

Cam ended the call and sat down on the sofa. Hopefully Rohan would be able to triangulate Georgie's cell phone signal and narrow down her location. She lived in the eastern suburbs. Anywhere in the vicinity of her street or the city would satisfy him. It would confirm she was where she said she was, and if so, he'd leave it at that.

The phone in his hand vibrated and even though the Caller ID was blocked, he answered straight away. "Cameron Dawson."

"Cam, it's Rohan. Good guess. She's with Telstra. The other good news is I've been able to approximate her location. She's heading west. The last ping we got on her phone was about three minutes ago from a tower near Emu Plains. I hope that's what you wanted to hear."

Cam's heart skipped a beat and then took off at a gallop. Blood rushed through his ears, almost deafening him to the rest of Rohan's comments.

"Something's wrong." His voice was husky with strain.

"Sorry?"

Cam cleared his throat and sucked in a desperate breath. He jumped off the couch and began to pace. "Something's wrong. She shouldn't be anywhere near Emu Plains. She lives in the eastern suburbs and she sent me a text to say she was meeting her mom in the city. The fact that you've tracked her cell phone heading west is all wrong. Are you sure your data is correct?"

Cam clung to the faint hope that Rohan would answer in the negative, but his sense of foreboding escalated when his colleague said, "I can't imagine why it would be wrong."

Panic started low in Cam's gut. *Why would Georgie be at Emu Plains and heading even further west?* After all that had happened that day, it just didn't make sense. He imagined she'd be home, coming to terms with the possibility some members of her family were criminals, and yet, according to her cell phone data, she was on the far western point of Sydney. There was nothing much after Emu Plains except...

"The Blue Mountains," he muttered and suddenly recalled her mentioning she'd grown up there. He was also sure he'd read something about that area while he'd been researching her parents and the adoption agency.

"Are you all right, Cam?"

"Rohan, I need another favor. Go to my desk and open the file labeled: Sydney Harbour Hospital. It should be right there near my phone."

"Hang on a sec. I'll go and see what I can find."

The line went silent and Cam tried not to count the seconds. A moment later, Rohan was back.

"Okay, I have the file. Now what?"

"Flick through it until you come to a printout from the Land and Property Information Office. It's toward the back."

"Yep, okay. I have that."

"Go through the list of property. There's a place located in the Blue Mountains. I can't remember exactly where and I need the address. Can you see it?"

The seconds ticked by and Cam did his best to hold onto his patience. If his hunch was correct, Georgie was on her way to her childhood home. He had no idea if she was traveling alone, but he needed to reassure himself she was all right. Her odd text messages had put him on edge and he wouldn't relax until he was sure she was fine.

"Wow, these people are certainly not without funds. I'd like to own even half of this property portfolio."

Cameron swallowed his impatience. "Just give me the Blue Mountains address."

"Fifty-eight Rawson Parade, Leura."

"You're sure?"

"That's what it says here."

Cam's heart rate jumped up a notch. "Thanks, mate. I owe you one."

"Is something the matter, Cam? Do you want me to put in a call to the station up there?"

"Right now, I'm not exactly sure what's going on, but my gut's telling me something's not right and I've learned to listen to it."

"I'm happy to call the boys up in Katoomba, give them a heads up."

Cam thought about it. Until he knew what was going on, there was no point alerting the local police. He didn't want to waste anyone's time, least of all some fellow officers.

"Thanks for the offer, Rohan, but I think I'll head up there on my own and see what I can find out. If I need backup, I'll call. Keep the address handy, just in case."

"Yeah, all right. Well, good luck and let me know if there's anything I can do."

Cam thanked him again and ended the call. A moment later, he strode back down the hall and halted outside Cynthia's bedroom. Knocking on the door, he waited for her to invite him in.

"Hey," she smiled. "What are you doing back here?"

"I'm sorry, honey, but I have to go out. Will you be all right here on your own?"

She rolled her eyes and shook her head. "I lived on the streets for two years, Cam. What do you think?"

"I know, but...you know. You're sixteen. You're still a kid."

"Cam, I'm *sixteen*. I'm nearly an adult."

He smiled. "Okay, but I'm not sure how long I'll be gone."

"I'll be fine. Go, okay?"

"All right." He started to back out of the room.

"Is this about Georgie?" Cynthia asked.

"Yes."

"Is she all right? I hope she's not in some kind of trouble."

Cam grimaced. "I'm not sure, yet, but that's why I have to go. I'm going to find her and make certain she's okay."

Cynthia's expression softened. "You're a good guy, Cameron Dawson."

Cam blushed under her warm regard, pleased that his little sister thought so.

"What are you waiting for? Go and save her," Cynthia urged. "All girls dream of being rescued by their knight in shining armor."

He looked at her. "Really?"

"Really."

"Do you?" he asked curiously.

Her expression softened. "Yes, and I know he's out there somewhere."

CHAPTER 24

Georgie risked a glance toward her aunt and was concerned to discover the deadly looking weapon in Rosemary's hands was still pointed at her head. She didn't even know her aunt, or anyone in her family, owned a gun. It frightened her to realize how little she knew the woman she'd grown up admiring.

Along with her mother, it was her Aunt Rosemary who'd inspired her to enter nursing. When she thought of how the two sisters had been spending their time, a wave of nausea rolled up from her stomach. She gasped aloud and tears burned behind her eyes. All of a sudden, she wondered if any of her sisters knew. She glanced at the rearview mirror to her mother, needing to know.

"Are Sasha, Clare and Montana involved, too?"

"No. To date we haven't had any need of their services, and of course, none of them followed us into the nursing field. But who knows what the future may bring? I'm sure when the time's right, we'll fill them in on our good deeds."

Georgie opened her mouth to utter another round of protest at the way her mother described their horrific and illegal undertakings, but then closed it again. It was obvious Marjorie was under some sick delusion that she was acting in the best interests of all concerned, and particularly, the babies. In her mind, she seemed to be saving the newborns from a fate far worse than death.

Georgie couldn't deny the life of a child born to a drug addict wouldn't be easy, but it wasn't up to individuals to make the decision to have the children removed. There were government agencies with specially trained people to assess each situation and deal with them in an open and honest manner. Georgie refused to acknowledge the little voice in her head that reminded her how, too often, the government resources were stretched to their limits and some families simply fell through the cracks.

On some weird level, she could understand why her mother and aunt had set out on this path, but it didn't make it right. Not one little bit. Curious as to how they'd started out, she glanced at her mother through the rearview mirror again.

"What made you decide you needed to involve yourself in stealing other peoples' babies?"

Her mother scowled. "We're not stealing them. We're giving them a better life!"

Georgie shrugged. "From what I've heard, it's stealing, but that's beside the point. You've been doing this for nearly forty years. Drugs and alcohol weren't even a problem back then. Not like it is now. Why were you stealing babies four decades ago?"

Rosemary let out a long drawn-out sigh, but the hand holding the gun didn't waver. "Oh, honey, we mightn't have had the level of drug abuse to deal with, but society back then had its own set of problems."

"Like what?" Georgie asked, hoping to distract the women from their apparent deadly goal upon their arrival at the Leura cottage.

Her mother continued. "The sixties and seventies were times of uninhibited, amoral behavior. There were plenty of girls willing to sleep with any man who happened to show them attention. Babies born out of wedlock to teenage moms were a common occurrence.

"Both Rosemary and I did our training under Sister Mary Margaret Hennessy, a nun from the local convent and matron of the hospital. Back in those days, many hospitals were run by religious orders. Ours was no different. It was Matron who first approached Rosemary about relocating children born of these mothers to more deserving and satisfactory homes."

Georgie shook her head, still unable to believe their mindset. "But, *why*? Just because a girl's fifteen and without a husband or partner doesn't mean she's an unfit mom. I'm sure I would have made a great mom, if I'd been given the chance.

"Many of the young women I've met over the past two years see the birth of their babies as a reason to try harder to make something of their

"Ladies, please. Perhaps it might be better to leave this...this family disagreement to some other time," Rosemary interrupted. "Georgie, your mother is right. Your situation was very different than our patients. Most of them are barely able to take care of themselves, let alone a baby. And I'm referencing the ones who actually want to try and improve their lot.

"You can't tell me you haven't wondered what happens to the hundreds of wretched young souls who leave the safety of our hospital ward in the company of their drug-addicted mothers— mothers who have neither the inclination nor willpower to change their desperate and dubious lifestyles."

Georgie kept her attention on the road. She wasn't prepared to let either woman know that she often despaired over the babies who were born to moms just like the ones Rosemary described. It didn't matter. Nothing justified their actions and nothing either of them said would change her mind.

"Why didn't you just approach each mom you thought fell into that category and talk about adoption?" she asked. "It's what thousands of single moms did back when you were young. It wasn't necessary to steal them, then or now! And to compound the tragedy by telling those poor moms their babies had died..." She shook her head and bit back a sob. "It's wrong! It's so wrong!"

Her aunt merely shrugged and another glance in the mirror showed Georgie her mother was equally unaffected by her daughter's despair. It was obvious she'd never make them see.

"Pull in over there," Rosemary snapped. "I don't want your car visible from the road."

Through the darkness, Georgie made out the dark hulk of her childhood home. The cottage was now used infrequently by her family, but it had always been kept in good repair. A man came twice a week to mow the lawns and keep the gardens under control. The last time Georgie had been there was for Christmas, nearly six months ago.

Thinking about that time when all her family had come together as one, to share the holidays and celebrate, she was filled with a deep sadness. Life would never be like that again—even if she managed to survive the next few moments and whatever else her mother and aunt had in store. As if she could sense her thoughts, Rosemary waved the gun in Georgie's direction.

"Get out of the car and keep your hands where I can see them."

Georgie did as she was told. The crazy gleam had returned to her aunt's eyes. It was almost as if she relished the idea of having her niece at her mercy. The thought sent a cold shiver down Georgie's spine. She glanced at her mother, hoping to find some sign that she wasn't supportive of Rosemary's dangerous plans— whatever they might be—but Marjorie didn't appear in the least concerned.

A little desperately, Georgie's thoughts turned to Cam and she wondered if he'd given any thought to her contradictory text messages. The possibility that he hadn't, caused panic to flare inside her.

What if he'd simply taken Rosemary's text for what it was and accepted that she'd gone to the movies? Even now, he could be asleep, blissfully unaware of her jeopardy. Her blood ran cold and her chest went tight. She swallowed a sob of desperation and tried not to think about it.

Despite the earlier threats, she was certain her aunt didn't plan to actually kill her. She'd known the woman her entire life. Her aunt had helped celebrate Georgie's every milestone. They were as close as an aunt and her niece could be. There was no way she would kill her, no matter what she said. And especially not in the presence of her mother.

For all the recent shocks Georgie had borne with respect to her mom, it still didn't change the fact they loved and cared for each other. Even the adoption had been forced upon Georgie because her mother cared. She cared about her future; she cared about her choices. She'd known better than Georgie that a baby would change everything.

Looking back, Georgie wished she'd been stronger, braver and had fought harder to keep her son, but she didn't blame her mother for forcing her to sign.

The feel of cold steel pressing against her back elicited a gasp and brought her attention crashing back to the present. Her aunt still held the wicked-looking weapon and was prodding her with the barrel of the gun in the direction of the paved walkway that led up to the front door. The carefully tended gardens that framed the path were dark shadows against the blackness of the night. Guided by memory and the faint light from the tiniest sliver of moon, Georgie stumbled forward.

The sudden onset of headlights from a vehicle turning into their drive lit up the path. Hope flared bright in Georgie's chest and she spun on her heel. *Cam!* A moment later, she recognized her father's silver Mercedes S Class Saloon. He drove past them and came to a halt outside the garage attached to the side of the house.

It wasn't Cameron, but she was just as relieved to see her dad. He could talk sense into the women and deal with the psychotic episode Rosemary appeared to be having, and perhaps her mother, too. It was the only thing that made sense. When they got back to the city, she'd insist both of them undergo comprehensive psych assessments.

"Keep moving," Rosemary growled and once again, Georgie felt the hard barrel of the gun in her back.

A car door slammed and she risked a glance in her father's direction. He headed toward them with a purposeful stride. A moment later, the place was flooded with light and Georgie guessed he must have triggered the sensors. He continued toward her with his arms outstretched and she couldn't hold back a loud gasp of relief.

"*Daddy!* Thank God you're here! Aunt

Rosemary's gone crazy and Mom's just plain scaring me! Careful, Aunt Rosemary's got a gun! I don't know what she's doing, but you need to talk to her."

In the middle of her monologue, she threw herself against him and held on tight. His arms wrapped around her. He held her briefly and then pressed a kiss against her hair and let her go. Georgie stared at him, confused. He averted his gaze.

"Dad?" she whispered. Her body flooded with uncertainty and dread, followed quickly by an overwhelming sense of panic.

"I'm sorry it's come to this, Georgie," he murmured and then frowned at his wife and sister-in-law. "Surely, there was no need for the gun?"

"Dad?" Georgie rasped again, filled with disbelief.

"I told you your father was part of this!" her mother crowed "Who do you think certified all the death certificates and obtained registrations of the births?"

Rosemary chuckled and then added, "I used to falsify them in the old days, under Matron's guidance, but this way's so much less risky... for everyone."

Georgie looked from her aunt to her parents and was filled with a fresh wave of fear and horror. Tears poured down her cheeks. "Daddy! *Nooo!* Not you, too! How *could* you!" The sobs came in earnest now and at first she didn't notice when her aunt raised the gun, her arms outstretched.

"Rosemary!" her father snapped. "What the hell

are you doing? Put that gun away before somebody gets hurt." He stepped forward and reached for the weapon.

Cam checked the satellite navigation screen mounted on the console of his car and made a sharp right. According to the GPS, the property owned by Georgie's mother lay directly up ahead. Slowing, he pulled over to the side and killed the engine and lights. A faint glimmer of illumination could be seen through the thick covering of bushes and trees.

Cam reached for the service revolver he'd left on the front seat and was grateful he'd taken the time to go via the station and sign it out. Though Rohan had expressed his reservations, Cam assured him it was purely a precautionary measure. He still had no idea what was going on with Georgie, but he believed in being prepared.

He'd left several other messages on her phone since the time she'd sent the last text, but he'd heard nothing. His last call had gone straight to her mailbox. He could only assume her phone had been switched off, but knowing she wasn't at the movies, he couldn't help but wonder why. His sense of foreboding grew.

Choosing his steps with care in the darkness, Cam picked his way toward the house. The evening was still and quiet. He shivered in the cold night air. Winter always came earlier in the mountains. Sometimes, they even saw snow—

The sound of a woman's cry broke the stillness and Cam's blood ran to ice.

Georgie!

His heart skipped a beat and then began to pound. He didn't know for sure it was her, but he wasn't hanging around waiting to find out. Sprinting now, he bolted in the direction of the noise and broke out of the trees. He found himself in a cleared area. Lights shone from the house directly ahead. He recognized Marjorie Whitely, even from the back. Frederick Rolleston was also there, next to Georgie. A short distance away Rosemary Lawson faced the three of them, holding a gun.

Cam's heart went into overdrive. Quickly, he dialed the station and was relieved when Rohan answered. As quietly, and with as few words as he could manage, Cam explained the situation and ordered the local cavalry.

Ducking low beside a thick hedge, he eased the safety off his gun. Raising himself just high enough so that he could see the people in front of him, he listened in disbelief.

"What the hell are you doing, Fred? Georgie needs to die. She knows too much."

"Don't be ridiculous!" the doctor snapped. "I don't care what she knows. We're not murderers. We can get her to see reason. Now, give me the gun."

Rosemary cackled and moved out of reach. "I don't think so, Fred. I started this and I'm going to finish it."

Frederick stepped in front of his daughter. "You'll have to shoot me first."

"Fred!" Marjorie gasped. "What are you doing?"

"I'm saving our daughter from your crazy sister. What are *you* doing?"

Marjorie looked from one to the other, appearing more and more confused. "Fred's right, Rosemary. Put the gun down. Murder was never part of our plan. We help people. We don't kill them."

"Your daughter's ruined everything!" Rosemary shouted, waving the gun around. "She must be removed. I can't take the risk that she'll blab to the police and spoil it for all of us. She's even dating a detective. Did you know that, Fred?"

Fred frowned and turned slightly to look at Georgie. "Is that true? You're seeing someone?"

Cam strained to hear Georgie's answer and felt a surge of relief when she responded in the affirmative.

"And you never told me?" her father exclaimed.

Georgie's reply was masked by her aunt's snort of impatience. "Who cares about her boyfriend? She's never going to see him again."

Cam heard the distinct click of the gun's safety being removed—and froze. *Fuck!* The thought reverberated around his head at the same instant his reflexes kicked in. With his mind spinning furiously, he tried to put together a plan of attack.

Over and over, he cursed under his breath, wondering how far away the local police were.

He was armed, but with the group of people standing so close together, he might not be able to get off a clear shot and he'd never risk Georgie getting hurt. He had to think of some way to distract them, or at least, get her out of the path of a stray bullet.

Careful to maintain his cover, Cam crept forward. A stick snapped under his boot and his heart leaped into his throat. Easing himself up high enough to see over the hedge, he noticed all four people now stared in his direction.

With his heart thumping hard enough to burst, Cam plotted his next move. As he watched, Rosemary advanced on the others.

"Unless you want to take the first bullet, you'll get out of my way, Fred."

Georgie's father didn't move. Rosemary came even closer.

"Fred!" Marjorie squeaked. "I think she's serious!"

"I have no intention of going to jail, Fred. If we let her live, that's where we'll all end up."

Frederick's shoulders slumped and Cam's breath caught in his throat. He waited for the man's response.

"Then so be it, Rosemary. I refuse to allow you to murder my daughter. She had nothing to do with this. Let the police arrest us! Let us be judged by our peers. You might be surprised how many of them will sympathize with our cause. They might even admire us for our courage."

Marjorie turned to her husband, her face filled with hope. "Really?"

Frederick shrugged. "Maybe."

"Don't listen to him! Rosemary shouted. "He's spinning you fairytales, dear sister. Now, step aside, or I swear I'll shoot you all!"

She rushed forward with her arms outstretched, the gun pointed toward the doctor. Right behind him was Georgie. With Cam's choices dissolving before his eyes, he stood and revealed himself.

"Drop the gun!" he shouted and almost simultaneously spied a puff of smoke coming from the end of Rosemary's pistol. A millisecond later, he heard the roar. At the same time, he squeezed the trigger and watched both Georgie and her aunt fall to the ground. His gaze shot to Georgie and his heart stood still.

CHAPTER 25

Georgie came awake slowly and then gasped at the sharp pain in her side. Muted light shone through the half-closed blinds. She moved slightly and a piercing headache stabbed at the back of her eyes. Cam materialized beside her, soothing her with quiet murmurings and a tender smile.

"How are you doing?" he whispered and leaned over to brush a strand of hair off her forehead.

"I feel like I've been hit by a bus," she croaked. "What happened?"

Cam frowned. "You don't remember?"

"Some of it."

"Your aunt—"

"Yes, I remember that part." She grimaced against another wave of pain, this time from the vicinity of her heart.

"You took a bullet in the chest, just below your collarbone. It went out through your shoulder. Luckily, it missed the artery."

"Was I shot by…my aunt?"

Cam's lips compressed and his expression turned grim. "Yes."

Georgie cried out in distress and closed her eyes. She couldn't bear to think about it. *What kind of aunt fired a bullet at her niece with the intention of seeing her dead?* Not the aunt she thought she'd known. And then there were her parents…

She shuddered and went cold all over. Icy tentacles of desolation clutched at her heart. She was grateful to be alive, but she couldn't imagine ever feeling warm again; feeling *anything*.

"Where is she?" she asked numbly.

Cam stared at her steadily in silence, as if contemplating what to say. She made an impatient sound in the back of her throat and clenched her fists. "Tell me," she said in a voice that brooked no argument.

"Your aunt was shot and killed during the incident."

Georgie gasped. "By…you?"

"Yes."

She tried to absorb the shock. "And my parents? Are they okay?"

"Yes. Your father was shielding you from your aunt and was grazed by the bullet that entered your chest, but he's fine, along with your mother."

"Where are they?"

Cam's expression turned grim. "They were arrested at the scene on a string of charges and were taken back to the City of Sydney Police Station. There will be a bail hearing for them later in the morning. There's no reason bail won't be granted, given the circumstances."

Though Georgie had been expecting bad news, Cam's words still rocked her to the core. Her aunt was dead. No doubt her parents would spend a good deal of what was left of their lives behind bars. Her family had been torn apart and would never be put back together again. It all seemed surreal and yet, it was now the reality of her life. "What about Uncle Bernard?" she asked dully. "I assume he's been arrested, too."

Cam's lips tightened and he nodded.

"Do my sisters know?"

"Yes."

"Where are they?"

"They're outside, in the waiting room. The doctors have been restricting your visitors, at least until you regained consciousness. You hit your head on a rock when you fell. You were so still, I thought you were dead." Cam paled. "I thought I'd lost you forever." His voice broke with the force of his emotion and he looked away.

Ignoring her pain, she reached out and touched him. He turned back toward her and clasped her hand in his. Pressing a soft kiss against her knuckles, he leaned closer, his voice still ragged.

"You can't imagine how terrified I felt, seeing you on the ground. The time we'd spent together... It just seemed way too short. I want us to spend the rest of our lives together, enjoying every moment that we can. Is it too soon to feel that way?"

Georgie stared up at him and a tiny sliver of warmth slid into her frozen heart. She shook her head and then winced at the pain, but managed to smile anyway. "No, it's not too soon. I... I feel the same."

Cam's eyes widened and gave her a hesitant smile. "Really? After everything we've been through?"

Georgie's heart clenched with pain at the thought of everything that had happened. She looked back at Cam. "You're not to blame."

Cam's expression filled with tenderness. "Thank you for being understanding. I'm not sure I would be so open in the circumstances."

Georgie shrugged. "They made their own choices many years ago. It had nothing to do with you. Or me."

Cam nodded. "I'm grateful you see it that way. I could learn some lessons from you on the art of forgiveness. I... I'm sorry about what I said about your baby and the...adoption. I'm sure you had good reasons for doing it."

Georgie stared at him. "I did."

"I should never have spoken to you like I did. It wasn't fair to assume you were like my birth mother."

"And how was she?"

Cam frowned and Georgie could see he was struggling to find an answer. The truth was, he had no idea why his birth mother had given him up for adoption and he probably never would. It was just one of the things he'd have to deal with—just like her son. The thought saddened her.

"Don't look so sad, Georgie. I'm so sorry we argued."

Forcing a smile, she reassured him again that she wasn't angry about their quarrel. Relief washed over his face and he pressed another kiss to the back of her hand.

"I love you, Georgie."

Her smiled widened. The sliver of warmth spread through her chest and kept going, all the way down to her toes. Despite the trauma and tragedy she'd recently experienced, happiness trickled into her heart. "I love you, too."

"So, you want to be with me...forever?"

"I do."

This time, Cam whooped his joy and looked like he wanted to take her in his arms. Instead, he squeezed her hand and another soft kiss, this one pressed against her lips.

He pulled away slowly, but continued to hold her hand. "The police raided the adoption agency a few hours ago. They found—"

"What time is it?"

"It's just gone after ten. The nurse was in here a little while ago to check on your vitals. She was pleased with the results."

Georgie absorbed that information and nodded. "What were you saying about the agency?"

A small smile lifted Cameron's lips. "You won't believe it, but the police found Cynthia's baby, along with two other infants."

Shock made Georgie momentarily speechless and then she found her voice. "You mean, they're *alive*?"

"Yes! The adoption agency was housed in a nondescript, two-storey building at Strathfield. The offices were located on the ground floor. The second storey had been outfitted as a nursery. From what I've been told, Josephine and the other two babies were still waiting for their adoptions to be finalized."

Georgie laughed with disbelief and then was forced to breathe through the pain. "I can't believe it! Cynthia must be ecstatic! Do you know who the other babies are?"

"Yes. All of the infants were being held under their original names. It made it easy to identify them. One of them belongs to Sandra Briggs; the other to Danielle Jamison."

"The premier's daughter?"

"Yes."

"Oh, my goodness! It's... It's simply unbelievable. I mean, I feel desperately sorry for those moms whose babies have disappeared, but at least we know now they didn't die. That has to be of some comfort. Do you think the police will be able to trace the other children and return them to their biological parents?"

Cam nodded. "I believe extensive records were kept by the agency, some dating back nearly forty years, right up to when the agency opened. It's going to take a lot of time to go through them and work out where each child is. Some of them of course, are now adults. It will probably be a matter of tracing the birth mothers and going from there. We'll have to wait and see."

"It could take years," Georgie said softly.

"Yes."

"What about...my son? Do you think... Do you think you could find him for me?"

Cameron stared down at her, his eyes dark with a tumult of emotion. "Do you want to?"

Georgie held his gaze steadily. "Yes, I think I do," she whispered.

Cam nodded. "I'll see what I can do."

"Thank you," Georgie breathed and then added, "You're going to be busy."

"Yes, and so will you."

Georgie cocked an eyebrow. "How do you figure that?"

"Don't you have a wedding to plan?"

Slowly, his words sank in. Surprise and elation rushed through her. "Are you proposing?"

Cameron took her hand in his. The tenderness and love on his face stole Georgie's breath.

"Georgie Whitely, will you marry me?"

Despite the turmoil and shock over the past few days and the dark months up ahead, Georgie's eyes teared up with happiness. "Yes, Cameron Dawson! Yes! Yes! Yes!"

EPILOGUE

Two months later

"Do you think we might be able to move the wedding forward?" Georgie murmured, plucking at a blade of grass.

Cam looked down at Georgie where she rested her head in his lap and wondered at her question. They were stretched out on a picnic rug, enjoying the late winter day. Cynthia and Josephine were not far away, playing on the swings. It felt so good to know his little sister had blossomed into the beautiful, young girl he remembered, albeit with a baby in tow. Having her and Josephine and Georgie in his life made him feel complete.

"Why is that?" he asked, playing with her hair.

"Well, my family has this thing about babies being born out of wedlock. With the wedding set for April, we could be cutting it close."

It took him a moment to comprehend what she was saying. When he did, he was flooded with surprise and disbelief. He pulled her up to face him, grinning madly. "You're *pregnant*?"

She grinned back. "Yes."

Throwing his arms around her, he hugged her tight. "How far along?"

"Six weeks."

"Six weeks! Why didn't you say anything?"

"I wasn't sure myself and I was scared to take a test. We both want a baby so badly. I didn't want to be disappointed. I finally got the courage to do it and two pink lines showed up right away."

Cameron grinned harder. "*Pink* lines? Does that mean it's a girl?"

Georgie chuckled. "No, silly. It doesn't work that way. The color of the lines isn't important. It's all about the number. Two lines means you're pregnant. You can't find out the sex until the twenty-week scan."

Cameron groaned in mock horror. "We have to wait *that* long?"

Georgie shook her head and smiled. "It's not so far away."

Flooded with happiness, Cameron thought his heart might burst. He couldn't have imagined life turning out so well. Adopted at birth and then thrown out of his home as a teen, his only thought had been survival and making it on his own. And he had. Now, he had a beautiful fiancée and a little sister, and a niece that he adored. Soon, he'd have a child of his own to raise and nurture and shower with his love. And he had the woman in his arms to thank for it.

Though she'd buried her aunt, was no closer to

finding her son and still had to face the ordeal of watching her parents and uncle go to trial, she'd risen above her adversities and managed to do it with a smile. She was a remarkable woman with more courage than he could ever imagine and he loved her with a fierceness that overwhelmed him.

Lowering his head, he kissed her soft lips, loving the feel of her against him. Surrounded by his family, he was where he belonged until the day he died. She was his and he was hers and together they'd conquer the world.

———————

Tammie Sinclair checked her mirrors and then moved into another lane. It was the end of another long night and she looked forward to getting home. Since the death of Rosemary Lawson and the arrest of Marjorie Whitely, Ward Seven was struggling for staff. Even so, she'd stopped looking over her shoulder. They'd have come for her by now if they suspected how much she knew.

It seemed like every shift had at least one casual agency nurse in attendance and Tammie had been forced to put in more of an effort than usual. She missed the nights when Rosemary would take over and bear the brunt of the workload herself. She might not have agreed with the fact Rosemary and her sister were stealing babies, but having the other nurse on night duty with her had sure made life easier.

Her phone rang to indicate an incoming call. Glancing at the screen, she smiled and answered it.

"Hi, babe. How are you doing?"

Her greeting was met with silence and then she heard a sob. Her heart skipped a beat.

"Wendy? Are you all right? Talk to me, honey. What's wrong?"

"Oh, Tammie. I'm...I'm bleeding."

Trying to control her panic, Tammie sucked in a quick breath. "Like, spotting?" she asked hopefully.

"No."

Fear congealed in her belly, but once again, she forced herself to remain calm. "Have you called the doctor?"

"Yes. He said there's nothing anyone can do."

Another desolate sob filled Tammie's ear. Tears filled her eyes. It felt like her heart had broken in two. If Wendy was having a miscarriage, their baby was no more.

Accelerating through the traffic, Tammie made it home in record time. Her fatigue forgotten, she raced into the house and found Wendy curled up on their bed. She ran to her and drew her into her arms, whispering words of comfort.

"I'm sorry, Tam. I'm so sorry!" Wendy sobbed.

"Hey, don't be silly. It's not your fault. Like the doctor said: It's just one of those things."

Wendy lifted her tear-stained face up to hers. "Maybe we're not meant to be parents."

Pain filled Tammie's heart. She couldn't imagine never being a mother. It's all she'd ever wanted to be. It's the reason she'd chosen to be a midwife. Midwifery was the only job she knew that brought her in close proximity of babies every day, until she was blessed with one of her own. She wasn't willing to let her dream die so easily.

"Would you... Would you ever consider adoption, Wen?"

Wendy stared up at her with eyes red and swollen from tears. "Adoption?"

"Yes. IVF hasn't worked for us so far. Perhaps it's time to consider other options?"

Wendy nodded slowly. "Adoption. Yes, maybe that's the way to go."

Tammie smiled. Relief and anticipation flooded through her. Her dream of being a mother was still alive. "I'm glad you think so. And you know what? I just happen to know an adoption agency."

Wendy looked up at her with hope in her eyes. "Really?"

"Yes. The directors used to be friends of mine. They've met with a little...misfortune of late, so it might take some time, but don't worry, I know everything there is to know about the adoption process. Trust me, babe, I know how to make it happen..."

NOTE TO READERS

I do hope you have enjoyed reading Georgie and Cameron's story. If you've enjoyed this story, please feel free to leave a review for The Baby Snatchers at Goodreads and your favorite digital retailer. Every review is very much appreciated.

If you would like to receive news on upcoming stories, release dates, book launches and other snippets, please feel free to sign up for my newsletter. You can do this by visiting my website at www.christaylorauthor.com.au and clicking on the "Subscribe to my Newsletter" link on the right.

The Final Bullet is the next book in the Sydney Harbour Hospital Series. Here's a sneak peek:

Detective Sergeant Lachlan Coleridge has seen it all. A veteran cop with more than fifteen years on the force, there's nothing much that surprises him. But when he comes across the charred bodies of two children while searching an illegal meth lab, he struggles to put the memory behind him. In desperation, he makes contact with a police appointed counselor.

Ava Wolfe is a psychiatrist currently attached to the New South Wales police service. Her heart aches for the darkly handsome detective who is in such urgent need of help. After years of exposure to the worst mankind can offer, Lachlan Coleridge's spirit has been ravaged beyond belief. She yearns to help him, but she's not sure that he'll let her...

To be a cop is to be tough—physically and mentally. There's no room for weakness. If it gets out that Lachlan's seeking help, any chance he has for promotion will be jeopardized. But he's drowning in a sea of pain; of darkness and confusion and it's only a matter of time before he topples into the abyss...

Can he trust the only woman who appears to understand him? Is he prepared to put his career on the line in return for saving his soul? Will he open up to Ava and let her help him...before it's too late?

The Final Bullet will be released on 1 May, 2016 and is available for pre-order from your favorite digital retailer.

ABOUT THE AUTHOR

Chris Taylor grew up on a farm in north-west New South Wales, Australia. She always had a thirst for stories and recalls writing her first book at the ripe old age of eight. Always a lover of romance and happily-ever-afters, a career in criminal law sparked her interest in intrigue and suspense. For Chris to be able to combine romance with suspense in her books is a dream come true.

Chris is married to Linden and is the mother of five children. If not behind her computer, you can find her doing the school run, taxiing children to swimming lessons, football, ballet and cricket. In her spare time, Chris loves to read her favorite authors who include Richard North Patterson, Sandra Brown, Kathleen E Woodiwiss and Jude Devereaux.

You can find out more about Chris and sign up for her newsletter at her website:

http://www.christaylorauthor.com.au